Dangerous Mission

Jenna Gunn

D1528422

To Mr. Gunn.
For all always being my protector and being the hottest husband ever while doing it.

About This Book

Inspiration for This Book

Hello reader,

Thank you so much for purchasing Dangerous Mission.

This book is a standalone HEA suspense romance with lots of open door spice. So get ready!

It's part of the Team Falcon Series in the Agile Security & Rescue world. Be sure to read the note at the bottom of this section about the content.

Happy reading.

Inspiration

As I'm a curious sort of person and ideas find me everywhere, I wanted to share what inspired me to write about cave rescue divers in this book.

Not long ago I watched a compelling movie—Thirteen Lives—about the cave rescue of a youth soccer team in Thailand. *Oh my heavens.* Let me tell you, this was a real nail-biter.

As a former diver myself and wife of a free diver, I was completely compelled by the rescue divers. In this book, I touch on the danger, and the need for such incredible, brave people.

One of my dear fellow authors shared this link with me to an article with the most beautiful cave diving photos, if you'd like to see, just follow this link. Smithsonian.com

Content Warning

Dangerous Mission is like my other books—romantic suspense—with strong and often complex characters that have experienced loss, emotional and physical injury, and heartbreak.

In this story our main female character is a rape survivor. She bears physical scars and confronts her abuser in this book. I didn't really set out to make this happen, but as the story unfolded, her pain came out in incredibly emotional, graphic ways. I wanted you to be aware of this so no one is taken off guard.

This book also deals with death—including a side character (not on the team!), but I also think this is important for you to know before you dive in.

While I don't consider my books dark, I do write grittier topics as they intertwine with suspense, crime, and danger.

Thank you again for being a supporter and part of my author world. I'm blessed to have each and every one of you with me along this journey.

XO, Jenna Gunn

Book Description

Can I survive letting a man like former SEAL Scout Silas in?

Will I survive if I don't?

One night of mayhem, one vending machine, and a slippery slope make a fine line between finding myself again and losing the remaining shards of my heart...

To a man my brother hates.

Who knew that Twinkies could be the downfall of the carefully constructed wall around your sanity?

Memphis "Scout" Silas wasn't supposed to happen.

The 6'5" SEAL with possessive eyes the color of razor blades and a dark past that rivals the Bermuda Triangle is a force I wasn't prepared for.

The job with my brother's company was supposed to be easy—work with Team Falcon to find the missing woman. But life gets complicated fast when Scout refuses to leave me to fight my battles alone.

Even if that puts him in my brother's crosshairs. But the real threat isn't the burdens we carry—the secrets that could destroy everything—it's the things we didn't see coming...

The fire between us included.

Readers who love action movies like the Bourne series and angsty suspense romances like those in the original Agile Series will find their next binge read with this HEA romance with protective military hero + off-limits + damaged past themes.

Note: This book contains subjects and themes that some readers may find upsetting.

Chapter One

Aria

The sick feeling in my gut worsens as the small plane dips.

"Griff..." I carefully rest my hand on my brother's damp shoulder. "Are you going to be okay?"

Not like he'd tell me if he wasn't going to be okay. Griff's tough as nails and more likely to jump out of this plane without a parachute than share his feelings.

When a groan is his only answer, my blood runs cold.

Lightning flashes ominously, backlighting the wing tip outside his window, casting him in an eerie halo.

No! *Not a halo.*

Griff's going to be fine.

He is not leaving this earth. I don't know what I'd do if...

Pain squeezes my heart like a vise.

"Is the pain worse?" My voice is weak and wobbly, when I need it to sound strong.

Jenna Gunn

"Yeah." He rocks in his seat, his elbows resting on his knees, his shoulders hunched forward. "Bad."

Panic sweeps through me, tightening my toes against the insoles in my shoes.

Griff is truly the hardest person I know. He's a Delta, a hardened combat veteran, a gunshot wound survivor, so the agony on his face makes my heart race and my mouth dry.

"Don't panic, A." He fists his hair. "I'll live. This isn't like you to be so upset. You're usually Ms. Sunshine."

"Well, I'm not always. Especially when you're hurting so badly. Truthfully, it scares me."

Swallowing, I look away. He does not need to deal with my emotions right now.

Griff squeezes my knee. "I'm not dying."

"It's just—"

"He's not going to be able to dive."

What the hell?

I want to turn around and smash something over Timothy Brundage's ugly head. What an asshole comment to make when my brother is in extreme physical duress.

Jesus.

I try to rein in my temper, but I'm not used to dealing with the kind of anger Brundage makes me feel. "Let's get on the ground without one of us expiring before we have this discussion."

Griff buries his head in his hands. "I know, I can't dive. *Fuck.* I know."

Griff isn't just a hard man, he's an honorable man. And when his company is hired to do a rescue dive, he's not stopping until the person he's hired to help is safe.

This situation is going to make him crazy.

I catch a glimpse of Brudange watching me, malice clear in his dull green eyes, the heat of his fury on my skin.

2

I exhale, my lungs shaking, and focus on Griff. *Brundage can go to hell.*

The next few minutes are wretched. My brother's pain increases more and more as we drop toward the runway, slicing through the clouds with rain hitting the fuselage like bullets.

I grab the armrests as the plane pitches and yaws. The storm is unrelenting. Wind makes the engine strain. Barely a few seconds pass between flashes of glaring light that tear through the cabin.

It's a scene straight out of a nightmare.

I've never been religious, but right now feels like a good time to make the sign of the cross over my heart. Maybe some guardian angel will hear.

My pulse alternately races and stalls. Stutters and jerks to a start again.

Please let us live.

Give me dark, cold water any day over stupid turbulence.

"Hang in there," Griff says with a dark laugh.

How can he be laughing when he's in agony?

"Just worry about yourself, big brother."

"I'm fine."

A yelp of pain from him makes me jump in my seat. Heart racing, my sweaty palms clutch the armrests. I've never felt more helpless in my life.

When I look at Brundage in the seat behind Griff, his eyes are closed.

"Brudgage, we have to do something!"

"Nothing we can do, but get on the ground."

Tears roll down my cheeks, tightening my throat until I can't breathe.

Griff moans, growls. Contorts on himself. I wrap my

arms around his shoulders. "This will be over soon. We'll get you to a doctor and everything will be okay."

Not only do I feel helpless, a wave of fear presses me back into my seat.

The weight of this job is going to be on my shoulders. Brundage is a liability.

Griff needs me. A woman is missing.

The pressure couldn't be higher.

And then the wing tip catches on the ground...

Chapter Two

SCOUT

The wipers slash violently back and forth. The storm a perfect background score for the whirring thoughts in my head. *How is it possible we haven't found this woman?*

The sound of my ringtone snaps me back and I blink the grit out of my eyes. I hit accept and refocus on the murky pool of light in front of the truck.

"Beast, what's up?"

"Where are you?"

My team leader sounds as tired as I feel.

I hit the volume button on the console to crank up his end of the call so I can hear him over the onslaught lashing the outside of the truck.

"About fifteen klicks from home base."

Voice blasting out of the speakers, he asks, "Near the airport?"

"Close enough."

"Good." He exhales a tired groan. "Do you mind picking up the DepthStrike team? Their plane should be landing any time now."

My eyes—seconds ago narrowed on the watery road—go wide and instantly dry as I almost run into the ditch.

"Did you say, *DepthStrike,* as in Kane's company?"

Sure as shit, Beast confirms the missile that just left the launcher and is coming straight at the center of my chest.

"Yeah, that's the one."

Fuck. Fucking fuck.

"Did you hear me?" His voice fades in and out because monsoon season and cell towers don't go together in Vandemora.

"I heard you."

A bomb couldn't have been louder. My ears are ringing.

"Camile and I can get them if it's better," Beast offers, clearly detecting something from my curt undertone. "You're just closer so I thought I'd see."

Scrubbing a hand over my open mouth, I consider telling him I quit.

Out. See ya if I see ya.

But my mouth betrays me, not my team. "No, get some sleep. We've all been up far too long. I'll pick up Kane and his divers and get them to the farm."

I'd never do that to Team Falcon or to the missing woman. I know my place and I'm needed here, no matter how jacked up I am.

Jesus. I knew a team was coming, I knew they would be arriving tonight. *How did I not know it was DepthStrike?*

Anxiety churning in my gut, I let off the gas as the truck tries to hydroplane.

Somehow I missed this fact because I've had my head in logistics preparations. And there's plenty of that going on.

I'm Agile Security & Rescue's liaison for the cave diving searches.

But I didn't know my head was buried in the sand.

Faaak. "Has it always been DepthStrike?" I ask, baffled.

"Yeah. They're the best. We spared no expense."

He's not wrong there. Kane's got a hell of a reputation. "Did you tell me that's who you hired?"

"I said the wrong name. I called them Deep something."

"Deep Attack," I mutter. "Now I remember."

Deep attack is right. *On my goddamned sanity*.

"Sorry, major fumble on that, but you know who they are."

"Copy, I'm on it," I reply, my voice tight, my stomach tighter. Squeezing out two more words, I end the call. "Signing off."

My fist returns to my mouth, only this time I mash it against my face hard, until I taste copper.

Griffon Kane, former Delta Force operator and witness to the worst moment in my life is coming to work on our case with us. Here. Now.

A glance at the GPS on the dash only makes everything worse. Six minutes out from the airport.

The dread almost chokes me as an uncomfortable tingle spreads across my skin. Shifting in the driver's seat, I tug at my shirt and adjust my cargo pants as I scan the dark watery road in front of me.

Someone would probably think I have fire ants in my clothes. Not far from it.

Of all the damned cave rescue groups in the world, it would be Griffon Kane's.

Fucking hell.

I swing the truck through a turn, making water push away from the tires in a slow wave that rushes toward the ditch. Serious as shit, this gets any worse and we're going to be using the snorkel this thing is equipped with.

Too bad it can't save me from drowning in my own personal mental hell.

Finally, the airport comes into sight.

But, what the fuck am I seeing?

A light is shooting upward in the air. Slicing through the sheets of rain, it disappears in the low clouds. That part's clear—the beam is coming from an upside-down plane.

But the men swarming around the plane with guns...

That's where shit gets crazy.

I don't know how long ago the Cessna carrying Griff's team crashed into the grass next to the runway. Or exactly how it got there, but it's pretty obvious this storm is a motherfucker.

I also don't know if anyone is alive in the wreckage, but I know the sight of the kind of rebels that terrorize Vandemora when I see them.

Gunning the engine, I ram the nose of my truck through the fence surrounding the airport's runway. The chain link scrapes the sides of the truck with a wail as it rips apart.

My headlights flash across the plane wreck as the truck bounces.

Heads whip my way.

That's right. Big dog's coming to the party.

Two of the four men jump in a small white truck and take off, swerving wildly across the wet grass, gunning for the open gate by the terminal.

Another man reaches into the plane and drags something out.

His buddy is waving wildly as I pin the gas pedal, heading right for them.

That's when I realize what he has isn't a bag of Griff's gear.

He's got a woman.

A young woman.

Bucking like an animal, she flails in his arms. Kicks wildly at his head.

I don't know how the guy is hanging on, but the bastard drags her away from the plane, toward the open passenger door of the waiting truck.

My vision narrows. My blood surges forcefully. The cold taste of adrenaline scores across my tongue.

I growl and tighten my hands on the wheel. "You just fucked with the wrong people, buddy."

I don't even slow down. I ram the truck, knowing it won't hit the man that's dragging the woman. Or the woman. Not that I give a flying fuck about the attacker, but with the truck out of the way, I've got room to work.

The sound of the collision is like a bomb. The impact jolts me hard enough to make me grunt.

Their truck will have gotten the worst of the hit thanks to the burly brush guard Agile's trucks have on the front.

Shaking the impact off, I throw off my seat belt and hit the ground running.

This asshole is about to regret getting up this morning.

He yells something at me as I grab a piece of bumper off the ground.

"Let her go."

He looks around wildly. Breathing hard, he yells, "Stop. I'll shoot her."

She whimpers, biting her lip as the man drags her into a chokehold.

Shit.

There's no way I'd risk taking a shot with him using her as a shield.

She meets my gaze with hers. There's a plea in her pretty brown eyes.

"Easy, sweetheart. I've got you."

Snarling, the man tightens his hold. "You're not getting her, I'm shooting her!"

Holding up my free hand, I steady my voice. "Then what?"

"Then... then, I'm shooting you."

"Right. Think about this. I'll be all over you in a second. You won't have time to shoot me too."

The eyes behind the mask get round. Dude is scared shitless right now.

Rightfully so. He's fucked. I'm not backing down. Ever.

"Let her go."

He shoves her aside, hard enough to send her crashing to the pavement. Her scream makes my skin tighten and my focus sharpen.

Now he's pointing his pistol at my chest.

"You're not getting away. You're trapped. There's a man behind you, holding a gun on you. He's going to take you out."

Faked out, he glances over his shoulder.

I lunge, knocking the gun away.

He twists and drops to the ground and comes up swinging.

Terror in her voice, the woman shouts at me. "Watch out! He has a knife!"

I use my improvised weapon to block him, and dance out of the way.

He ducks when I swing the piece of hard plastic bumper at his head.

Fucker's surprisingly fast. He's not focused though, and that will be his downfall.

Moving quickly, I advance on him, keeping my breath steady and my weight balanced.

His eyes flick to my right and back. Stealing a look at the truck I rammed.

"Looking for backup?"

He curses under his breath.

"Your buddy's probably got a concussion. If he's alive. I hit the truck hard."

Desperate, the man slashes out at me with the five-inch blade of his field knife. He lowers his guard as he does.

The plastic bumper piece hisses through the air as I swing. A jagged end catches the side of his face, gashing open his mask and his skin.

He roars and stumbles back.

"You liked that?"

He clutches the side of his face with one hand. "Fuck you!"

I charge him. Taking him to the ground.

He slashes at me, screaming.

My patience is done.

I flip him over on his back, pining his knife-hand to the ground. Just in time to hear a truck engine roar to life and get blinded by a crooked headlight.

Chapter Three

Aria

Oh my god. Oh my god.

I scream, hit the gas and squeeze my eyes closed.

I know it's coming. I know—

Slam!

Holy crap, how did that truck get up so much speed and hit me with such force?

Slam!

Is that me screaming?

Slam!

Covering my head, I duck down in the driver's seat.

Oh my god. I've gone through a black hole and landed in a terminator movie.

Slam!

I hold my breath, waiting on the next horrible impact, covering my face with my arms.

"Aria!"

Next to me, the driver's door rips open.

"Aria! Goddamnit, are you okay?"

What?!

My brother's voice barely cuts through the ringing in my ears. When I sit up, he's there, reaching for me. Rain blows into the cab of the truck through the opening, soaking me again.

Dazed, I raise arms that feel like noodles.

It's over. It's over. I chant, coaxing my body down.

But Griff makes another kind of alarm race through me. He looks like literal hell. There's a gash on his forehead. The broad width of his shoulders is rounded now, hunched and his eyes are squinted in pain.

"Griff, holy Jesus. Are you okay?"

Not only is my brother sick, he's been in a plane crash.

"I'll live."

Nervous, I ask, "Did I save the man?"

He laughs, squeezes my arms and winces. "Yeah, hot mess, you saved him. It took me for-fucking-ever to get out of the plane, my damned ankle was trapped."

"Oh, thank god, you're okay. When that man tried to drag me away, all I could think about was that you were sick and possibly injured."

I lean into my brother's arms, my whole body vibrating from the tsunami of adrenaline inside me. "Is Brundage injured?"

"No, but he's not getting out without the help of some serious heavy equipment."

I realize that the man who saved me is standing behind Griff with rain pounding around him.

Outlined by darkness, he's a monstrous stone column.

His hands fisted by his thighs. Piercing me with two eerie ice-blue eyes that cut through the darkness.

The look on his face is one step shy of furious.

"You're okay," I say roughly.

Griff steps back when he realizes where I'm looking.

Locked on me like I'm a target, the stranger roars, "Are you *fucking crazy*, woman?"

Apparently. Because who in their right mind does what I just did?

I blow out a shaky breath and sag back into the driver's seat of the stranger's truck, beginning to shiver from being soaked to the bone. "I wasn't going to let that guy run over you."

His body is statue-still, but his eyes take in everything about me.

The intensity is unnerving.

Giving myself a shake, I ask a dreaded question. "What happened to both of those men?"

His expression darkens beneath the brim of his baseball cap. "I took care of them."

Uh. Yikes.

My heart flops around behind my ribs. "As in killed?"

"They were going to kill you."

Gulp.

Griff squeezes my wrist. "Thank god Scout showed up. I couldn't get out to help you."

A violent shudder rolls through me as they both watch me. When tears rise to my lashes, I have to look away.

"Thank you." My words come out hoarse.

It's impossible to control the shake in my hands as I wipe my eyes.

When I look at the stranger again, he's not angry, he's blank.

Cold.

Like he was there and now he's not. Totally checked out.

Intense, awkward silence stretches out around us. The only sounds is the rain hammering down on the tarmac.

Finally, Scout's shoulders rise and fall before he tips his chin up a notch. "Thank you. Don't ever do any *fucking* thing like that again."

The tension eases enough for me to take a quick inhale. "Hopefully I'll never have to, but you're welcome."

I drag my eyes away from the withering glare he's giving me and focus on my brother. "Griff, we need to get you to a doctor."

He slowly nods, surprising me. "This fucking earache is killing me."

"Scout," I call across the space between us, "Do you know where we can get medical care for him at this time of the night?"

"I can make some calls."

Griff rubs the side of his neck as he looks at the upside down plane. "Thanks, feels like I've got an icepick in the side of my head. But first we need to deal with that. The pilot is okay, but shaken up badly, and one of our team is trapped in there."

Scout has a strange look on his face when he asks, "Who is diving with your team?"

"Aria." Griff hooks a thumb my way, then with a displeased sound, he motions toward the plane. "Brundage is the other diver. We're going to have to cut him out. He's not injured, but we're going to have to move some metal to get his big ass free."

Scout, whoever the hell he is, gives me one more cold, angry look before he walks away. "Let's get this done."

15

Chapter Four

SCOUT

Griffon Kane. Former Delta, current cause of my irate anger.

Motherfucker. Of course he'd have a girlfriend that looks like she does and acts like she does.

Lucky bastard.

Some assholes just have everything.

Some assholes like me get the fuck-stick our whole life.

For Christ sake, she jumped in a truck and put her damned self in harm's way to save my sorry ass.

A stranger.

I can't think about that now—shit needs to be done. People extracted. Medical help for Griff.

Sleep, for fuck sake.

God.

I need to lock myself in a dark room for a week.

When was the last time I slept?

Feels like years ago.

I rub the back of my neck, and try to ignore the weight of my bones. It's a real bitch when the adrenaline wears off before you're done with your work.

When I duck down and shove my head inside the plane, the rain sounds like jackhammers on the upturned belly.

This weather is unrelenting. I thought the heat was bad before, but now with the wet season upon us, I'm starting to hate rain.

A set of angry eyes slash my way as I look around inside. Griff said his diver's *big* ass was stuck—the man was right. This dude is a fireplug. They must have lubed him up to get him in the plane to start with.

Glaring at me, he rattles the seat that's blocking him from the exit. "You gonna get me out of here?"

"Depends. Where's the pilot?"

"Crawled out there while the circus was going on." He slashes a hand through the air. "Fuck if I know where he is."

I duck back out and look around.

Oh, hell.

The sight of a foot sticking out from under the plane has me frowning.

"Hey, buddy. You okay?"

When I crouch down and look under the upside down plane wing the man skitters back like a crab. Two owlish eyes peer out of a ghost-white face.

"Hey, man, I'm one of the good guys. Let's get you out of here. You're in shock."

"No! Get back! I'm armed."

He jabs something at me.

"Whoa!"

I hold up my hands and try not to breathe at him. I've

17

never been shot by a flare gun, and I sure as hell don't plan on trying it now.

I've got enough burn scars.

"How about I back away? You can come out when you're ready."

I take a few steps back as Griff slogs his way over to me, water splashing from his boots. His hand is clasped over his ear, his color is bad, and he's groaning.

For a man like him to look like he does, it must be bad. Proven by the fact that when he reaches my side, he lurches forward and pukes.

Yuck. "Oh, you fucker, that's gross. Could you do that somewhere else?"

He wipes his mouth with the back of his hand. "Like on your boots?"

"Get out of here. Go make sure your girlfriend doesn't get into any more trouble. I'm going to see what I've got in the truck to use to cut your guy out of there."

Banging comes from inside the plane. "Fucking hurry up you assholes!"

I'm pretty sure Griff doesn't hear the other man's demand, he's puking his guts up again.

This time, I grab Griff's arm and pull him toward my truck. What's left of my truck. Technically not my truck. Agile Security & Rescue's truck.

The second one our team has destroyed since we arrived in Vandemora.

The last one blew up.

This one is doing a Grand Canyon impression on its passenger side.

Guess I should be glad that dent is not in my head.

Thanks to her.

When I look up, she's watching us. Standing in the rain, shivering.

The touch of her gaze is visceral. Heat tightens my skin below my wet clothing, which stokes my anger.

As I approach, she looks away. Which is a damned good thing. She should be nervous around me.

I snap at her. "Keep your boyfriend on lock. I've got enough to deal with."

She stands back as I open the rear door and push Griff into the seat, praying he doesn't throw up inside. The last thing I need is to be fighting my gag reflex all the way back to the ranch.

"Do me a favor, open the door if you're going to hurl, got it?"

He grumbles, but there's no fight in him. Another indication of the fact the man is practically dead on his feet.

Jesus that says a lot. Deltas are hard to take down. Just don't ask me to admit that to one of them....

When I close him inside, I head for the back of the truck, leaving her. If she's not smart enough to get out of the rain, that's not my fault.

She's Griff's problem.

Not mine.

Definitely *not mine*.

So why does it bother me so bad that she's freezing, drenched, and rattled all to hell?

I fling up the door to the cap on the back of the truck and drop the tailgate. At least both still work. But inside, is a different story. Tools and gear are everywhere, tossed around like kid's toys thrown down on a playground.

God. Another pain in the ass.

"Can I help you?"

That small voice drives a burr right under my skin. I

curse silently in my head, then look down at her, and I curse some more.

The pretty brunette with the blue lips, soaked hair, and the soulful brown eyes is smiling at me.

God, those eyes.

Men do stupid things over women who look at you with a gaze like that.

Other men.

Not me. Ever.

Then why the hell does it feel like I just stepped onto a frozen lake with cracked ice?

I sound rough and very much like an asshole when I speak. "No. You need to deal with Griff until I can get this done."

With great effort, I focus back on the mountain of disheveled gear in the truck. Ignoring her. Everything about her.

Until she says, "He's not my boyfriend."

My head swivels around so fast my vision blurs.

"What?"

Not the most intelligent response, but that's all I got.

"Griff's not my boyfriend."

I process this as she looks up at me.

Fuck. *Why is she telling me this?*

"Sure looked like it."

Her smile turns into a grin. A cute as hell one.

"Oh, because he hugged me."

This news that she's not in fact Griff's girlfriend is the worst news I've heard all night. Maybe ever. When she was *his* girl that was one thing.

Now she's not.

Now she's a twenty-something with a gorgeous face, a

smoking body, and a weird, idiotic bravery that made her save my life.

Yeah, I'm in deep here.

Take that back. I'm drowning when she laughs.

The sound is pure as metal tapping on a crystal glass.

I inhale abruptly.

I exhale slowly.

Pray to wake up from this weird, fucked up dream.

The woman was almost kidnapped, had to save my ass by vehicular sacrifice, and her coworker looks like he's about to step on death's doorstep...yet she's able to laugh.

That's grit.

My dick likes that way too much.

Goddammit.

I force myself to look away with a violent jerk of my head—shove aside a couple of boxes with too much force—silently ripping myself a new asshole.

Finally, I spot the case that the metal saw is stored in. *Thank fuck.* I grab it and flip open the latch so hard hinge breaks. Like I'm about to.

I've got the hots for the girl that works for my...frenemy? And I'm exactly the kind of man that would shatter that sweet smile and leave her in tatters.

There's never been a time when a man needs to tear some shit up more than right now.

Chapter Five

Aria

Well...

He's hot. In a dark, broody, dangerous kind of way.

He's also strange. In an unpredictable wild animal kind of way.

The kind that has you walking too close before you realize you're about to be eaten.

I shake myself loose from my thoughts as Scout strides toward the plane.

Long legs. Lean hips. Strong thighs. Not to mention shoulders that can carry the weight of the world.

Aye, yai, yai. I'm a sucker for a man that moves like that.

When I climb in the driver's seat—because the passenger side is totally screwed—Griff mutters something from the back seat.

"What was that?" I ask. "My ears are still ringing."

When I turn around to look at Griff, his eyes are closed, his jaw is clenched, and his hands are fisted on his lap.

My heart squeezes. I wish I could do something for him, but don't know what to do.

"Should I look around in the truck for a first aid kit? Maybe they have some pain pills."

"Yeah," he replies in a ragged tone. "But A, I need to tell you something. Stay away from Scout. I saw how he was looking at you. He's bad news..."

Hm.

I should probably focus on the bad news part, but instead I have a different question. "How do you know him?"

"Our team worked on a mission with his SEAL Team a few years ago."

That explains a lot. He's a SEAL. An enigma.

Much like Griff.

I don't know much about my brother's career. Only the small details he's shared, which were few and far between.

Enough to satisfy me, but not enough to worry me. Even though that is exactly what I did. Constantly.

Sometimes, I both hate and appreciate that he was protecting me from the ugly details of his life. Even though I was watching it change him.

"Deltas and SEALs work together?"

His tone turns gruff as he shifts in the back seat. "Sometimes. All you need to know is, he's trouble."

Okay, so this subject is a revolving door and I know when I need to get off.

"Don't get upset, Griff. You don't have to worry about whatever he is. He saved my life. I returned the favor. I'm not in any hurry to get involved with a man again."

This is the truth in every way.

Too bad my body is obviously starting to think otherwise. A fact that baffles me, given what that monster did to me.

"Good. Stay clear." Griff slits his eyes open and pins me with a warning glare that only a brother can give. "Scout's a bomb with a faulty fuse. I can't believe Agile hired him."

Biting my tongue, I stare out into the rainy night.

Curiosity almost has me asking more, but I decide to let the subject go.

Scout can be whatever he is. I can enjoy the view and keep myself safe.

One bad judgment call nearly got me killed. So, no thank you. I'm one and done.

A shudder makes me wrap my arms around myself. Cold pulses deep in my marrow. Not because my clothing is plastered to me, my hair is hanging in wet strings, and my boots are literally full of water.

This kind of cold doesn't go away when you're dry.

It hides in the scars around your wrists...

And comes out to haunt you when your guard is down.

Mouth going dry, heart rate speeding, it feels like the truck cab is closing in on me.

I can't let my brother see. Trying to sound normal, I reach for the door handle. "I'm going to search the back of the truck for a first aid kit and some pain medicine for you."

But when I step out of the truck, the unmistakable sound of racing engines makes me forget my past like it's nothing more than dust in the wind. My blood runs colder than the rain.

Chapter Six

SCOUT

When two sets of headlights cut across the runway, I start to move for cover. What kind of trouble have we got now?

God knows, it just keeps on coming.

Then a glint of light catches on something blue on the roof of the first truck—an unlit law enforcement light bar. Behind it is an ambulance.

A few seconds later a third vehicle arrives.

Based on the height and angle of the lights, I'd say it's Agile's other truck—the replacement for the one that blew up.

Boots hit the pavement and a shadowy figure starts moving around.

"Yo, Scout."

I turn toward the voice and lift a hand as a familiar federal agent strides toward me. He snorts as his hawk-like eyes take in the scene.

The small white and black plane is lying inertly on its top. The damaged trucks are parked haphazardly. Plastic and glass parts are all over the ground. A gun and a knife are lying in the rain.

Clearly, a lot has happened.

Shaking his head, he rests a hand on his service revolver. "Didn't expect to see you again so soon."

I lift a shoulder. "What can I say? Trouble follows me."

He adjusts the collar of his raincoat, pulling it higher. "Sorry it took me so long to get here. How many bodies?"

"Two. Behind the other truck."

"Both rebels?"

I glance toward the two prone forms. "I guess. Armed. Not too smart. Our team had a run in with some in Santa Rosa. Seems like a similar type."

He listens intently as I give him a two minute rundown of what happened.

"I don't like it." He frowns, turning introspective for a beat. "I especially hate that they tried to grab a woman. That's an escalation from what we've seen before."

A memory of the man dragging Aria from the plane flashes through my mind. It flares my anger again. "I don't know what their intention was, but it wasn't good."

I turn my attention toward the truck where Aria is waiting with Griff. Her shadowed face can barely be seen through the gloom and rain.

But I don't have to see her to know she's watching us talk.

An electric sensation stirs at the nape of my neck. It's been there the whole time she's been watching.

My sixth sense pokes at me, but the message is muddy and the vague warning makes me crazy. I can't stand chaos.

He tips his chin and focuses on the plane again as the

other member of Griff's dive team jerks bags out of the cargo area. *Jackass attitude still on display.*

"Where's the pilot?"

"He's hiding under the wing, crawled into a hole underneath."

"Madres Dios." He leans down, squinting through the darkness, even though we're twenty yards away. "Is he in shock?"

"That and maybe concussed too. But the real problem is he's armed with a flare."

Resting his hands on his hips as rain runs down his Vandemora Federal Agent jacket, Torres shakes his head slowly. "I'm going to let the ambulance people take care of that."

"Yeah, that's why he's still under there. I wasn't ready to tangle with him. I had enough fun for one night. Maybe when he sees their medical uniforms he'll feel safe enough to come out."

"Hey guys." My teammate, Justice, strides through the puddles. "Man, what the hell, Scout?"

I chuckle darkly. "You missed the party."

"I can see that, what a mess. Looks like a demolition derby."

For a few seconds, Agent Torres, Justice and I watch Brundage work. I should probably offer to help, but he's grouchy as fuck and I've had enough. I'm out of gas.

Justice is on it though, he takes off at a trot to assist moving the dive equipment. Because that's the kind of guy he is. Always ready to jump in and help.

Agent Torres, leans against the hood of his SUV. "How do you think that happened?"

"Probably just got too close to the edge of the runway. The ground is soft."

"The bandits must have heard it come in for a landing. Who was onboard?"

"Three plus the pilot. That guy, last name Brundage. The other two are in my truck."

"They okay?"

"She's fine. He's sick as fuck. Needs medical care."

"Not injured?"

"Something with his ear."

His eyes turn reflective, then he nods. "Isn't this the team of rescue divers your company brought in?"

"Affirmative."

With a shake of his head, he mutters, "Well, shit."

"My feelings exactly. Think you can get him in that ambulance and get him some medical care?"

"Yeah, no problem."

"Good. I'm going to see if I can get my company truck back to Karma."

Before he goes, Torres thumps a hand on my back. "Do me a favor, keep the rubber side down."

"That's my plan. That, and getting some fucking sleep. I'm dead on my feet."

He stops and looks at me. "Are you sure you can get back?"

"I'll stop and sleep if I have to."

"Copy that." He tugs at his hood again, fighting the rain. "I'll call tomorrow and we can finalize the report."

I throw up a hand and take off toward the truck.

Now I just need to get rid of Griff and his girl.

Chapter Seven

Aria

Where would it be? There has to be a first aid kit in here...

Operators don't go around without substantial medical supplies.

I scoot deeper into the rear cargo area of the truck, lifting aside a heavy box.

"What are you doing?"

Holy dammit! Waving my hand in front of my face, I wheeze, "How about a little warning. You gave me a heart attack. I can't take any more adrenaline dumps tonight."

The man's pale eyes glance around at the gear surrounding me. The ticking in his jaw matches the flicker of tendons in his clenched hands. "What are you doing?"

Heart pumping like mad, I lick my lips. I'm so on edge it feels like I'm going to crack open.

"I'm looking for your first aid kit."

His head tilts and he studies me with eyes that are so pure and clear that diamonds would be jealous.

"Did you reorganize all of this?"

Oh. Oops. I didn't think about him being upset.

My cheeks begin to heat. "Yeah, I... I'm so sorry. I know some people are funny about their stuff. I was just looking for some pain relievers for Griff."

His expression is unreadable.

What is it with this guy? He gives poker face a whole new level of meaning.

My pulse speeds even more. His gaze is palpable on my skin.

The skin that's now under a jacket that belongs to *him*. One I found in his gear.

Awkward.

I shift and put a box down that was open on my lap. His box.

"I borrowed your coat."

No answer.

Yikes.

"Are you upset?"

His mouth compresses, the icy blue of his eyes punches through the dim light like knives. "I'm too fucking tired to care."

I can relate. But the true extent of his fatigue hits me. He's a walking zombie. "Scout, you should lie down."

He looks around the truck, even considers the ground as if he might obey my command. I swear I see him swaying on his feet.

"It's tempting. Come on. Get out of there. The ambulance is taking you and Griff."

I scoot toward him, sliding a few things aside to make a path. "Really?"

"I'm not one to joke around. Would have thought you figured that out by now."

I keep my mouth shut this time. Scout is angry, and rightly so. He's had a terrible night. I mean he had to…

Gulp. A shiver races down my arms.

I can't even think about what he did to protect me.

When I scoot forward enough to reach the edge of the tailgate he grabs me and lifts me down.

G-good lord.

He's really strong. He didn't even blow out a breath.

"Thank you."

Standing close enough for our breath to mingle in the rain-soaked air, he pierces me with a stare so hard it feels like he's slapped me.

As if a magnet has snared me, I can't move. Brows notches, his silvery gaze slips back and forth between my eyes. Searching?

No. Something harder than that. Accusing.

A hole in the ground would be welcome right now. Yep, just disappearing sounds like a great idea.

"I'll get Griff and head to the ambulance."

He silently watches me go as I slip by him, but his eyes are like battering rams on my back.

Skin tingling from my waist to the nape of my neck, I hurry to the driver's side passenger door. As I tug it open against a gust of wind that makes rain swirl around me. "Come on, G, let's get you to the ambulance."

Griff mutters and with great effort he climbs from the truck.

"Are you dizzy?"

"Yeah, I'm a shit show. Feels like my guts are going to come out through my mouth."

"Oh my god. Okay, let's get you to the ambulance as fast as we can."

I take his arm and we hurry as fast as a turtle toward the back door of the big vehicle. Inside, through the glass, the pilot is visible. His arms are waving around, a look of horror on his face.

I give Griff's arm a squeeze. "Looks like we're going to have company. The pilot is in there."

"At this point I don't care if Ozzy Osborne is in there with bat blood on his face."

"Ick."

He stops and curses. "Fuck, this hurts like a mother-fucker. Have I told you this feels like a goddamned icepick hooked to a battery is stuck in the side of my head?"

"No. And that visual is just gross. I'm sorry you're hurting so badly." I refrain from giving him a hard time about his foul mouth.

Not that it's ever worked before. Griff is Griff.

"Hang on. Let me get the door open."

He stands silently beside me as I fight with the handle on the Ambulance door. After a few seconds of tugging, it pops open and a rush of warm, welcoming air rushes over my face.

"In you go."

I start to climb in behind Griff and the paramedic stops me. "No room."

It is tight with the pilot and two paramedic-people.

"Oh. I can't go?"

"No, we are at capacity."

Griff crawls onto the bench, flops over and curls up. I almost faint from the sight of my big, strong, brother lying in the fetal position with his hand over his eyes.

I drop my voice to a whisper as I take a hesitant step back. "Will you please take care of him?"

"Yes, yes. Now close the door."

I've barely had time to step off the back bumper when the vehicle lurches forward, makes a turn and speeds off toward the airport exit.

I stare as the taillights disappear into the rain.

Well...

I guess I'm staying here.

Feeling off-kilter and still buzzed from adrenaline, I spin around and scan the scene of carnage.

Turns out the ambulance crew isn't the only ones that have left.

Chapter Eight

SCOUT

It takes ten minutes to drive five miles. Between the hellacious rain and thick fog that's settling in, there's no way to go faster.

And then there's the metal shit flapping on the truck.

It's getting worse. I might be sleeping on the side of the road after all.

The sound of my phone ringing pulls me out of my blurry-eyed stare. Déjà vu hits me. This is exactly how this started when Beast called.

God bless. *What now?*

It's an unknown number, but given the shit night we've had, I'm not going to ignore it.

It might not be a set of digits I recognize, but a familiar angry voice ramps up the second I accept the call.

"It's Griff."

No shit. I'd recognize that asshole tone anywhere.

I ease off the accelerator, an ominous feeling settling into my gut. "You're on the way to the hospital, right?"

"Yeah."

"What's up?"

"I've got to say something and I'm regretting not doing it when we were face to face so you could see how serious I am about this."

Drama much? "What, Kane? Spit it out."

"Stay the fuck away from my sister."

That's out of left field.

"I'm sorry, I'm going on forty hours with no sleep, you're going to have to explain how and why I'd have something to do with your sister who is some goddamned place in the United States."

The phone crackles with static.

"Griff, are you there, you bastard?"

His voice fades in and out. I can't understand a single word. But I get the tone. He's irate.

As I'm muttering, it hits me—*holy shit*—Griff thinks he might die from whatever is going on with his head. He thinks I'll be the one to deliver the news to his sister.

That's why he's warning me off.

The call fails, a loud beep confirms the connection has dropped.

Rubbing my eyes, I try to focus on the road. It's much harder than it was a few moments ago. Everything is a blur of water spots and inky black sky.

My body is shutting down.

I'm going to have to sleep.

Taking my foot off the accelerator, I ease the truck off the road. The frame groans as the tires cross a small ditch. This truck is fucked, Beast is going to be nuclear that the team has killed two of Agile's vehicles.

When I check my phone there's one tiny bar of signal. I toss it on the console. It's going to have to wait. Griff probably won't die.

I guess.

Not that dying is the worst thing that can happen.

I lean the seat back. Shut my eyes and fall away into the blackness.

Chapter Nine

Aria

Rain runs down my nose, across my lips and into the valley between my breasts. In other words it awful.

I've got to take cover. But I refuse to get in the truck the men who attacked us drove.

I just won't.

And the plane gives me the creeps. I mean we almost died in there. I'm not sure I'll even be able to fly home to Florida when this job is over.

I'll have to go by boat. Who cares if it takes weeks and I have to sleep in the cargo hold?

I squint through the rain and spot a small building at the end of the runway. The far end.

I'm not great with estimating distances but the only place in sight is at least a half mile away.

Dropping my head, I tug up the hood of the borrowed

coat that I didn't return. The one that smells like cedar and sex appeal.

Oh god. *I did not just think that!*

Trudging through the deep puddles, I count to five hundred, just so my mind does not have time to think about Scout's gigantic hands around my waist.

Hot, strong, massive hands.

Seriously, how can I even think about the opposite sex with any level of interest after what my ex did to me?

My ovaries are stupid.

By the time I get to the small metal building, I'm irritated and exhausted and desperate to find shelter from the storm.

I'm also more than a little ticked at Mother Nature for both the weird hormonal reaction I'm having to Scout and the unrelenting rain.

Give a girl a break, for god's sake.

But alas, no break for me. The door is locked.

After trying the knob a few times, I make a very unladylike growl at the door. "Seriously, couldn't you just be unlocked and make this easy for me?"

When there's no divine answer, I start looking around for a rock.

Who knows, maybe a fairy will have left me a key.

Or maybe... I'm going to bust the stupid window out of that door.

No cop would ever arrest me for breaking in after the night I have had.

When I finally spot a rock that is the size of a very large, size fifteen running shoe, I know I've hit pay dirt. My brother's shoes are fifteens. Scout's looked bigger.

Stop! Stop. Stop. Big hands and big feet do not mean anything to me. Nothing. Less than nothing.

I pick up the rock, testing its weight in my rain-soaked, shriveled-up hands. Yep, this should do.

Hurrying back to the door, I look around one last time. I'm not sure why, because no one is here. They all left. But the good girl in me makes me feel seriously reckless right now.

Get over it. There's no stopping me now. I'm going to grow gills and get hypothermia if I don't get out of this weather.

Plus, there could be a vending machine inside. *Please, let there be.* Me and my rock are going to have a party.

I raise it over my shoulder and stumble back. Oh. It's really heavy. That's not going to work.

I swing it to the side and rock back and forth. Okay, this is better. Like a two handed lob. Baseball bat style.

"One. Two... Three!"

The rock leaves my hand, sails through the air and crashes into the door...

And falls to the ground. Without hitting the glass.

"Shit!"

My mother would be totally mortified if she saw me right now.

Elenor Kane would wiggle her prim self over and swat me on the ass for cursing like she did when I was a five year old and Griff thought it was funny to teach me all the wrong words.

"Well guess what, Mom!" I shout at no one. "I'm over it. I'm done! I've had the worst day ever."

I grab the rock and hurl it at the door at the exact moment a bolt of lightning hits the building.

Chapter Ten

SCOUT

I jolt out of a dead sleep. Fuck. My knees slam the dash, my elbow hits the window.

Goddamn phone.

It's lying on the floor blinking.

"You hung up on me."

Griffon Kane is still angry.

"So you're not dead."

There's a loud huff on the other end of the line. "Of course I'm not dead. Did you hear what I said about my sister?"

"Did you hear what I said?"

"No," he snaps.

"I said I don't even know where your fucking sister is."

"What do you mean?"

I close my eyes and pray for the cell tower to be blown over.

"I mean, your sister is back stateside. She's the last person in the world I'm going to see. You're not fucking dying. You've got an inner ear infection. They're a bitch. It happens when you dive. You know this."

Griff starts yelling. Then someone yells at him to keep his voice down.

Growling, he returns to the call. "Scout, my sister is with you."

I might be out of my head from exhaustion, but I am one hundred percent certain no one is with me. "Not me."

"Scout, Aria's my goddamned sister."

I almost drop the phone when my hand spasms. "Wait a goddamn minute. She's the sister you used to talk about?"

This woman is Griffon Kane's baby sister—the one he was as protective as a badger over.

"Yeah, asshole."

I stare at the windshield. "Oh my god, now I get it. You're afraid I'm going to try to fuck your sister."

"About time your brain came back online."

"She's barely of age."

"She's twenty one, Scout. But the point is, I don't want you so much as breathing in her direction."

Too damned late.

"Look. I'm not sure why this couldn't wait until tomorrow. I'm dog fucking tired. You and your sister are on the way to the hospital, and I'm going back to sleep."

"She's not with me. They made her get out of the ambulance. Tell me she's with you. Tell me she's not somewhere alone." His voice gets really loud. "Scared and ALONE!"

The fog in my head vanishes in a second. "No. Not with me. I hope she's with Justice and Brundage."

Two minutes later my call to Justice has failed and I'm

driving like a maniac in a destroyed truck on a road that's covered in water.

Griff wouldn't stop yelling, so I hung up.

I hadn't gone far when I collapsed, so I'm less than six minutes out from the airport at this speed.

Come on!

Fuck.

I don't even let myself think about the fact that Aria is Griff's sister.

Not his girlfriend.

Okay, I do think about it. But I shouldn't. *Ever.*

She's...

Griff's sister.

Ten years younger than me.

Innocent as hell.

So wrong on every level.

When I swing the left turn into the airport's driveway, a startled sound wrenches out of me.

My mouth drops open, I blink to clear my gritty-eyed vision.

No. This is not happening.

Flames are dancing behind a small window on the side of the structure. The red and orange glow as real as anything a man can ever see. But that's not what has my heart leaping into my throat.

It's the sight of Aria running into the building.

Chapter Eleven

Aria

I hate fires.

"Oh god. Not this!"

When we had career day in high school, I went with the fire department and quickly confirmed that I like water. *Not flames.* And definitely not smoke. After our demonstration of controlled burns, I had a whole new appreciation for people who do that job. Other people.

So, what the heck am I doing?

"Come on!" I smack my wet rain coat on a burning computer. "You are not burning this building down!"

A rush of air races across my skin, making me scream.

My body is suddenly airborne and there's a steel band wrapped around my waist.

My scream morphs into a yell. "Let me—"

"It's me."

An announcement I don't need because in the midst of screaming and yelling for him to let me go, I got a hit of his scent. My new favorite addiction.

Warm, earthy and apparently the best things my ovaries have ever smelled.

"Wait, no!" I shout when I realize he's carrying me outside.

"Aria, hold still!"

"No! I'm putting out the fire. We have to—"

Scout plants me on the sidewalk, growls something I can't understand and stalks off.

I race after him.

He spins around and shoves a finger in my face. "You *will* wait outside."

"I want to help you!"

He growls, his icy eyes slice me as he grabs my wrist. "Goddamn, I don't understand you, woman."

He practically drags me through the building, grabs a fire extinguisher on the way, and goes to the office where the burning computer smells like an environmental disaster in the making.

Like some kind of expert, he puts the fire out in five seconds flat using the industrial-sized extinguisher. All while making it look like the gigantic canister weighs nothing.

Why didn't I think to do that?

Then he turns to look at me.

I shrink back. He looks unhinged.

"You didn't tell me you are Griff's baby sister."

My blinking is probably a clue I have no idea what he's talking about. His comment is so out of left field my poor overworked brain can't computer. *I mean compute.*

Much like the smoking desktop's carcass, my wiring is shot.

Waiting for me to do something, he just pins me with his arctic ferocity.

I offer a nervous shrug. "I didn't know I needed to tell you that."

He walks past me without a word.

Jesus. This guy!

I need an app that interprets glares, grunts, and weird loaded silences.

Fueled by anger, I follow him back toward the front of the building. When he stops suddenly, I have to jump to the side to avoid slamming into his gigantic back.

His voice is a low growly tone. "Did you..."

When I see what he's looking at, I cringe. The rock and a lot of broken glass.

"I had to break the window."

With a slow shake of his head, he tugs off his hat. "And did you set the computer on fire for heat?"

"What?" I gasp. "Oh my god, no! There was a lightning strike."

He swivels his gaze toward me. It's silver as the moon and full of disbelief.

I hold up my hand, scout's honor style. "I'm serious, the building got struck."

He puts his hat back on and tugs it down so his eyes are in shadow again.

How can he make me feel so confused and so guilty with one slicing look?

Even though I don't owe him a thing, the man can probably get a confession out of a tin can.

I throw up both hands. "I got left behind. I was sick of being in the rain and I couldn't sleep in the plane. That's just too... I don't know how to explain exactly, but the idea of getting in that plane is too much. And I couldn't get in that other truck."

After repressing a gag, I say, "Double ick. So... I convinced myself there must be a vending machine in here. I was starving. Then a bolt of lightning hit the building. And the computer caught on fire."

He walks off.

Again.

I stare at his very fine, very masculine butt as he disappears down a hallway.

What the hell? *Extra* what the hell?

He just walked off and I was officially undressing the man with my eyes.

The sound of breaking glass makes me jump.

When he emerges from wherever he was, he throws something at me.

Plastic crinkles when it bounces off my chest and lands on the floor.

The only light in the building is from a small emergency exit sign which must have a battery because I'm pretty sure the electrical system in the place would be fried.

But I can see that package as clear as day.

"Oreos!" A laugh bursts out of me. "I want to kiss you right now. These are going to taste like heaven."

My stomach lets out a grumble as I grab the pack off the floor and climb up to sit on the desk like I own the place. Not the crazy woman I feel like.

I'm so excited to eat, I can hardly get the wrapper open.

"I haven't had these in ages. Who would have guessed they'd have them in Vandemora?"

He makes a gruff sound. When I glance at him, he's

tearing open a package of Twinkies with his teeth. Staring at me.

Right at me.

Oh...*Ah*.

Yeah, that's not sexy. Not at all.

Lie, girl, lie.

My face suddenly feels like it's windburned.

Scout burned.

I'm losing it over here. Maybe it's my blood sugar.

Thank god, I finally win the battle and get the wrapper open. Otherwise I might melt into a puddle and flow off the desk onto the floor.

Keeping my head down, I carefully take a bite of a cookie, restraining myself so I don't scarf it like a piggy, even though I want to inhale those little cream filled devils.

That would be mortifying.

I duck my head and chew, making sure to keep my mouth closed, my groans of pleasure at bay, and my hand tight on the other cookies so I don't have to eat them off the floor if they fall.

Because I would.

I so would.

Scout would probably tell my brother. I'd never live that down.

When I pop the second cookie in my mouth, I close my eyes and savor it. So freaking good.

The lunch I ate when we stopped to refuel the plane was burned up hours ago. All the stress didn't help. I probably plowed through five-thousand calories alone when I was fighting that horrible man.

The man Scout took out.

Ooof.

Okay, no thinking about that whole nightmare.

47

Think about chocolate.

Or chocolate food product and white waxy filling that somehow works its way into your heart and not in the heart disease way. The way where you can't explain why seeing the package just makes you happy...

Humans are weird.

I'm squarely included in that camp and I'm thinking Scout is too since he's making a sound of pleasure in his throat as he eats Twinkies. A lot of them.

When he's finished, he mutters, "Fuck, I needed that."

I crumple up the empty Oreo wrapper and look over at him...

Just in time to watch him face plant on the floor.

Chapter Twelve

Aria

I leap off of the desk so fast, my feet tangle on themselves sending me to my knees on the carpet. "Scout! Oh my god, Scout!"

He's motionless.

Think, Aria!

ABC... Airway, breathing, clothing?

No! No, that's not it. Airway, breathing, circulation. You know CPR, for Christ's sake.

I'm a trained rescue diver.

But this... this is *freaking me out!*

Hands hovering over him, I can't figure out where to touch him. I whisper, "Scout, can you hear me?"

He sighs.

Is that good?

I lean over, holding my wet hair back and put my face as close as I can to his face.

His eyelids flutter. Soft, warm puffs of air cross my skin.

He's breathing. *Thank, god.*

"Are you okay?"

His sigh is deeper this time, rumbling from somewhere deep in his chest. I think this is a good sound, but...

What if I'm wrong?

Panic makes my heart rate spike again. My hand is trembling when I rest it on his back. The muscles beneath his wet T-shirt are warm and sculpted.

"Are you sleeping?"

"Exhausted."

One gravelly word.

I sag and close my eyes. He's so tired he collapsed.

I'm right there with him. If you're listening, God, no more scares tonight. This girl needs a break.

Carefully, I pull my hand back and look at Scout. Really *look* at him. As if you could when a lion was locked behind glass.

Thick, dark beard covers a strong jaw. His lashes are short, dense and black as ink. A faint white scar crosses the bridge of his nose. Another on the crest of his cheek. Small crinkle-lines fan out at the corners of his eyes. A deep furrow scores between two masculine brows.

I fight myself for a few seconds, avoiding looking at his lips.

I already know they look soft, but hard. A contradiction.

So fitting for him.

When I cave to the urge and study the lines of his mouth, a tingle builds in my own lips.

What would a man like Scout kiss like?

Slowly with precision or would he attack, knocking the senses right out of your brain?

He'd kiss like an animal, I decide.

All snarls and nips, and commanding thrusts of a tongue that takes what it wants.

I close my eyes and a little groan slips out of me. Heat pulses in places that have been cold for hours. A welcome tingle sets up shop in my lower belly.

How can I think about kissing a man? I swore I was going to be celibate forever.

Squeezing my eyes closed, I expect to be assaulted by terrifying memories. But that's not the vision that appears.

It's Scout looking at me through those icy, mesmerizing eyes. So cold they burn right down to the center of me.

I scoot away from him, needing the space.

When I stand up, my wet clothing binds against my skin. Cold and unforgiving. I need to get out of these.

Scout has clothing in his truck.

With one more glance to make sure he's okay, I see something different. An exhausted man that's so wiped out he doesn't even know the world exists right now.

He needs me now.

I needed him earlier.

It's my turn to take care of him.

It takes less than five minutes to rummage through his truck and find what I need. I'm wrapping up my raid when I hear a phone ringing.

The number on the screen is instantly recognizable and sends a wave of relief through me.

"Griff! Are you okay?"

He lashes out. "Aria, what are you doing on Scout's phone?"

"It's a long story. Are you at the hospital?"

51

He's silent long enough for me to know he's winding up to unleash. "Aria—"

"Griff, please tell me what's going on."

With a grumble, he relents. "I'm in a city called Carollia. It's the closest place with a specialist. I've gotten something for pain, I'll be seeing the ENT in a few hours. Now where the hell are you?"

"I'm..." Sighing, I pinch the bridge of my nose. "I'm at the airport. I'm fine. Look, I need to go."

"What the hell are you doing answering Scout's phone?"

"He's busy."

Sleeping.

I grimace. Griff sees through lies like they're made of Saran Wrap.

I need to get off this phone.

Trying to sound cheery, I say, "Get some rest, brother. I'm fine. I'm safe. I'm going to try to get some sleep so I can start planning the dives as soon as I can meet with the rest of the Agile Security team."

I can hear his extreme unhappiness through the line without him saying a word.

Then he lets loose. "Fuck, I can't believe this is happening."

Well, neither can I, but I don't say that aloud. "Just rest. You'll get well more quickly."

"I guess." He snorts and mutters, "Remember what I said about Scout. I'm really angry right now that you're with him. He's the last person I want you to be around."

I feel compelled to point out one very important fact. "Griff, he saved my life."

"He's a fucking SEAL, that's what they're trained to do. He does that shit in his sleep."

Oookay. This is a pointless conversation. "Griff, please, take a breath. I'm fine. Nothing is going to happen to me."

"You need to watch your back around him. I'm serious, A, he's a liability. I won't take any chances with you. The way that fucker was looking at you made my blood boil."

God. Griff is over the top. And he doesn't even know about what happened with Adam. If he did he'd really lose his mind.

Chapter Thirteen

SCOUT

A peel of thunder wakes me, launching me from sleep to high alert in a fraction of a second.

I'm on my feet by the time I register that it is already daylight, I'm in a strange place, and two people are staring at me.

Dammit. Not just two people.

My boss and his woman.

Gruff as a pissed off dog, I scowl at them. "You two should know better than to sneak up on someone like me."

I drop my hands from a fighting stance to hang by my sides.

They both look past me with such looks of shock, I whirl around, expecting to find a mountain lion about to attack me.

But that would have been easy.

Instead, I find Aria on the floor wearing one of my

favorite T-shirts, with sleep tangled hair and a blanket pooling around her lap.

Sitting where I just leapt off the ground from.

Holy fuck.

God.

Damn.

What have I done?

A flash of hot, then cold rushes over my skin. The scars on my legs tighten as the hair raises all over my body.

I point in the general direction of the front door of the small ass airport terminal. "Get. Out!"

Aria startles and scrambles to her knees, causing the blanket to drop away from her hips. Her bare thighs make an appearance causing my heart to leap out of my chest.

Oh no. No. *No fucking way.*

Behind me, Beast and Camile are making a hasty retreat, their footsteps loud on broken glass. The metal door slams closed, sending an echoed boom through the terminal.

From the looks of things, Aria's about to take off with them too. "Not you!"

She slowly stands up, and when she does, something falls out from within the fold of the blanket and clunks on the ground.

Wide eyed, she freezes.

A taser. My taser.

A tremble shakes her slender shoulders beneath my T-shirt. The one that looks sexy as hell draping over her sweet feminine curves.

But the orange object on the ground is almost as alarming

If my muscles weren't locked in place from disbelief, I'd scrub my hand over my eyes.

This cannot be real.

Reaching down, Aria snatches the blanket up and holds it to her chest like a shield. Her eyes skate to the taser and back to me fast as lightning.

"I know this looks bad." She licks her lips, "It's not what you think. And right now, I think you should take a few breaths to try to calm down."

"I'm breathing. Can't you hear me snorting like a wild animal?"

"That's what I meant." She cringes and waves her hand at my chest. "It's not good for you to be so upset."

"Upset?" I snap, "I burned the bridge to that particular emotion when I saw you don't have any pants on. And that was before I saw a fucking taser hit the floor."

Her brows go up as she bites her lip.

Blink. Blink.

Those doe eyes of hers never leave my face.

"I promise I didn't shoot you with that thing. I don't even know how."

Her teeth return to her bottom lip, this time hard enough to blanch the color.

Sexy AF.

My blood surges and something short circuits in an already overloaded motherboard in my head.

I'm going to be smoking like that goddamned computer.

When I speak again, I sound like I'm on the crazy train, I've been snorting coke, and I'm channeling a heavy metal singer all at once. "I woke up with a woman sleeping next to me that might have tasered me, who has no pants on, and I have no memory of what fucking happened!"

The building's metal walls are an echo chamber.

She puffs up her cheeks and blows out a slow breath. Color blooms around her neck and climbs up to rest on the curves of her face—sweet pink color like the inside of a woman's thighs when your beard scrapes the tender skin.

I do a quick body scan of my muscles. Doesn't feel like I've been tasered.

Ask me how I know…

But still.

I'm out of patience for whatever game is happening right now. "What happened, Aria?"

She's treading carefully when she speaks. "You fell asleep."

I chose this inopportune time to look down at my fly to make sure my pants are zipped.

Thank god they are, and my dick is safely locked inside, because not only is it a serious mind fuck not to remember why or how she's sleeping next to me, if I had sex with her and fell asleep in the middle of that, I need to be put out to pasture.

"I'm sorry… God. I feel like I'm saying that all the time with you. I brought the taser inside because those men could have had friends." She holds my gaze even though she's nervous. "I didn't know if I could… shoot someone with your pistol because I'm not a very good shot. But I really hope you're not mad that I got a change of clothes out of your truck and that I got a blanket for…us."

That last word croaks out of her.

Us.

Right. There is no us. Never will be. No matter how beautiful I think the woman is.

Looking down at her hands, she mutters something too low for me to hear. Then she tries to move past me.

"This conversation is not over." I move to block her path, by inserting my six-four frame in her path. "I'm not mad that you got yourself into dry clothes and got a blanket.

The rest of this is what's freaking me out. I don't like unknowns, so I need for you to explain exactly what happened. How did we..."

When she looks up at me, the deep brown warmth of her eyes sucks me right in, snatches the air out of my chest.

Drowns me and buoys me at once.

This is not happening.

This can't be happening.

I can't...

I cannot be with a woman that would expect things from me.

It's impossible.

I'm not that man. I'll never be.

A bitter taste slides down my throat, scorching a path to the marrow in all my bones. Every damned one of them.

"I need to know," I say in a rough voice. "Aria, you need to explain what the hell happened between us *right* now."

Chapter Fourteen

Aria

Nothing. Nothing happened, but the crazy thing is, I wish it did. I wish he had curled up around me and chased my demons away.

Even if just for a single night.

But no. And now he's furious. A very pissed off, very deadly looking SEAL.

Surely, he's had more than a few crazy things happen to him. But the man looks so unhinged right now.

As if waking up—fully clothed—next to me is somehow the final straw that breaks his back, as if everything he's ever faced was manageable until now.

Me.

Little old me.

It hurts like I've been slapped to think I'm the reason for his extreme distress.

His eyes are filled with the chaos brewing inside of him, flicking between confusion and anger. I'm surprised the tension crackling in the air isn't shooting off sparks.

"You collapsed," I say carefully, with pain surfacing in my stinging eyes.

His expression tightens even more when that seems impossible. A thousand things pass behind the crystal windows he sees the world through.

"No way. No. I've been to hell and back, and I've never collapsed. No. Fucking. Way."

Careful, Aria. He's triggered.

We both had a bad night. The last thing I need right now is to make this situation worse. We have to work together.

"I'm sorry, Scout. I know this has to be confusing and I am sure with all your high-price training, this scenario does not add up. But I saw it with my own eyes." Meeting his gaze, I soften my voice, "You had just eaten a Twinkie and you kind of crumpled—sort of fell. You landed face down on the carpet. It was as shocking to me then, as it is to you right now."

He huffs and blinks rapidly, looking right through me, as if there is zero chance of that information being true.

"Right there." I motion toward the carpeted expanse in front of the desk. "You're too big for me to move. Not that there was anywhere to take you. No comfy accommodations here. They don't even have a couch in their lounge. At least you didn't land on the broken glass."

Scout's body has gone scary-still.

He was always impossibly big, but now he's scary-viking size.

"Did you touch me?"

For a beat, his question confuses me.

"Of course, I was afraid you needed CPR."

Then it hits me. I realize what he's asking. *Oh my god.* "Not inappropriately. I would never."

The angle of his jaw tenses, his cold gaze gets even icier. "Tell me exactly where you touched me."

Heart thudding, stomach knotting, I step back. "I promise I didn't do anything bad. I made sure you were breathing."

I cover my mouth with my hand, trying to remember exactly where I touched him. "Your neck first to check your pulse. I put my hand on your back to make sure you were breathing steadily. Not under your shirt. I took your hat off."

Definitely not telling him I brushed my fingers through his thick, soft, dark-blond hair.

He steps closer, making me crane my neck to match his gaze.

Voice rough, he asks, "What did I do?"

"You were just sleeping. You said one word —exhausted."

For a while we just stand. Looking at each other as heat pushes off of him and my nerves fray.

"I passed out... I've never had anything like that happen."

"You were a walking zombie, pale skin, dark circles under your eyes. When did you last sleep?"

"Days."

I tilt my head, my heart softening as I take in his strong, handsome face. "That's terrible. You can't do that. It's dangerous. What if you were driving?"

He scrubs both hands over his face. "Are you sure I was sleeping?"

I take a steadying breath. No man wants to think he's

been vulnerable and unaware. Out of control. Especially him. It doesn't take a genius to recognize that he's got to be in charge.

But something bad has happened to Scout before and this whole thing has been a trigger for him.

God knows I have mine.

"I know you're upset you collapsed. I would be too, if I couldn't remember anything. But I promise you, I was worried about you. I took care of you. I only wanted to make sure you were safe."

He looks down at the spot where we were lying as if he's looking for a chalk outline like a coroner would make around a corpse in old movies.

But there's hardly any evidence.

His hat is on the ground. The taser too. My discarded, wet boots are a few feet away. They leaked so much they made a ring on the carpet.

Beyond that, there's nothing.

But I know the experience might as well have left a crater for the effect it has on him.

Feeling awkward, I take a few steps toward the hallway. "I'll just go change."

"What did I do?"

I raise my gaze to his face again. "I'm not sure what you mean."

"Did I pull away when you touched me?" His body flinches as he searches my face. "Did I...look like I was in distress?"

Frown deepening, I twist my hands together. "No. You sighed. Then you dropped into a hard sleep. Didn't move until those people woke us up."

His pale blue gaze drops to the side. The cords of his throat work as he swallows.

He's in so much distress, the tension around him could cause the floor to collapse with its weight.

"What is it, Scout?"

For a rough few seconds, he works through some emotion. Shallow breaths make his chest pump. His hands open and close.

My heart hurts for him. But hugging him is clearly off the table.

Finally, he rasps out a reply. "I don't like to be touched."

There it is.

Not the root, but the ugly vine that came from whatever experience he had.

An ache spreads in my throat, making my voice soft and strained. "I'm sorry, if I'd have known that, I would never have touched you. Truthfully, not that I'm making this about me, but I don't like to be touched either."

The silence that follows makes a cold chill run down my spine.

I step past him, heading for the bathroom at the back of the terminal where my clothes are hanging over the stall door. But something stops me—a resolute feeling blooms in my gut.

When I turn back, he's frozen in place, staring at the floor. His hands are wrapped around the back of his neck.

"I take that back, Scout. If you're ever in danger again, I'd touch you. I'd do whatever it took to make sure you were safe, and then I'd deal with your emotions after. I won't apologize for taking care of you again, but I'll be there for whatever wreckage is left afterwards."

Chapter Fifteen

SCOUT

I'm hanging by a thread when I shove open the door and stride out into the weak morning light.

Aria took care of me.

What the living hell?

I barely notice the rain has stopped for the fog in my head. When I glance up, it's clear this break in the weather is only a small reprieve. Soon we're going to have more rain filling flooded caves that we need to search for the missing woman.

That's what I need to be focused on. Not the fact that Aria slept next to me. Touched me. Cared that I was safe.

Fuming, I jerk open the driver's door of the truck.

"Hey, Scout!"

When I look to my right, following the unwelcome voice, I curse. *Dammit.* With all the chaos inside, I forgot my boss is here.

I can't exactly ignore him and Camile. That would be a total dick move, but I'm so strung out and spun up, that would be the smart thing to do.

Beast climbs out of the rental truck he's been driving and takes a few measured steps toward me. Camile hops out of the passenger side and heads for the terminal without looking my way.

Damage control.

Divide and conquer.

He leans a hand on the truck's roof. "You okay, brother?"

That's some nerve.

"Do I look like I'm okay?"

His frown deepens as he inspects me from head to boot. "You look like you finally got some sleep."

"Guess I needed it. She said I collapsed."

Beast gives me a suspicious look. "I hope after, not during."

"Fuck you. I didn't sleep with her. I mean I slept with her, I didn't get in her pants."

Shit, just saying such a callous remark about Aria makes my gut go sour. I really am a jackass.

His left brow goes up as an almost grin tugs at his mouth. "Wouldn't fault you if you did."

I stride away, before I tear his head off, rounding the truck to the fucked-all-to-hell side. This bitch needs a bodyshop like I need a cup of coffee.

When he follows me, I give him a look that leaves no doubt I'm unhappy. "Well you should fault me."

"What's that mean?"

"She's Griff's little sister for starters."

He stares at me. Shakes his head. Whistles. The trifecta of shock.

"That explains why he's been blowing up my phone trying to find you two."

I rest my hands on the hood and hang my head. "That's gonna be a problem."

"Only if you let it be."

I bang my fist against the dented metal. "You don't know Griff."

"I know plenty of men like him."

As I look at Beast, I laugh darkly. "Then you know if he thinks the wrong guy so much as sniffs around his sister he's going to want blood."

"What if you prove you're not the wrong guy?"

Pushing off the truck, I fist my hands in my hair. Which reminds me, I need my damned hat.

"That's impossible. I am the wrong guy."

"You've been a tight-lipped asshole since you joined the team. I think it's about time you let me in on what's going on with you."

That's a hard no.

"There's nothing going on with me."

"Then why—"

"Look, I respect the hell out of you as team lead. You're a great SEAL. An outstanding boss."

As he studies me, I kick the broken running board, breaking the dangling part loose. After it clangs to the ground, I turn to face Beast.

"But you are not picking apart my sex life. Or anything else about me. I do my job. I get results. You need me to be locked on. Every minute that passes, is another minute that our missing woman needs us."

"You're right. We do need you locked on." Beast crosses his arms and leans against the truck. The fender groans under his weight. "But I need to know you're okay."

"I'm fine. The truck is not."

The light in his eyes goes hard. I know this topic is far from over, but he cuts me a moment of slack.

Maybe I look as unhinged as I feel.

"You assholes keep destroying our trucks."

I feel a presence at my elbow—the small feminine kind that smells good and makes my wiring light up—causing me to grit my teeth.

Aria holds her hands up toward me. My baseball cap is in her palms. It's filled with packs of Twinkies and a plastic bottle of water.

"You should eat and drink water."

After she shoves the contraband goods at me, she turns to give Beast a lift of her chin. "Technically, I wrecked the truck. Or the bad guy did. He rammed me four times. I got in the way to save your boy's life. Since I know it's expensive to replace someone like him, I think that should knock down the cost for me to replace this behemoth. But send me a bill for the balance."

By the time she finishes, her hands are on her hips.

Beast chuckles.

I do nothing but stare at her because I can't get a damned thing in my mouth to work.

With one more glittering glare in my direction, she turns to leave. "I'll be in your boss's truck since it's clear you don't want my company this morning."

My mouth slides open as my forehead wrinkles.

Hellcat.

When she walks away, Beast grins so hard his face might crack. "Sassy. I like her already. I think I'll make you two ride back to the ranch together."

67

Chapter Sixteen

Aria

Well that was awkward.

God, what was I thinking?

Scout makes me so anxious that my mouth just does its own thing. I'm possessed by some sassy monster—probably wearing red stilettos—that is laughing right now as it sits on my shoulder.

Well, I'm not laughing. I definitely don't wear stilettos. And I'm hanging by a thread. What a freaking nightmare. All of it.

Camile is standing by the other truck.

Thank heavens, she and Beast are here. I have an escape from the grumpy commando. They're saving me from having to sit in a passenger seat next to a man that's making my heart hurt and my head spin.

Stupid, I know.

But I'm kind of a mess when it comes to men.

I groan silently, as I close the last few feet of distance to where Camile is standing next to a blue pick up truck.

She's looking beyond my shoulder with a sly grin on her face. "Girl, I don't know what you said, but those boys are both catching flies right now."

I shrug both shoulders as my face heats. "I said I'd be riding with you two since Scout clearly doesn't want company this morning."

"Scout never wants company." Glancing at me, she chuckles softly. "That's just how he is. Don't take it personally."

For some reason her remark really bothers me. I climb in the back seat, as I worry at my lip with my teeth. "Do you know why?"

"Because he's in the badass club?"

"That's for sure." I brush my hand over my face, massaging the tightness in my forehead. The events of last night are making my whole body stiff. "I guess you're right. Griff, my brother, isn't exactly easy to get along with, either."

"Beast has more than a few sharp edges, but I found the key to his heart. Anyway, he talked to your brother earlier. Have you gotten an update on his condition this morning?"

"No. Did he say how he was?"

"This is third hand information. He saw a specialist, and he's getting some pretty heavy antibiotics."

"I should call him, but my phone must be in the gear that went with Brundage and your other guy. Have you seen him, he's got sandy red hair?"

"Yep." She scrunches her nose. "That man is not a morning person."

"Seriously." I blow out a breath. "That man does not

69

have a time of day. He's also in the grumpy operator club, but..."

She turns to look at me over her shoulder from the front passenger seat, waiting on me to continue.

Should I air my dirty laundry?

"Now that Griff is out of commission, it's going to be just the two of us—me and Brundage—diving together to help hunt for the missing woman. The man has never liked me. "

She looks me over with a quick, impatient inspection. "You? What's not to like?"

"Plenty, I guess. I think he doesn't want me in the boys' club."

Camile's eyes soften. "I've been there. But I can tell you with one hundred percent certainty the men of Agile Security & Rescue are not like that. Even if Scout acts like he stepped in a fire ant nest, he's very respectful. All of the men are."

"Must be nice to work with guys like that," I mutter. "The dive rescue world is full of oversized egos and lots of bad attitudes."

"I'll tell Beast to see if he can smooth the way for you on this—"

She stops mid-sentence. "Uh. Oh. This doesn't look good."

I pull my unseeing gaze away from the side window and focus on her man.

Wearing a scowl on his lips with a dark, piercing gaze, he's standing several yards in front of the truck. Crooking his finger.

Me?

Nerves fluttering, I lean forward between the seats. "Who does he want to come out there?"

"Hmmmm. I don't know, but I don't like his expression. When he gets that determined look on his face, things get testy. Hang tight, I'll find out."

She slides from the truck and marches toward him with her red ponytail snapping.

For several seconds they talk with him looking down at her upturned face and his hand gently wrapped around her elbow.

They make a great looking couple. He's got stars in his eyes when he looks at her.

I should look away. Jealousy is the last thing I need to be dealing with this morning. I've already got enough of an emotional cocktail in me to give me a hangover that will last for days.

But...I don't stop watching.

Camile's so small compared to him, but her energy is just as commanding. I have a feeling she gives as good as she gets.

Like right now. Full of sass, she drops her hands on her hips and glares up at him. He leans close and says something next to her ear.

It's not hard to imagine he would have a sexy whisper with the deep voice he's got.

No matter what frustrating thing he's saying, I bet it sends shivers down her spine.

When he steps back, he watches her with every ounce of his energy.

It's enviable—the way he gives her his all.

But my thoughts about them are swiped away when she casts one look my way with a pensive expression tightening her eyes.

My heart sinks.

Whatever happened out there was about me.

Damn. What now?

I fully plan on questioning her when she returns, but Beast loops an arm around Camile's neck, guiding her away.

I sag backward into the seat, unease weighing me down.

It's petty of me to feel deserted.

But that's exactly the sensation inside of me.

Not that I thought Camile was suddenly a BFF, but she was kind enough to come check on me in the airport terminal—offering words of support and help carrying the supplies I pilfered from Scout's truck.

Maybe he was scolding her for that.

But why?

I'm so lost in my head, looking down at my cuticles when the driver's door suddenly opens.

The hat full of snack cakes lands on the center console. The water bottle bounces and thumps into the passenger side floor well.

"Nice mic drop. Now get your ass up here in the passenger seat. I'm not a chauffeur."

Chapter Seventeen

SCOUT

Revenge is a real bitch. That was my warning to Beast when he said he was taking the busted up truck for a repair estimate and that Aria and I were to proceed to the farm in his vehicle for an urgent meeting.

Unfortunately, my barely veiled threat didn't even make him flinch.

Big bastard.

It's hard to scare someone who's just as equally skilled an operator as you are.

So here I am. Unhappy as fuck. Getting in a truck with the one woman I want a thousand miles from me.

"Aria, did you hear me?"

Her shocked expression morphs in front of my eyes. The soft curve of her kissable mouth becomes a hard slash. "Yeah, I heard you. How about saying, *please?*"

Energy crackles up my spine and shoots out of my eyes. The nerve of this tiny creature continues to dismay me.

With a lift of her chin, she holds my gaze. "I can just sit back here. That way you won't have to be disturbed by my nearness and your mean-mug attitude won't rub off on me."

I hang my head as I rub my jaw. "Fuck."

"And I don't like that word."

Closing my eyes, I pray for another lightning strike. This time with me square in the path. "Okay, let me see if I can dial my X-rated SEAL vocabulary back to PG for her highness. How about *freak*."

She huffs.

"What, is that too offensive for your delicate little ears? How about Foo-foo?"

"Oh my god. You're insufferable."

She's right. I am. "Get up here."

"You didn't say, please."

I climb into the truck, slam the door and hit the start button. "I'm not going to. We're at a standoff."

From the backseat, a tight voice says, "So be it."

I throw the truck into reverse and hit the gas too hard, causing the Ford to lurch.

Aria squeals. "You maniac!"

"You have no idea. Buckle up."

Her grumble is really close to my ear. Close enough that a warm breath brushes over my neck.

Alarm bells go off in cells I didn't know I had. The warning racing from my head to my toes and lighting up several very inconvenient places in between.

I refuse to look at her to see what she's doing. Shit, I shouldn't even breathe that soft, feminine scent. The salt on her skin, the hint of rain from last night.

When she squeezes through the gap between the front

seats, the hat full of Twinkies fly into my lap and her tit brushes my shoulder.

At least I think that's what it was.

It was warm and soft and round. Not like anything on my body.

Clenching the wheel, I ignore, ignore, ignore.

She wiggles her way up to the front, making a soft little sound in her throat as she drops into the passenger seat.

Why, god? *Why me?*

I tear open the wrapper on one of the snack cakes with my teeth, because I'm going to bite my tongue off otherwise.

Goddamnit. Why does she have to look like that?

Girl next door. Oversized eyes as sweet as melted chocolate. Cupid's-fucking-bow and all. The sleep tangles in her hair don't help one bit. If she was anyone else—a woman in one of the clubs I go to—she wouldn't stand a chance.

I'd be all over her.

But that's never gonna happen.

Boring a hole in the side of my head with her inspection, she asks, "What did you say?"

Fuck. *Did I say something out loud?*

I shove a creme-filled cake in my mouth, choking on the dry ass thing.

It goes down like sawdust rolled in peanut butter.

I drive and swallow audibly. Praying I don't need a medical intervention—which she might not be willing to provide—given the way I've treated her this morning.

My voice is a croak. "Where's that bottle of water?"

"The one you threw on the floor when you tossed your hat in the truck?"

"That one."

She hands me the bottle, and even twists the lid off for me.

Shit.

This girl.

"Thanks."

A tiny gasp beside me makes me loose my concentration and look at her.

Eyes wide, she clutches her throat. "Oh my god. Did that hurt?"

I shove another cake into my mouth to block my grin.

Those big brown eyes aren't tender now, they're full of spitfire. "Seriously, did it hurt you to say thanks?"

"Does it hurt you to be quiet?" I mutter around a mouthful of food. This time, I chase it with half of the bottle of water.

With a huff, she crosses her arms. "God, they must have given you two when they handed out assholes."

Water shoots out of my nose all over the steering wheel.

Chapter Eighteen

Aria

I'm suppressing a laugh and failing miserably at it when he turns to look at me. I give him a little shrug and head tilt. "Guess you got my point."

"That was one hundred percent your fault. You could have caused me to wreck."

When I start laughing, it's hard to breathe. Or talk.

"It's not my fault you're a jerk. And based on what I heard, you probably don't want to wreck another company truck. Beast is already punishing you by making you drive with me. Imagine what he'd do if you wrecked this one? He'd probably make us share a bedroom."

We both go a little wide-eyed.

Then Scout growls. It's a surly sound that makes the hairs on my nape stir. "I'd like to see him try. He might be big, but he's not that fucking mean."

He flashes an abrupt smile. Bright. Hot. And utterly destructive.

"Sorry if I upset your *widdle* ears with my profanity. Let me try again. He's not that foo-foo mean."

I shake my head, making a rough sound in my throat. It's not the ridiculous thing he says, it's the smile.

God. *This is just cruel.*

He's gorgeous. Everything about him. The scars, the tooth that's a little bit crooked, the dark scruffy beard along his jaw.

How can a stone-faced killer have a smile that knocks the wind out of your lungs?

He lays his head back against the headrest as he drives, casting looks at me with humor softening his expression. His eyes are bright, clear and pale as the morning sky in Iceland. His dark-blond—almost caramel—hair, just a little longer than military standard, is ruffled from his hat and sleeping. The beard is neatly trimmed though and is a dozen shades darker.

It's also much rougher to the fingertips.

"I can see your brother in you. But on you it's not just straight up smarts, you're cheeky."

I shrug and smile at him, with my fingers tingling from the memory of touching the thick forest of his hair, feeling the heat of his skin below. "I don't know, I just say it like I see it."

I just hope I don't slip up and say exactly how much I like what I see.

He takes a drink from the water bottle, looking at me over the top as he does.

When he's done, he licks his lips.

A shiver races down to my squeezed legs.

Oh, boy. That was hot.

He rasps, "Guess we have that much in common, at least."

I snatch one of the packages of Twinkies out of his hat, which is sitting on his lap. *Cream filled treat anyone?*

Choking, I try to play off the heat that sears across my cheeks. "That and we're going to have a sugar high this morning."

Desperate for a change of subject, I rip open the package with my fingers—not my teeth. "I'm starving. But I'm ready for something that doesn't come out of a vending machine."

His gaze flicks to mine. There's something hot in the way he's looking at me. When he glances at my lips, I get so overheated I wonder if I'm sitting on a bed of coals.

"Oh, you!" I toss the plastic wrapper at him. "Stop. I wasn't talking about sex."

"You sure?"

I'm the one trying to swallow now. "I'm sure. I gave up that particular sport."

As he drives he cuts his eyes to me a few more times. "That's the strangest thing a beautiful young woman has ever said to me."

I stop mid bite and clear my throat.

Beautiful?

"Not really strange. I mean..." I let my words die.

"You don't have to explain if you don't want to."

No, I should say something.

"I had a bad relationship."

After making a gruff sound he looks at the road again. This time his eyes are narrowed. "Haven't we all? It doesn't mean you have to stop having sex."

What?

That remark makes no sense from a man that doesn't like to be touched.

His phone picks a great time to ring. For both our sake, before we open a can of worms that neither of us want to deal with.

He lifts the sleek black device, slides his man-sized thumb that would feel really good in tight, wet places, and puts it to his ear.

Something in my brain sizzles. But it takes zero-point-one seconds to tell it's Griff on the call.

I cringe as my brother yells something really profane.

Scout doesn't utter a single word. He hits the End button and tosses the phone in the cup holder.

I stare at the silent device. "Wait! What? You hung up on him."

"Didn't have anything to say."

So matter-of-fact.

This time it's my turn to smile. "Wow, just like that?"

"That's me, buttercup. I don't waste my time on espousing hot air."

I turn to look at him. More closely this time.

Beautiful.

He called me beautiful. Actually said the word.

I drag my gaze away, but a small smile lingers on my lips. "I'll remember that."

A glow of pleasure builds in my chest, slides down to my tummy where it warms me. I might have given up on the horizontal olympics, but it sure feels nice to have a man like him give a compliment that's not hot air.

When his phone rings again, the ringtone is different.

His expression darkens this time as he picks up the call. After listening for a beat, he says, "Copy that. We're almost there."

My warm glow is chased away by concern.

"What's wrong?"

"The professor who has been advising us on the caves said you need to dive today. The rain we're going to get tonight will cut us off from one of the main entrances. It's going to be dangerous today, but tomorrow that area will be out of the question."

He pauses, looking troubled when he glances over. "Are you up for it after what happened last night?"

Even though something tenses inside of me I nod. This is why we're here. This is what we do. We rescue people from caves that are filled with water.

"Brundage and I can handle it."

I just know it's going to be ugly dealing with the man.

My nerves are humming by the time Scout and I pull up to a ranch house on an agave farm.

Scout catches my confusion. "This is our temporary headquarters."

The place looks like a normal house, minus all the SUVs and trucks parked outside. They don't look so normal. The blacked out windows, winches on oversized bumpers, snorkels for deep water, gear strapped on top, and insignias on the sides make it look like a CSI crime scene on steroids.

Brundage is outside. At his feet, are several bags of our dive gear. He stares at me through the windshield with open disdain.

"He always like that with you?"

It takes me a second to register Scout's question. "I just started working with Griff's company. Brundage is... slowly adjusting."

When I reach for my door handle, Scout clicks the lock button so I can't open it.

I whip my head around to look at him.

He's staring at Brundage, but he speaks to me. "You let me know if you want me to step in."

Gripping the door handle, I try to interpret his expression. "What do you mean?"

"Whatever you want that to mean."

With an aggressive jab, he hits the button again and my door unlocks.

Chapter Nineteen

SCOUT

There are a half-dozen people meeting around the dining table when we walk in. The entire group stops what they're doing to look at us as move through the foyer.

Immediately the mood hits me wrong.

This whole situation with a missing woman and flooded caves is jacked. But for some reason, having Aria by my side adds a new level of tension that abrades my nerves.

Justice, my teammate, smiles at us. It means nothing.

We could be on the deck of the Titanic getting ready for the cold plunge from hell and he'd be cheesing it up. The man is always smiling, no matter how FUBAR things are.

"Glad to see you two."

I grunt as I look over the room. Justice sits next to a man wearing a shirt and tie. Not only is the fifty-something man the sore thumb in a house full of operators, he seems out of place in Vandemora—the country has casual down to a science.

On the other side of the table, two Russian mercenaries wearing head-to-toe black clothing and the expressions of assassins sit shoulder to shoulder. Taking up too damned much space.

They tip their chins, then give Aria unguarded once over.

Fuckers.

I still haven't figured out exactly how their team got rolled into ours. But that's a problem for another time. After giving them a back-the-fuck-off glare, I cut my gaze to the last two.

Rounding out the side of the table closest to me are two guys who could be college students. They look like kinder-gartners compared to the over-muscled alphas I run with.

I hook a thumb to my right. "Everyone, this is Aria Kane. She's one of our rescue divers."

That tense vibe I sensed when I walked in intensifies.

It's very evident that the non-Agile people were expecting a man to be the second diver. First there's shock, then there's unease in their expressions. That pisses me right the hell off.

Beside me, Aria inhales quietly and stands taller.

I'm so angry on her behalf, I have to bite my tongue to keep from unloading. I mean, *what the fuck?*

"I presume you've met my teammate, Joe Brundage, already." Aria motions to the man standing off to my left. "My brother, Griffon Kane, the owner of DepthStrike, is getting medical treatment. But he will be joining us as soon as he can."

Her tone is stone-cold professional and confirms that this isn't the first time she's dealt with this bullshit.

More staring follows. More pissing me off.

The protector in me wants to put my arm around her, but that shit would just get her even more disrespect. It would probably also send me into shock, so there's that.

I keep my arm in my own space and motion Aria and her teammate toward the seats, but I remain standing. "Sit. The clock is ticking, we've got a case to solve."

Brundage throws himself into the dining room chair on the opposite side of the table. His glare is so hard on Aria, I consider reaching across and acquainting him with my fist.

Justice gives me a double take. "*Oookay.* Scout, did you have a chance to talk with Beast about the most recent developments with the weather?"

"Yes. I don't like it."

One damned bit. We're already under the gun with the mission, and to add the pressure of the rainfall and rising water in the caves makes me edgy as fuck.

Now I'm the one getting the uneasy looks. "The divers were in a plane crash last night. This feels rushed. We need to get into that cave, but we're going to do it the right way."

"They have to dive today," the man in the tie pronounces.

What the fuck? I focus my angry energy on him. "So I've heard. But I need to know exactly why."

Smoothing his tie, he puffs up his chest. "Aria and Mr. Brundage, I'm Professor Mason, one of the advisor Agile Security & Rescue hired. These gentlemen are with me."

The two younger men each lift a hand.

Kindergartners.

Probably follow him around like baby ducks, too.

The professor continues as he points. "That's Shane, he's completing a Ph.D. in geology. The other guy is our doctor from the university clinic, Doctor Morales."

"And?" My tone is rude and I could give a damn.

Professor Annoying looks down his nose. "We all agree that your divers have to dive today. As you know the weather is deteriorating."

Clenching my jaw, I consider all the ways I could twist that tie around his neck to extinguish the flow of air.

Justice clears his throat and I realize I'm staring at the man like he's got a target on his chest.

I snap, my tone overly loud. "You're not calling the shots here."

Aria startles in front of me, making me realize exactly how loud I was.

If I was a different man, I'd rest a hand on her shoulder to soothe her tension. But that's not who I am. Instead, I clench the back of Aria's chair as the professor turns red.

Behind me, the deep familiar voice of our team leader breaks the heavy silence. "Actually, Aria is making the call."

I crane my neck toward Beast who is assessing the room with the keen eye of an operator who has seen a lot of shit. "Aria's making the call on what?"

On silent feet, he moves into the room and crosses his burly arms over a chest that's almost as wide as mine. "I just spoke to Griffon Kane. Aria's the diver in charge of this operation."

Concern crawls up my spine. For a beat everyone is silent.

But Aria's reaction is easy for me to spot even from where I'm standing behind her. Her color blanches. Her mouth slides open, but she quickly closes it and tightens her shoulders.

Just in time for Brundage to shoot forward and slam both his hands on the table in front of her.

I'm already lunging for him when he snarls, "The fuck she is. I'm senior to her!"

Chapter Twenty

Aria

I leap back as Scout launches his six and a half feet of body in front of me. *Holy what?*

It happens fast—air choosing across my face, tangling my hair around me. The scuffle of feet is loud in the small dining room. Big arms slice space around me. It's like being caught in a mosh pit only this isn't for fun.

Snarls and a tidal wave of testosterone consume the entire dining room.

When I snap back to my senses, Brundage's neck is clutched in Scout's hand. There are two men in black wrangling my coworker's arms behind his back. Everyone's breathing hard.

On my side of the table, things are much calmer. Scout's teammate has my arm, guiding me away from the fray as he chuckles. "That went south fast."

I try to look over my shoulder, but he blocks my view with his height as he whisks me through the living room, into the kitchen, and out the back door.

I'm a little winded and a lot shocked. "You're not kidding, that was crazy."

"Let's get some fresh air while they take care of that situation."

Wow. *Just wow.* I wheeze when I speak. "Scout is an animal. I mean I knew he was. I saw him last night, but this was like watching a snake strike."

"Yeah, he's like that. Silent, but very deadly."

Inside my head there's a raving crazy woman trying to make sense of this strange reality that I've fallen into.

I blow out a breath and take a few unsteady steps across the patio. Justice stands nearby, his compassionate gaze following me. "You want to talk about that?"

Rubbing my arms, I shiver. "My coworker's reaction was alarming. But truthfully, finding out my brother wants me to be the team leader is a shock to me as well."

"You've worked with them for a while?"

My legs are shaky, so I take a seat in one of the patio chairs. "On a few dives. I just joined my brother's company a few months ago."

Justice looks at me for a beat as he rubs along his jaw. He's usually smiling, but not now. "Scout's wired tight today."

"Camile said he always is."

"True that." He grins. "But this was extra special."

My heart thumps a little harder. I've never had a man go caveman for me. It was equal parts alarming and thrilling.

Still clutching my chest, I fight to get my racing heart under control. "He was kind of protective, huh?"

Justice looks away, but his grin deepens. "Kind of, sweetheart, that man was ready to kill your teammate for disrespecting you."

For me.

I laugh harshly. "Is it sick that I really like that?"

Justice pulls out a chair and sits down. He doesn't say anything, but there's a look in his eyes. A humorous knowing.

It drives my curiosity crazy. "What are you thinking?"

"I'm not going to ruin the fun."

I widen my eyes and throw up my hands. "How can you call this fun? Things are in chaos. Everything!"

As he leans back, he turns thoughtful. "I'm beginning to realize that's when it happens."

Oh my god.

"Can you please not be cryptic right now? I was in a plane crash. Someone tried to kidnap me. I had to stop a man from running Scout over by sacrificing one of your trucks." I bury my face in my hands and peek at him between my fingers. "I got left behind at the airport. I had to break into a building that got hit by lightning. There was a fire. I tried to put it out, but failed. And then your coworker collapsed and I had to lie next to him all night long because I was afraid he wasn't breathing—"

He hinges forward, all humor gone "You did *what?*"

Exhaling tiredly, I drop my hands and lean back in the chair. After rubbing my face too hard, I groan. "Even telling you all of that is tiring. It sounds like I've been starring in an action movie gone wrong."

"No, back up. What was that last part?"

I frown at him. "The lightning and the fire?"

His eyes are dancing as he leans close. "No, the part

about you laying next to Scout all night long. Does he know that?"

"Um. Yes, why?"

Justice's brows rock up. There's not an ounce of humor behind his dark brown eyes. "And he didn't freak?"

"Oh yeah, he freaked. We talked it out."

He's staring at me so hard, a tingle forms at my nape. "What? Please, you're making me really nervous."

"I'll be back."

He stands up and walks away without looking back.

Chapter Twenty One

SCOUT

Still breathing hard, I take off through the house. "Where is she?"

Justice, who just came through the door, moves through the kitchen until he's planted in front of me. He looks me over, head to toe and back again.

Is he mute?

"Where. Is. She?"

"Out on the patio." He glances toward the dining room. "You okay?"

"I'm fucking fine, but I'll be better when I see—"

He grins. "Take a breath, brother. There are no threats to her out there. You need to take it easy."

"Fuck easy."

He tilts his head, dark gaze boring into me. "I want you to do me a favor."

"I want *you* to do *me* a favor. Get. Out. Of. My. Way."

"I want you to let her in."

The line between my brows grows tight. "The hell are you talking about?"

"You'll know."

He steps aside, moving around me and leaving me staring at the space where he was standing.

Let her in.

No. He's not talking about that.

No fucking way.

I give myself a mental shake and stalk through the laundry room-slash-mudroom and out the back door.

When I shove the door open, my stomach falls. It's the relief on her face when she sees me that almost makes me trip over my own feet.

She rises, keeping her gaze locked on me as she wipes her palms on her pants legs.

Lips rolled in between her teeth, she takes a dozen steps and closes the distance between us. When she's toe-to-toe with me, she tilts her pretty face up.

Ten beats of my chugging heart pass.

"Thank you for defending me."

Swallow. Swallow. Breathe.

"Of course I defended you."

Her gaze softens as she glances at my lips.

No. Fucking hell. Don't look at me like that.

I'm not. I can't.

I'll never be the man that deserves for her to look at me like that.

With my chest constricted, I step back. Anger seeps into my tone. "He's not diving with you."

When I turn and walk away, her feet tap quickly on the patio stones behind me.

There's a sharp tug on my shirt sleeve. "Scout! You can't

pull the plug on the mission."

Against my better judgment, I turn around to look down at her. She's fisting my shirt. But she is not touching my skin.

The fire in her eyes sets something inside me ablaze. A dangerous fuel that has no place in my life.

With color brightening her cheeks, she inhales quickly. "I'm here to do a job. That woman your team is looking for could be dying in that cave right now. She needs us to set personal bullshit aside. You heard the professor. We have to dive today or the chance to explore that chamber is gone."

"I know." My voice is rough as fuck.

Rife with confusion, my brain tries to lock onto anything that makes sense.

Worry tugs her brows together as she searches my face. "Griff is out for who knows how long. Brundage has to dive with me."

Tension spreads through my body at lightning speed until I'm wound like a coil. "No. He won't be getting into the water with you. I don't trust your life to him."

Shock echoes through her gaze. "But..."

"I'm taking his place."

Chapter Twenty Two

Aria

You could knock me over with a feather right now.

A hundred reasons why this is not happening come to mind—Scout is not replacing Brundage.

"That's not possible. Cave diving is incredibly dangerous. You can't just..."

Scout looks at me like I've slapped him and called him a pansy.

"I was a United States Navy SEAL for more than a decade, Aria." His angular jaw hardens. "I trained in the harshest underwater environments in the world. Including caves. I've been in more dangerous diving environments than that asshole ever has."

I can't suppress a shiver that races down my arms, turning my fingertips cold.

SEALs are competent divers.

I've been on rescues with them before. But...

With fear crawling up my throat, I fist his shirt sleeve more tightly. "This situation is not good, the cave could be incredibly dangerous. I don't want anything to happen to you."

His reply is instant. "Then we will make a good team."

The gravity of that remark hits hard.

Us.

We.

Team.

The electric current he threw into the air with that remark lands between us.

I always feel concerned for any other person I dive with. This is totally different.

Unexplainable. Confounding. Alarming.

"Scout. I don't know..."

"I'm your only option. That man is not going anywhere with you."

Well.

For a long beat, I stare as weird sensations fill my body. Rushing through my blood, cross-wired signals.

I want to scream. I want to throw myself into his arms. I want to yell at the Universe demanding to know what the heck is happening right now.

Rubbing my forehead, I look away. God, I need a shower and some real food. I'm not thinking clearly.

His voice rumbles around me, vibrating my over-sensitized nerve endings. "The question is, are you fit to dive today, Aria?"

Dragging my attention back to him, I let go of his shirt. "Sorry, what did you say?"

Scout is wearing an uncompromising expression. He's

erected a wall of alpha control that a torpedo couldn't penetrate.

"You're not diving until you have a physical. The plane crash could have given you a mild concussion."

"I'm fine, I don't have a headache. Well, I kind of do, but that's just from tension."

He shifts, looming over me, making me realize just how small I am compared to him. Scout could probably toss me over his shoulder and run a marathon.

My body finds this alarmingly attractive, which baffles me.

Gruffly, he says, "I'm not compromising on this. The doctor in there that looks like he's young enough to be my son is going to give you a physical to make sure you're safe to dive."

I do a double take. "You have a son?"

"No. I was being sarcastic." His eyes rove over me as they glitter with frustration. "He's young. Just like you."

I'm not sure what his point is. "So what? I'm younger than you."

"I was in the Teams before you were even in middle school."

Incredulous, I frown at him. "That's not true."

"Wanna bet me?" He lifts a brow.

"How old are you?"

Those icy eyes glitter beneath the brim of his hat. "Old enough to know better."

Chapter Twenty Three

SCOUT

I watch something dawn in her eyes. She wasn't tracking, but now she knows exactly what I'm talking about.

Our age gap. The fact that this *is* sexual tension between us. And I'm ten years older than her.

Enough age difference to ignite a war with her brother.

Hell, a war inside myself. I don't have sex with girls. They can't take what I want.

Sexual tension or not, there's a whole assload of reasons I will not be acting on any crazy impulses.

Her brother.

My job.

The fucked up past and future that is Memphis 'Scout' Silas. In other words, my goddamned life.

But a trembling breath leaves her lungs and brushes over my skin like a wind signaling danger.

Within seconds the ache inside me turns into a roaring hurricane gale.

My mouth goes dry, my tongue swipes my lip.

Fuck. "Aria," I warn in a gruff tone. As if she knows that I'm one second from doing something bad.

The storm grows and grows inside me until my abs are clenched and my muscles are burning. Heavy lust pulses through me, twists my bones, pretzeling my will. Making me crazier than I've ever felt in my life.

"I'm twenty one. I'm not a kid."

Fisting my hands next to my thighs, I fight the urge to punch myself in the dick.

"Close enough."

"That's a lot like them thinking I can't dive well because I'm a woman."

"This is nothing like that," I rasp, my hackles rising. But fuck if I can tear my gaze off her mouth.

Kissing Aria would be a disaster.

But, god bless whoever made her…

Those pretty brown eyes.

The way she gives me hell. The sweet line of her neck.

The sweeter smell of her skin. Curves for days packed in a strong little package.

But that's not it.

That would be so damned simple. I could just jerk off or solve this problem when I get back stateside with some rando brown-eyed brunette.

But the evil asshole called logic in my head laughs at me. She's so much more than a fuck.

So goddamned much more than a tight, wet pussy and a few hours of distraction.

Skating her tongue over her bottom lips, she sighs. "You feel it, don't you?"

"No." Yes. Fuck, yes.

It's as if my bone marrow is jonesing for a hit of her.

The long kind. Days. Weeks. Months.

And the only damned solution is to drown myself in her nectar.

Fucking mother fucking hell.

Forcing myself to swallow, I stare at the one thing that could bring me down.

Her.

Not a bullet, not burning alive, not all the chaos and nightmare of being on active duty for all those years didn't destroy me.

But this...

Is not happening.

Aria is not happening. For the love of all sanity. I am not kissing a woman that I can't and won't touch.

I *never* kiss women.

Rule number one in the Scout Silas playbook: no kissing because kissing leads to touching.

Rule two: no touching with hands or mouth.

Rule three: Orgasms will happen.

Supposedly, I can fuck like a goddamned pornstar according to the women I've had. They didn't complain about any of my demands or my rules.

It's simply a mutual release. Contractual in a way.

Nothing more.

That's how sex clubs work. At least the ones I belong to.

The kind of place that Aria would never step foot inside.

She'd be horrified.

Worst of all, the thought of seeing her look at me with disgust in her eyes would break me.

I'm never going to see that expression on her face

because she's never going to find out about my stupid fucking hangups.

I step back a few paces from her and train my eyes on a spot beyond her shoulder because I'm not man enough to look into her eyes any longer.

"I'll go get Griff's gear set up. You find the doc and get that clearance. Eat something for fuck sake." I warn, "You try to get out of it, I'll know."

Aria doesn't move.

Hands fisted on the curve of her hips, she stares at me. My skin feels every second of her narrow-eyed scrutiny.

"What just happened, Scout?"

More than you'll ever know.

An admission of how fucked up I am. How my life will never be the pretty happy-ever-after that my teammates have found.

The realization that I'll be seventy-five—god willing my dick still gets hard—and fixing my carnal needs with a woman's body that will never know or care to know my name, or know anything about me beyond the fact that I've got a big cock and know how to use it.

Damned depressing.

Yeah. That's my life.

Forcing my jaw to relax before the bone breaks, I slice my angry gaze to hers. "You don't want to know."

She drops her hands and strides to me, hair swaying, mouth set in a determined line. "Why are you trying to tell me what to think?"

What the hell? I give her a scowl as I clench my teeth. "I'm not."

"You've done that multiple times."

This woman...I suck in air and blow out a rough sound. "Are you always so challenging?"

Electric silence grows between, thickening the humid Vandemora morning air.

"Did you hear me?"

"Yeah, King Scout, ruler of the world, he who espouses his reasoning upon all. He whose word is the last word."

What. The. Hell?

Throat tight, I stare at her in disbelief. "Seriously? You're attacking me right now?"

"Challenging. That's the word you used. And it doesn't take a doctorate to know that you're not used to it and it bothers you."

"Are you like this with everyone? If you are, now I know why your brother is so hard to get along with."

She blinks and snaps back with fire. "That was rude!"

"It's the truth. You and your brother must have the same genetic predisposition for being—"

She fills the blank. "Spirited."

I snort.

Her frown deepens and her voice drops low, and husky. "You can't survive in the world I walk around in without backbone."

Something about that remark unravels part of my anger.

She's right. If she deals with dickheads like Brundage all the time...fuck.

"I get it. But you seem to be determined to push all my damned buttons. All the damned time."

"I am determined."

I pull my hat off, scratch my head, and slam the ball cap back on. "Oh great. What did I do to deserve this honor?"

After looking me over, she seems to have decided something. "You're a puzzle and I'm determined to figure out the pieces. Besides, I think you need a friend."

Ha. Friend?

No. Double hell no.

This is not good. I've obviously stepped in it this time getting tangled up with her and need to figure out a way to backtrack fucking pronto. "Get your ass inside the house."

She gives me one final inspection and walks past me. When she reaches the back door of the house, she looks back at me, her dark brown hair sliding along her shoulders.

"You don't get to tell me what to do, King Scout." Lifting her chin, she hides all of the other emotions except determination. "I'm doing this because I'm here for a job. And don't think this conversation is over. I'm not dropping it. So use this time to figure out how you're going to drop the BS and tell me what just happened. We've saved each other's lives. How many people can say that?"

I don't reply.

Voice low and coarse, she says, "The least we can do is be honest with each other."

When the door slams behind her, I unglue my feet and go after her.

Chapter Twenty Four

Aria

Oh my freaking goodness.

Breathe. Walk. Keep moving.

Legs shaking, heart skipping, I step into the house and fall back against the washing machine.

I don't know what is happening to me. I'm hot. I'm cold. I'm pissed, I'm alarmed. I'm...disoriented.

The total effect is not a good feeling. If the doctor examined me right now, he'd cancel the dive. No way he'd let a crazy person suit up and go into a cave under fifty feet of water.

I need to get myself under control.

When the door flies open, I close my eyes and groan silently. In the next heartbeat Scout's in front of me.

Too close.

Warm, with the scent of masculinity and rain lingering on him.

But all he does is breathe heavily. At me.

This fires up my attitude.

"It's kind of small in here for a grumpy King and an irritated peasant."

He looks up at the ceiling of laundry room and mutters, "Fuck."

"Is that the only word you got? Because if you remember..."

When he lowers his gaze to mine, his pale blue eyes are more alive than I've ever seen them.

My complaint is instantly stolen.

Along with my ability to draw in a breath.

When he reaches up and touches my cheek with the back of his knuckles, my breath returns in a rush and my sanity shoots out of the top of my head like a bottle rocket.

His fingers brush lower, down my neck.

Time freezes. His touch is so shocking that every single one of my muscles, tiny to large, are locked up. As if by moving even the smallest amount, I might shatter whatever is happening.

Finally, a quiver moves through me.

My toes curl in my boots.

The way his gaze is locked on his hand makes my throat sting with emotion.

I've never felt a more charged moment in my life.

Heat curls off his fingers, sinking deep into my hungry skin—so hungry for his hand, it's a kind of desperation.

Raspy, he speaks in a low tone. "I can't believe you."

What? "Me?"

"Yeah, you, Aria *Kane*." He emphasizes the last word.

In the blink of an eye, the connection is gone. The energy around him shifts, turning cool.

All the little lines on his face tense as his eyes narrow. His hand snaps away from my neck, like he's touched a hot stove burner.

But it's too late. It's been done. I'm trembling from it.

He's going to bolt—I know it in my heart. He's going to lock down and leave. It's Scout's M.O. and I'm beginning to know the plays before they happen.

This time I know the effect of his withdrawal is going to hit me even harder. I brace myself for the wake of stinging cold.

Ten heartbeats pass as I wait.

But when he moves, it's not to leave. Both of his arms rise up and he cages me in by resting his forearms on the cabinet above the washing machine.

Whoa. Hello curveball.

I don't know what's about to happen right now, but my body is one hundred percent onboard with him moving closer. Pressing all of his tall, muscled frame into me.

But he doesn't. He keeps his distance, except for moving his mouth closer to my ear. And he says nothing. Every one of his exhales stir my hair.

It's agonizing. Yet I don't ever want him to move.

The function of my lungs reduces to dizzying pants. Each of my heartbeats makes my knees weaker. My hands curl as I fight to keep from touching him.

I need to feel his skin like I need air.

In a low, rough voice, he slays the silence. "You're making me fucking crazy, Aria. After we dive today, we're going to put an end to this bullshit, whatever it is."

Mouth going instantly dry, I suffer through a series of palpitations.

"Okay," I lamely reply in a choked voice.

Okay?

Okay? Gah! Couldn't I even ask what he means? Is he promising a good end, or a bad end?

I'm seriously confused right now. Not enough oxygen is getting to my brain. Or maybe my vagina is using it all up.

God knows it's been getting a workout with all the pulsing going on below my belt.

I'll be a kegel olympian after this. Not to mention the organ in my chest. Anticipation isn't for the faint of heart.

From somewhere on the other side of his body, in another part of the house, I hear my name being called. "Aria!"

The sound is so surprising and I'm so keyed up, I startle, bumping my head on his arm, thrusting my hips forward, knocking against Scout's erection.

His hard, monstrosity of an erection, that is so big it has to be a registered weapon.

Gulp.

Scout's boss continues talking from somewhere in the house. "Aria, your brother's on the phone and needs to talk to you!"

Oh my god!

I whisper hiss, "I cannot talk right now. I'm not even sure my legs will work."

The other man bellows, "Aria!"

Before I realize what's happening, Scout's palm is wrapped around the side of my throat in a firm, but gentle grip. The heat from that hand scorches my skin, making me shiver.

His voice drops to a growl. "Fuck Griff, he can wait."

Whoa, baby. The hand on the throat thing is seriously hot.

The way he's touching me is so commanding, so freaking taboo-feeling that I'm in serious danger of losing control of my actions. It's a fight to keep my hands down.

Scout's burning gaze slides across my features. His hard expression is as fierce as any Viking warrior. I'm so gone when this man looks at me.

I rasp out the only thing I can put together. "I need to go..."

All of my words are so shaky, you'd think the damned washing machine behind me was on the spin cycle.

Scout's eyes burn hotter as if my distress is gasoline. "What's wrong, little one. Are you scared now?"

Yes. Very.

I'm scared that I'm not afraid of him. I'm scared of the violent reaction in my womb. I'm scared that I can even be attracted after what happened.

I swallow and find my voice. "No. Let go."

He laughs darkly.

The pressure of his hand falls away from my neck, making my skin flash cold, but his piercing crystal eyes stay locked on my lips.

Unblinking he stares.

I don't know Scout well, but it feels like the armor is down and what's behind it might be more than I can handle...

He's big.

He's clearly dominant.

And I'm in no way interested in being a victim of a man's abuse again.

But even if my brain is screaming for me to run, my body has other plans.

Hot, dirty, plans that involve him.

I feel whatever this man is, from the icy slice of his

108

razor-sharp edge, down to the pit of my stomach where some carnal need decides his dominance is just fine.

God. Run, Aria run. Before you make another mistake. You might not survive this one.

A grumble from behind Scout, blocked from my view by his shoulders, has my eyes going wide. I shrink down, not wanting anyone to see the mess I am.

His boss makes an annoyed sound. "Oh you two. Christ, like two teenagers, can't you wait—"

Scout's body revs up. Vibrating with anger, hulking over me protectively, he turns to snarl at his boss. "Get. Fucking. Lost."

Chapter Twenty Five

SCOUT

What's happening right here, right now is between us. As fucked up as it is, it's between Aria and me. Not my fucking nosy ass team leader. Or anybody else for that fucking matter.

Hand tingling from her skin, cock throbbing, brain in the spin cycle, I glare at Beast.

He looks me over good. Seeing something that concerns him if the tightening of his brows is what I think it is.

Fuck his attempt to check me.

I don't need to be checked.

My shit is in order. I hate chaos. Every moment of every day, I do my damndest to control it.

Unblinking, I let him see just how fucking serious I am 'bout him getting lost.

Even though I know in the pit of my twisted gut this is

dangerous madness. Dancing with the devil that has my blackened soul.

Beast blinks first. Holds up his palm stop-sign-style. "Easy, brother. She needs to take this call."

I grate out a reply as I put my gaze back on Aria, where it should have been all along. "In a damned minute."

He says, "We're short on time."

Something I know well, but can't seem to get a handle on this god blessed situation. The proverbial tires have been coming off the bus since the dive team's plane landed last night. When Aria crashed into my life in the most literal sense of the word.

Fucking hell.

I grit my teeth and count to one because counting to ten wouldn't do a damn bit of good. "We're on it. But until you walk away, that's not happening."

In my peripheral vision, I watch Beast shake his head as he presses the phone to his thigh. "Aria, my cell's going to be on the kitchen counter. Griffon needs to talk to you about your equipment."

From beneath my barricading arms, she makes a sound that's close to a word, but not exactly.

Beast finally gets a clue and gets his damned feet moving.

Son of a bitch. This disaster scene between Aria and me is partly his fault for forcing me to drive back with her. I can't be alone with the woman.

She's off-limits, she's too young.

She's...

Impossible.

When I step back, I adjust my cock because if I don't the head is going to stick out of the waistband of my tactical pants.

Balls. I'm hard as a baseball bat.

As I rearrange, I don't even bother to hide what she's already felt.

I keep my angry gaze locked on her face as I lay the attitude on heavy. "Yep, this is me, babe. One hundred percent the man you do not want to fuck around with."

Her throat works as she swallows. But she's so silent that I can practically hear her pulse surging.

Every little thing about her makes my blood sing.

Those doe eyes are wide enough for me to fall into and never be able to climb out.

Beautiful. *Heart stopping beautiful.*

And scared out of her mind.

Her flingers rise up to her throat and touch the place where my hand was wrapped around her neck as her cheeks go pale and her chest movement gets erratic.

That's when I remember... Aria doesn't like to be touched.

Goddammit. I groan and curse myself silently. She doesn't like to be touched and I wrapped my hand around her throat like she's a fucking sub and I'm about do dominate her.

God. *What have I done?*

I scrub my hand roughly over my eyes and hope that when I open them I find out I've been on an acid trip.

But it's not a drug induced vision and she's still hemmed in by me, looking like she's on the verge of an emotional cataclysm.

I'm such an asshole. Selfish bastard. Crazed motherfucker.

"I'm sorry I touched you. It won't happen again. I'm going outside. You go find that damned doctor, and if he clears you, we're mobilizing the team. And eat something other than junk food, for god's sake."

As I'm walking through the house, her voice cuts through the noise in my head as she takes the call.

"Hey Griff, yeah. I'm fine. My phone is lost somewhere in my gear. Everything's happening fast. Listen, Scout's going to replace Brundage and—"

Aria's voice abruptly dies. I halt mid-stride and turn to look at her. She's pinching the bridge of her nose, looking at the floor with the phone pressed to her ear.

Goddammit. The sight of her, rumpled clothes, tired eyes, tangled hair, dealing with her brother's bullshit attitude sets me off.

When I stride up to her, she gives me a weak version of a back-off glance. I hold out my hand as Griff yells so loud on the other end of the line that there's no need for putting him on speaker phone.

Such is Griffon Kane.

One volume. One speed. Full fucking blast.

"Griff, hey..." Aria raises her voice as she closes her eyes, locking me out.

More yelling from Griffon.

She raises her voice higher. "Griff, if you'll just—"

I grab the phone from her hand. Her eyes flare in alarm and she tries to reach for it, but I'm too tall.

He's still going on. And on. And fucking on.

Out of patience, I yell into the microphone. "Kane. Shut your damned mouth!"

For about four seconds he has to regroup and I can picture his head rupturing. Then he spits fire. "You! What the?! Why are *you* close enough to my sister to interrupt her phone call?"

"Protecting her."

Two hard words full of a thousand meanings.

He's silent for a flat second. Voice going low and dangerous, he enunciates his next words carefully. "What does that mean?"

It means I'm about to throw down the gauntlet.

I'm about to own this.

About to cross a line that can't be uncrossed.

"Exactly what I said. I'm protecting Aria," I reply, matching his tone as I lock eyes with the woman that's started a war. "You're done talking to her like that and Brundage has been fired as far as I'm concerned. That ego-driven idiot will never get in the water with her again. And if I have my way he won't ever be in the same room she's in."

Who knows what's going to happen after the call, but one thing is certain: Griffon Kane will want my head on a stake.

Chapter Twenty Six

Aria

Scout passes me the phone and leaves.

Just walks out. Talk about a mic drop...

Wow.

Jesus. The man knows how to make a mess of things. And I'm not just talking about what's going on inside of me.

It takes a few breaths before I can get my vocal cords working again.

Even then, I try to speak, but I only croak. "Griff, you needed to tell me something about the equipment?"

I've never heard the exact tone that my brother uses as he proceeds to remind me about some gear he packed. He's eerily cold. Voice almost monotone, every word a razor's edge of precision.

But, I'm well aware that the storms that come in quiet are sometimes the most devastating.

When he's done, he hangs up without saying goodbye.

I've known my brother for twenty-one years and of those, I remember thousands of phone calls with him. Many of them scolding me about something any brother would do, just because they want to be a pain. But never can I remember him hanging up on me without some kind of closing remark.

And since he's been a Ranger, it's always been. *"Watch your six, baby sis."*

By the time I disconnect, I'm so rattled that I pocket the phone instead of returning it to Beast.

"You gonna give my phone back?"

I blink and realize I've been staring blankly at a wall and I have no idea how much time has passed. "God, I'm sorry. Here you go."

"You okay?"

When I shove my hand in my tangled hair, he steps closer.

"If you want me to pull Scout off the case, I will. Justice is fully capable of diving with you too. He is a former SEAL also, and he's fully certified for cave diving. I am too, but I've got a meeting that I really need to go to. And trust me, I'd much rather be diving than meeting with the feds."

I'm obviously not thinking clearly because my reply makes no sense given the context of the last thirty minutes.

"No, Scout wants to dive."

He studies me. "But are you good with putting your life in his hands?"

"I already have." I push my hair back and give my head a small shake. "He has done nothing but look out for me since he arrived at the airport last night. Things are just tense... for obvious reasons with Griff."

Resting a hand on the counter, the SEAL considers

something before he replies. "Copy that. But I want you to remember you're the diver in charge."

"Right, well then, Scout is my second diver. Is the doctor still here? King Scout is demanding I get a physical before we go."

"King Scout?" It's said with a chuckle as Beast's brows rise up. "I'll have to remember that one. Has he heard you call him that?"

"Yep."

Beast flashes a grin and looks away. "Alright then. The doctor and the professor are in the office. First door on the right, down that hall."

Ten minutes later, I'm still inside my head.

"You're cleared to dive. Just remember if you start to feel off—"

"I know the drill, I don't have a death wish," I reply numbly to the ridiculously young doctor who has just given me a neurological exam, listened to my heart, and made me do fifty jumping jacks while he stared at my boobs.

Real fun.

Almost as much fun as twenty minutes later when I climb into the truck with Scout, Justice and a dark-eyed man that I'm pretty sure is an assassin and eats barbed wire for breakfast.

It's a real party if you're into brooding operators.

Which I'm not.

Only my stupid ovaries are.

Not all alpha SEALs. Just one.

The one who pinned me in with his gigantic arms, and overly warm body. The one who made my skin go electric from the way his exhales skimmed over my neck. The man that destroyed me with his hand on my throat in a possessive grip.

And it was only around my neck. But I could feel it *everywhere.*

Lord, it's hot in here.

Shifting in my seat, I rub my hand over the place where his fingers curled commandingly around my throat.

I've never been touched by a man like that.

Turning my face toward the flow of air coming in the window, I close my eyes. It's a dangerous thing to do.

The overload of hormones in my body is demanding a fantasy. Guess who's the star?

"Aria."

I jump at my name and open my eyes to find Scout flicking his gaze to me in the rearview as he drives too fast.

My face is hot, my legs squeezed, my fingers still clutched around my neck. In other words, guilty looking as hell.

Voice deep and rough, Scout demanded, "Did you hear me?"

"No," I squeak.

God, that was pathetic.

Justice swings his head my way and smirks.

When I punch him in the arm he chuckles.

Dropping my hand to my leg, where I clench my thigh, I put on a neutral façade and look Scout's reflection dead in the eye. "What did you say?"

Chapter Twenty Seven

SCOUT

Fuck if I know.

I focus on the road, clenching the wheel and remind myself to get castrated.

Rory laughs darkly as he looks over at me from the passenger seat where he's taking up too damned much room. "What *did* you say?"

"Nothing."

Not a goddamn thing.

Jesus. The look on Aria's face! The way her hand was around her own throat where I was touching her...

Biting the inside of my cheek, I focus on keeping the truck between the edges of the road, out of the rain-swollen ditches.

It took a damned half hour for my erection to go down and seeing her like that made the bastard start throbbing again.

I glance at the screen on the dash. Focusing on the map for a fraction of a second. Thank god we're less than one minute away from our destination according to the GPS.

Rory picks this time to stick his crooked nose into my business. "I heard something and it sounded like—"

Delivered with a glare, I growl, "Shut it, Rory."

When our turn appears, I hit the gas to speed up when I should be slowing down. I've got to get the hell out of this truck.

The sooner this job is over the better.

Luckily, when we roll onto the secondary road near the cave entrance it's a shit show that requires my full attention.

The feds are already on site. Trucks and SUVs are stuffed into the ditch on both sides of the road. People in tactical gear are milling around. A makeshift operational base has been set up.

"No cops as expected." Rory half grins. "Glad we're not dealing with Chief Willometa any more."

"Crooked bastard," I mutter. "I just hope the feds are on the up and up now that they're all up in our business."

He studies the scene through the windshield, quiet and calculating. "You think they're not?"

"I'm just a suspicious bastard. I like all the i's dotted and t's crossed and I don't know who all the players are now. I do think Agent Torres is one of the good guys."

"He's still a fed."

Rory casts a glance my way, and I wonder again why a team of former Russian military guys are in Vandemora. But I won't fault their help. They were key in helping us deal with Marianna's trouble and cracking the illegal operations involving the local police chief wide open.

Without another word, the stone-faced bastard exits the truck and heads to the rear to start unloading gear.

I make the mistake of glancing in the rear view mirror. "I'm coming around to open your door."

Aria, who has been tensely quiet since our eyes met in the mirror, looks royally displeased. "Why?"

"Because that's what men do."

She grumbles and sighs, "Oh, brother. King Scout and his rules..."

But she waits on me, and that makes me feel strangely happy. Happier than it should.

I've always worked to be a gentleman, not that I had a role model. Exact opposite actually, but there were enough men around to show me how a woman should be treated.

When I swing the rear passenger door open, Aria's eyes are set, her jaw is tight. There's a strength in her spine.

She looks at me pointedly. "Let's get to work."

Sexy AF. I like her in this mode.

Hell, I like her in *every* mode.

I keep my hands very far away from her, but I don't let her out of the truck. Instead, I lean my forearm on the top edge of the door. "Are you sure you're up for this?"

She nods, glances beyond me. "Yes. I'm sorry for all the drama. Are you ready?"

"I'm always ready."

She suppresses a small grin. "Alright King. Let's get this done."

"Memphis," I say before I can understand why it feels important to tell her this.

She pauses. Thinks. "Is that where you're from?"

I shove my hands into my front pockets. Why does my face feel like I got too close to a damned campfire?

A sound rumbles through my chest and I think about changing the subject. "No. That's my name."

This time when she raises her gaze to mine, it's softer. "I like it. Memphis. That's nice"

"Well, it wasn't an easy name as a kid. Appreciate having a nickname."

"People are mean. It wasn't your fault." She slides out of the truck and stands before me. Close but not touching. "Besides, Memphis is a good name, a strong name."

The compliment doesn't escape me. Why is this woman so damned nice to me?

I realize I'm frowning extra hard, and that says something. This particular expression feels different.

She's still looking at me curiously. "How did you get that nickname?"

This is not the time to be standing around talking, and here I am again. *Shit. We've got work to do, and here I am telling her my story.*

I step back. "It was a map thing. I'm good with maps, always have been. It was kind of an obsession to find my way in the woods when I didn't want to be in my screwed up home."

Those deep brown eyes melt. She rolls her lips inward. Holding something back.

A solid concrete lump lands at the base of my throat.

The energy between us changes, and not in a good way.

I'm equipped for conflict, not...

Tenderness.

"You were right about us." I chew the inside of my own mouth as I look away. "We do owe each other the truth since we are about to go into a cave where we could die."

As if she knows I'm not done, or she's baiting me to continue, she just watches me with her brows lifted and drawn together. Curious concern.

But when I try to speak I can't.

I'm not able to admit to her what happened on the patio or in the laundry room. Because I'm not ready to hate myself any more than I already do.

Instead, I offer an apology. "I've probably handled things wrong."

Fuck. That wasn't an apology. It was an admission of guilt. A pathetic one at that.

She stops me by lifting a delicate hand. It hovers in the air, but doesn't touch. "You handled things the way you do. I handle things the way I do. We're not the same person."

Rory plows around the corner of the truck, stopping to drop his hands on his hips. "Guys, we might have a situation."

Jesus Christ. I clench my hands inside my pockets "What now?"

He's looking across the opening at a cluster of men standing by a truck. "Look what's on the ground over there."

I'm already in motion.

Chapter Twenty Eight

Aria

Once again Scout left so abruptly, my head is almost spinning.

Rory pushes a duffel bag into my hands. "Come on. He can deal with that. We can go down to the cave entrance and get set up."

"What's wrong?"

Rory's unreadable exterior is harder than usual. "Don't worry about that. Scout and Justice can deal with it. You just need to go over your dive gear."

I blow out a breath, fist my hair in my hand, and follow him around the back of the truck. "You're right."

It's not my job to worry about whatever political mess is swirling around the missing woman's case. I'm here for one job. To dive.

Rory and I spend the next few minutes going over

everything and deciding what gear needs to go down to the cave.

I zip up one of the bags and stand from where I was crouching. "Looks good. I think that's all we need."

"I'll come back for the tanks." He hefts the largest pack onto his shoulder. "Someone set up a staging area over by the cave for you. There's a canopy and a place to change into your wetsuit. Can you manage that small bag?"

I hold up the small duffel that's got my mask and fins. "This is nothing."

"If you want, I can carry that too."

I laugh and give him a glare. "I'm small. I'm not weak."

"Never said you are. You must be strong to deal with Scout."

The man isn't joking. Scout's a tough case.

I follow Rory, carefully watching the muddy ground as I walk, to make sure I don't fall. It's a treacherous climb down to the staging area. Water is rushing down the hillside into a muddy pond that's already at capacity.

"Here let me help." Rory extends a hand and steadies me as I try to navigate a steep section. "This trail is going to be filled with water soon."

Nerves tingle along my spine as I look around. "This is a sketchy situation."

The entrance to the cave sits at the bottom of a muddy incline. The whole area is bowl-shaped so all water pours down toward the cave.

I wish Griff was here.

Rory must pick up on my unease. "You're the one that makes the call. If you don't want to dive, your word goes."

I try to shake off my worry. A woman might be trapped. It's been days since her backpack was found by the entrance to the cave.

"No, we can do it. This is a short, straight-forward dive. Just one short passage and one chamber. We should be in and out in no time. But like the professor said, we should go soon. This area is going to be impossible to navigate if the water gets any deeper."

I'm so busy talking, my foot catches in the mud sending me off balance. "Oh!"

When I slide into Rory, he simply locks an arm around me. "Steady now."

He's a gigantic wall of muscle on two very long legs. Rory is also incredibly good looking with dark hair, obsidian eyes, and a five o'clock shadow that most women probably throw themselves at his feet to feel on her inner thighs. But I'm not the least bit aroused by him.

Instead, I'm eager to get away from his hold. Claustrophobia instantly sets in.

"I'm fine."

Heart beating a little too fast, I shift the bag to my other shoulder and try to smile.

He looks at me suspiciously. "You sure you're good?"

I've heard Rory speaking Russian. To my novice ear, it sounds like his native tongue. But his English is so smooth, I question where he's really from.

"Fine, really. That was close. Thanks for the catch. I think I'd be better off sliding down on my stomach. I don't know how you can walk on this."

"Years of training."

I grumble at him as my feet try to go in two different directions. "I don't know what you were training for."

"Everything."

I blink. *Okay.*

Rory forges down the hillside without missing a beat

and my curiosity about the man grows until it gets the best of me. "Where are you from?"

"Everywhere."

Typical. I laugh. "Someone's been watching too many Jason Bourne movies," I tease.

"Watching? Those moves are inspired by men like me."

When I roll my narrowed eyes, he chuckles. It's such a rusty sound.

How long has it been since he's really laughed?

Rory reminds me of Scout. I know the kind. Just like Griff. All of the men have that hard edge to them, but Scout's is next level.

And his barrier is by far the only one that makes my breath feel tight.

Which reminds me that he's MIA and must be stuck dealing with something.

"Rory, what did you see up there?"

Guiding me down to the only even terrain, an opening by the cave entrance, he doesn't reply.

"Why can't you use a robot?" he asks instead.

"A robot?" I sit my gear bag down on the tarp that's been stretched over the ground under a rain canopy. "Oh you mean an UUV—unmanned underwater vehicle. They work in some cases, but not all. It's better to get a human in there, especially when it's time sensitive."

I realize he's very still, watching me. The tingle on my spine grows. "What's wrong?"

He's not really looking at me, more looking through me, "Nothing."

"You might be an operative, but you're terrible at lying."

He glances at the cave, his nearly black irises flashing in the cloudy morning light. "Just concerned."

I don't tell him I've been getting non-stop tingles on the back of my neck. Instead I focus on getting my gear ready.

"In this business it's good to be cautious. Now where's the map? I want to go over it again before I get changed into my wetsuit."

He unzips the outer pocket on the bag he carried and extracts a laminated document. "Don't go near the water," he warns as he passes me the map. "I'm going up to get the tanks."

"Don't worry, I'll be right here. You guys are worse than a bunch of mother hens."

"I'm not letting anything happen to you on my watch. Scout would take it out in blood."

After the way Scout talked to Griff, I wouldn't be surprised.

My stomach knots as soon as I think about the impending nightmare—the clash of titan's that's going to take place as soon as Griffon gets out of the hospital.

And that worry doesn't even include the blowback from what happens with Brundage.

God. I'm in a hornet's nest.

And it's all because of me.

I glance up the trail and see Scout descending through the slippery ravine.

My heart flutters, but when he glances up, the anger on his face makes my heart sink.

Chapter Twenty Nine

SCOUT

Focus on the mission. Focus. On. The. Mission.

Aria tunes into my energy immediately. "Is everything okay?"

No. Everything is a fucking disaster. But that seems to be the M.O. in Vandemora, so it's no surprise.

I take the map from her hand and stare down at the lines. Maps have always been my solace, but right now, the image blurs as Aria's proximity punctures my normally impenetrable forcefield. "Fine. Are you ready to get geared up?"

"Yeah, just look over Griff's gear. It should all fit you fine."

I turn my back to her and go through the equipment. Griffon Kane is damn near exactly my same size. It still doesn't mean I like diving in someone else's gear.

But it is what it is. There's no time to be a whiney ass about it. If there's one thing I learned in the Teams it's to adapt and move forward.

"Everything looks good." I stand up and jerk my shirt off.

Behind me Aria sucks air. "Oh, I didn't realize you were going to... um..."

Shit. Twisting at the waist, I look back at her.

Suddenly quiet, she presses her hand to her mouth as she looks at me.

I doubt she saw the scars on my ribs, but I turn my back to her quickly anyway as I kick my boots off with more force than needed. "You knew I was getting undressed. You don't expect me to wear my clothes under my wetsuit?"

Her voice is distant when she replies. "Of course not. I just didn't expect to see you—" she clears her throat. "Naked."

"Wasn't naked."

The air pulses with her unease.

Finally, she says, "You know what I mean. I didn't know you were going to just rip your shirt off."

Fucking hell.

My hands fall still on my cargo pants. I got so wrapped up in Aria, I forgot about my damned scars. Some people are upset by old wounds. Which is why no one sees mine.

"Are you looking now?"

"No," she squeaks.

I rip open the button and jerk down the zipper, facing away from her. The scars on my legs are a whole different nightmare. Something she'll never see.

Anger pulses along my nerves as I toss the cargos and my boxer briefs onto the tarp, and pull on the legs of the wetsuit one by one. Behind me, the rustle of clothing and little sound of exertion remind me that Aria's doing the same.

My cock starts to wake up which just makes me even angrier. How can I be this fucked up?

But all I can think about is whether she's wearing a swimsuit beneath her wetsuit, or going naked.

If she's getting completely undressed, someone could see her.

My head snaps up and I scan the hillside. "Aria, where's Rory?"

There's no one in sight. I exhale sharply, puzzling at the possessive feeling tightening my lungs.

She murmurs, "Bringing the tanks down."

I finish pulling on the tight sleeves and adjust the neck of Griff Kane's wetsuit and turn around just in time to catch sight of a bare shoulder.

No strap. No bra. Definitely no swimsuit. Just smooth bare skin.

Before I realize it, Rory's sliding into the tent carrying two sets of tanks. He glances at my face, then at Aria.

With one shake of his head, he sums every single thing about this situation up. I'm screwed.

"Okay, I'm dressed." Her delicate voice glides into my ear and tightens my pressed lips into a fused line.

When Aria whirls around to find me staring, she freezes.

"Oh," she says quietly. "You were fast."

I snap myself in line and start strapping on a dive knife. "Let's get this done."

She eyes me suspiciously. "Are you sure you're okay with this?"

"Diving?"

That's when I see a shiver wrack her body. Voice full of worry, she says, "Yes. The water's going to be super murky. It's going to be challenging. I don't think it will take us long, but it's going to be stressful."

I check both sets of tanks and lift her gear so she can slide it on. When she turns around to look at me, it hits me —I don't want her diving.

No, it's not diving. It's specifically going into the dangerous cave.

If we were on a wreck dive in beautiful Caribbean waters, I'd be all about it.

"Scout..." She steps cautiously toward me. "What's that look on your face?"

"This is me trying to figure out if Justice can fit in your gear."

"What?" Aria crinkles her nose. "Why?"

"Because I don't want you—"

Anger flashes in her pretty brown eyes, turning them hard. "Oh no. Not you. You're not going to be one of those men that says I'm not a good diver because I'm a woman."

Before I realize what I'm doing, I tug her toward me by the straps of her gear. "This has nothing to do with you being a woman."

Okay, it has everything to do with her being a woman. The one I want to protect. The same fucking woman that's making me a dangerous liability.

Face tilted up, she inspects my face. "What then?"

"I want you safe."

Her pretty eyes soften again. Just like they did before and my body reacts the same way.

The harsh glow inside me eases, but a new fire tunnels through me.

With a sharp shake of her head, she tugs out of my hold. "Let's go. We've got each other's backs. We've got a job to do."

God. This woman.

What the hell am I going to do?

Chapter Thirty

Aria

Once I'm in dive mode, I'm good.

My mind stops racing, the thoughts about Scout's moody protectiveness fade into the background.

The vision of his scars slips deep, tucking away in a place I can unpack later.

Everything has to wait.

Water presses in on me as I slip into the pool and the hiss of my breath in my ears calms me. I've done this thousands of times.

The water is my home. Almost more than terra firma. Here, things are methodical and orderly. That's how you stay safe.

By the book. Do everything the way it's planned. There's a contingency for everything. On the surface, emotions make a mess of everything.

Scout signals me with his hand, asking if I'm good one more time before we move to the area of the cave's mouth where we'll descend into the blackness.

I reply with an okay sign.

He pulls his mouthpiece away. "You know ASL?"

I give him a thumbs up. He puts his regulator back in his mouth, exhales and then leads the way, swimming gracefully into the yawning cave mouth with long scissor kicks of his fins.

We pause one more time in the cool water, testing our equipment, giving each other hand signals.

Scout manages the line that we'll spool out to mark our path in and out. We'll follow it when we return. It's something you always cave dive with.

As my pulse speeds, I take a few slow breaths. *You know how to do this.*

Simple. I do this all the time.

Scout quickly proves he's efficient and calm. His eyes relaxed behind his mask as we check our lights one by one. Our back up lights get a double check too.

Then we kick up our fins and descend head first.

Blackness reaches up for us.

He glances back to check on me. I keep kicking my fins, following him into the darkness. Trusting him.

Thank god, it's not Brundage diving with me. I've never liked being in the water with him. I didn't realize exactly how much until now.

We settle into a slow, steady pace. I check my watch, we've been down for six minutes. The dive computer reports all the details of our depth, time, and air.

So far, so good. The tunnel is just like I expected. Wide enough for two people. Tall enough for someone to stand up inside if it wasn't flooded.

We should be approaching the first chamber any second—

I kick, but something's got my leg.

What? How is that possible?

I tug again and something definitely has my ankle.

Scout! I scream in my head.

Dammit. This is when I wish I had a radio, but diving with a full face mask and radios isn't an option in this environment.

I tap on my tank with the metal tool I have just for this purpose—to alert another diver that you need their attention. The sharp ping rings through the water.

I hit it again and again.

Come on, Scout!

The beam of his light gets farther away from me, the flip of his fins growing harder to see.

Wiggling, I try to get my leg loose, but realize the line he's spooling out has gotten caught on my fin. He should feel me tugging the line. He'll know something's wrong.

But there's current in the water. He might not feel it.

Breathe slow. Relax. It's nothing to be alarmed over.

Things like this happen.

I twist around, trying to free myself, but my other fin catches on a rock and wedges.

Oh, great.

I can ditch my fins, but I need to keep my gear. Swimming without fins is twice as hard.

Struggling, my pulse rate kicks up. The throb in my throat matches the beat inside my ears.

I twist around one more time trying to free my right leg, even though my left fin is caught. That's when everything goes to hell in a handbasket.

The hose to my regulator bursts.

Millions of bubbles surround my face, like I've been shot in the face with champagne. Panic explodes inside me.

My light slips out of my hand, falling a few inches to dangle on my wrist on the strap.

Calm. Aria. Calm. You know what to do.

I'm trained. Divers prepare for this kind of thing. That doesn't mean it's not scary as hell.

I scramble for my backup regulator—my octopus—but I'm so disoriented by the bubbles in the moving water, I can't find it.

It has to be here. Right here. On a loop under my neck...

Easy... Easy. You've got this.

My lungs squeeze. I need air.

I feel around, but my fingers are shaking badly.

Then I feel a rush of water. I flinch. But a hand touches my face, gripping my chin.

Scout pushes his octopus regulator into my mouth.

Oh my god. *Oh. My. God.*

He saved me.

I suck in a few breaths, telling myself to go slow. His arm brushes my neck as he reaches past my shoulder. Gentle tugging tells me he's turning off my tank to stop the escape of the air.

As the bubbles stop, the water slowly returns to the gray-green haze it was moments before my mishap. And as it does, his face comes into view in the circle of light.

My stomach clenches when he looks in my eyes, followed by a warm rush of relief rolling through me all the way to my toes.

His calm eyes are everything.

The anchor in the storm.

He stays right with me. Breathing slowly. Giving me something to pace.

The entire time, he holds the regulator, pressing it to my mouth, making sure I have what I need.

Finally, with a shaking hand, I give him the okay sign.

He eases back and uses sign language to communicate to me. *What happened?*

I motion to my leg.

His eyes flash and I can see the scowl in them as he reaches for the line around my ankle. Then he frees my other fin.

When he's got me loose, he signs to me again. *The chamber is just ahead. Let's go. There's air.*

The airline to his octopus is roughly seven feet long, so we have to stay close, chest to chest. Gripping my harness with one hand, he tilts me forward and begins to slowly kick. He scans the darkness with the beam of his light. Pulling us deeper into the cave system.

A blue glow starts to form ahead.

Shaking, I focus on the opening to the chamber as it comes into clear view. The water is clearer here. Less current.

Scout said there's air, meaning there's a room, a chamber of some sort. We can check my gear and get my equipment running again.

Seconds later, we glide through the opening, propelled by his strong kicks.

Water whooshes around us as we break the surface.

Above us an opening shows the blue-gray sky. Water ripples around us as we bob in the deep pool. Blue waves bounce off the sienna-colored walls and black rocks. The air is sweet and musty.

Life-giving air. I draw in a few more steadying lungfulls. Almost giddy from relief.

Scout turns off his light and moves toward me, making more ripples spread from his shoulders. "You okay?"

"I'm good."

He shakes his head as he pushes his mask up onto the top of his wetsuit covered head. "You gave me a hard scare back there."

I laugh even though the terror is still making my insides tremble. "Try being in my shoes."

Unimpressed, he frowns at me. "What the fuck happened with your regulator?"

I reach for the hose. "I have no idea. It's just ruptured..."

Tugging me forward, Scout moves us to a cluster of large slab rocks. He pushes me up onto the ledge. Then he proceeds to slide up onto the rock like a predatory animal. All grace and muscle.

Every single outline of his toned body is highlighted by the slick, wet neoprene of his dive suit.

"You're staring."

"Oh. I guess you're right." I don't bother to apologize. Why should I?

Taking off his fins, he moves to crouch next to me. After removing his gloves he inspects my gear. "Did you look all of this over before we started?"

"I did."

His silence makes me uneasy. "What's wrong?"

Tugging on the hose, he carefully inspects the place where it leaked. "I don't like this."

His jaw is tight, his hood is pushed back, and he looks every bit of the lethal SEAL that he is.

The sight of him steals my breath.

Maybe it's the enchanting setting. The water dripping

from his rugged jaw... the rugged masculinity of this incredibly capable man.

Or maybe it's just the fact that I saw a few moments of my life flashing back there in the midst of all those bubbles.

I must make a sound because his gaze falls to my mouth.

Heat infuses every cell in my body. It's an intoxicating feeling, especially mixed with the adrenaline of the mishap.

I've never been an adrenaline junky like my brother, but I think I might crave whatever this is.

I push my hood back, freeing my burning face, letting the cool air of the cave rush against the back of my neck, beneath my braided hair. "What are you thinking?"

My voice is raspy as all get out.

His eyelids lower a fraction over his pale, ice-blue irises. He exhales slowly and my skin goosebumps from the sound.

"I'm thinking that you've got the most kissable mouth I've ever seen."

I reach out for him, but halt my hand mid air. I almost forgot, he doesn't like to be touched.

But I do think he likes to touch me.

"Can I touch your arm?"

His gaze falls to my hand, but he doesn't pull back. He also doesn't say no.

This must mean yes.

Moving slowly, I reach for his wrist, grab the neoprene covered thickness of it and bring his cool fingers to my face.

"Then kiss me," I whisper as I lean my cheek into his palm.

The sound that comes from his throat is primal, the roughness echoing off the water and cave walls.

He looks me dead in the eyes and lowers his mouth until we're a centimeter apart. "Fuck, I shouldn't... but damned if I can stop myself."

Then he crushes my mouth, plowing the damp contour of his lips against mine with a growl in his throat. With a commanding thrust of his tongue he takes charge.

Diving deep into me with a hot, rough stroke.

I blink once in shock, then close my eyes as I absorb every ounce of pleasure I can grab.

He growls into my throat, a sound that sears a path to the very pit of my body. Tremors of pleasure unleash and race down my extremities.

Sweet lord above.

The taste of him invades my mind, erasing every kiss before this one.

Scout's flavor—danger laced with something dark and untamed—is exactly what I expected. The bite of dark chocolate with the heat of strong bourbon.

"Aria..." He rasps against my mouth.

But I can't respond. All I'm capable of is feeling.

But it's not enough. I'm desperate to feel more. Damn these wetsuits.

The urge to fist his hair and press my hardening nipples against him makes me shake. I want his skin on mine. I want the weight of him pressing me down.

I am out of my head.

I've never in my life thought something like that.

Every twist of his tongue with mine is hotter and hotter until it burns up all of the oxygen. I rip my mouth away gasping.

"My-my god," I wheeze.

After the nightmare a few months ago, I didn't think I could ever feel alive like this. But heavens above, I'm so charged, I feel like I've got nuclear energy in my veins.

Scout stands up from his crouched position, looking down at me from his full height. As my heart races, he hovers over me with an intensity of which I've never seen, and definitely never felt.

Then, his expression slams closed. In the blink of an eye, the stone warrior facade is back.

He looks beyond my shoulder and goes rigid from heat to toe. "Oh hell, what is that?"

Chapter Thirty One

SCOUT

Aria scrambles to her feet, "What's wrong?"

I swing my flashlight across the wall at the top of the chamber. A massive swath of the cave is covered in ancient art.

Reeling from the double impact of kissing Aria when I should stay arms length away and the situation in the tunnel, it's hard to get my head around what I'm seeing.

She laughs softly. "That's amazing. I've never seen any cave art in person."

"No one mentioned it to me, but we were all focused on the fact that the caves were flooding and the only sign of the missing woman was by the entrance."

I shine my spotlight across the northwest corner of the chamber. "Very impressive art at that."

I move along the wall, pointing my light into a darker

recess. "This is a first for me too. Not that I've spent a lot of time in caves."

Behind me Aria makes a sound of appreciation that makes my skin tingle. "Well, I have and I've still never seen art in person."

We stand for a few seconds in silence as we use our lights to look around.

Animals, human handprints, and elaborate geometric shapes in red and black cover the smooth surfaces. Thousands of years old, protected by the mountain.

The darkness cocoons around us. Almost intimate.

My lips are still stinging, my pulse still erratic behind my sternum. Kissing Aria was a mistake. Good as all fuck, but a mistake that's going to lead to all kinds of problems.

"Scout, there's more there."

Her sweet, soft voice pierces my growing angst.

When I swing the light to the right, I stiffen and narrow my eyes. This time, it's not the art that has my attention. It's another clue. A piece of blue webbing and a green rope.

For a few seconds, scenarios play out in my head. Very few of them are good.

"I'm glad we spotted the art, because there's a clue that could be related to the case. You see the climbing harness?"

Aria moves across the rock ledge to stand next to me. "Where?"

I swing the light, circling the area. "Right there. Blue harness. There's a line draped over a projection of rock."

She cranes her neck and looks at the ceiling where the hole opens to the sky, an opening the size of a tractor-trailer tire, revealing clouds above it.

Looking around again, she asks, "Do you think someone came down through the opening?"

"That's my guess. Which means they could have come or gone after the flooding. Given that the harness and rope are just carelessly discarded, I'm guessing that it fell through the hole or someone threw it in."

Or someone fell out of the rigging.

A morbid, but real possibility. Especially if they didn't know what they were doing or didn't have the right gear.

She looks at me suddenly. "You said they might have thrown their rope and harness in. As if they were hiding it..."

I force myself not to look at the beautiful, bright woman beside me. It's too much.

The sane, rational part of me wants her in ways I can't explain. The broken, angry part of me knows I can't have her.

Words husky, I offer her a taste of praise when I want to give her a hell of a lot more than just a few hollow words. "Smart girl. You could be right."

"I'm glad we didn't find a body." Wrapping her arms around herself, she makes an uncomfortable sound in her throat. "I've only retrieved living people during rescues. No postmortem recoveries. I know it will happen someday. But I'm glad we didn't find her."

Yet.

But I don't vocalize that it could still happen. Taking one more look at the rope and harness, I memorize the location compared to the opening in the ceiling of the cave.

"We need to have a good look below the water before we leave."

She moves back to her gear and picks up her mask and snorkel. "Do you think that harness belongs to her—the woman you guys called MZ?"

145

"Could belong to anyone. I have lots of questions for the professor and his contacts about the frequency of people coming and going from these caves."

Looking around the space, Aria taps her chin with her gloved hand. "Why would she be in here?"

For a beat, I mull over the situation with my team's case.

Technically, Aria's working on this mission with us, so it's not a total breach of confidentiality to read her in on some of the details. I also know her brother's company is solid. That's the reason Agile would have hired them.

Quickly reaching my decision, I turn to face her. "What I'm going to tell you is not to be shared with anyone."

Her expression turns serious, her hand falling to her side. "Of course. I understand."

"The missing woman is an archeologist. We don't know her exact reason for being in Vandemora yet. But I'm trying to work that out. She was known to be visiting some archeology sites in the country, including caves."

"So, she would study history?"

"Generally yes, but there are a lot of nuances to what archeologists specialize in." I pull up my wetsuit hood, adjusting it around my face and move to my equipment. "Let's wrap this. I need to get someone to the upper entrance of the cave to see what they can find before the rain sets in again."

"Do you think something bad happened to her?"

I don't want to give much airtime to that, but we're all uneasy. "Several days ago, we were doing some recon in the capital and saw a woman that resembled her being forced into a car. We chased them, but didn't get her before they disappeared. Since then we've run into dead ends.'

Aria's color blanches, and her hands tighten on her

snorkel. "I know that has to be hard on you and your coworkers."

Copy that. But hard doesn't feel like the right word. Frustration simmers in my veins. "It's never good when you fail to save someone."

"Did she look scared?"

"She didn't look at us."

Aria considers that for a beat. "But did her body language look like she was in distress?"

As the memory replays in my head—the blond woman being forced into a car by two men—my body tenses and adrenaline starts to flow, just like it did that night. "She didn't look relaxed."

Biting the corner of her lip, Aria's expression softens, "I hope you find her, Scout."

"So do I. I've got a thing about women being in trouble."

Her eyes drop to the ground. "About that. I need to thank you for taking such a strong stance for me about Brundage."

"I'd do it again in an instant."

She adjusts the snorkel's attachment on her dive mask, thinking for a few seconds as she toys with it. "Do you really think Griff will fire him?"

"If Griff ever wants another rescue job, he will. I'll make sure word spreads that he's got a dangerous, loose cannon on his team if he doesn't. That man is never getting near you in the water again."

She slides her fins on her feet and drops off the rock ledge into the water. As I pass her tanks down to her, her brow is tight. "I have to admit, I'm a little nervous about what happens when Griffon gets to town."

"I'm not."

Aria makes a startled sound as she frantically looks around in the water. "What—are you expecting someone?"

I grab her arm and tug her toward me as water starts to swirl around us. "Nope." But I'm already pulling my dive knife free of its sheath.

Chapter Thirty Two

Aria

An eruption of bubbles causes a flare of panic inside of me. For a beat I wonder if the cave is being inundated by some new water source, but soon the glow of a handheld light creates a circle in the water below us.

Scout pushes me toward the ledge. "Move over there."

"Are you worried?" I squeak, as if the Loch Ness monster could be making those bubbles.

"I can handle anyone. You don't need to be afraid."

Said so confidently. I watch the man that kissed me turn into the warrior in a single beat of my stressed heart.

The light grows brighter as I back away from the growing field of bubbles. "What the heck is another diver doing in here?"

"Causing trouble."

"Maybe it's one of your men."

"Doubt that."

Oh how right he is. Nothing could have prepared me for the face that emerges from the gloomy water a few seconds later.

I wish it was Loch Ness instead.

"Keith!?" I fumble for words as anger rips through my veins like razor blades. "What are *you* doing here?"

Dark blue eyes locked on me, Keith gives me an evil smirk. "Aria, what do you think I'm doing?"

My throat is nearly glued shut from my fury. "Diving in a cave where you have no business being."

He pulls off his mask, and tugs off his hood, revealing his jet black hair and the scar on his forehead. The tiny white line on his skin he tells people he got in combat, but I know is from passing out drunk and hitting his head on a coffee table years after he was out of the Army.

Scout slices a look between us. "I take it you two know each other."

"We worked together before I joined Griff's company," I grit out. "Scout, we should go. The rain is going to be starting soon."

Keith lazily swims toward me with his usual smartass expression on his pale face. "Don't want to hang out while I do some recon on the cave? Maybe I'll find the missing woman and get the big payout."

I grit my teeth and fight the urge to tell Keith off.

Scout inserts himself between us, then answers for me since I'm already geared up. "You missed the party. Where's your dive buddy? Hate for you to have an accident."

Like with a dive knife at the end of a SEAL's arm?

Not the least bit concerned, Keith smiles. "He's coming."

Scout's tone is almost as icy as his pale eyes . "You were told to leave."

The difference between two men has never been more stark. Keith's dull, soulless gaze flicks over Scout's face as he floats lazily in the water. "What's it to you?"

Scout is not lazy. Or relaxed. "I'm the fucking lead on this aspect of the investigation. That's what it is to me."

"Then you should have hired Blue Guard for the job."

I spit my regulator out as fire races up my spine. "They didn't hire your team, Keith. They hired Griff. You need to get lost."

Keith makes a point of looking around dramatically. "Don't see your big bad brother. Given that you've got some two-bit backup diver, figured a real rescue team needed to step in."

A low growl from Scout has my skin prickling.

"You've had your warning. I'll have the feds remove you for tampering with my investigation."

With a creepy smile, Keith looks around the cave. "Just diving in a public cave. Good luck on getting me removed for that."

Chapter Thirty Three

SCOUT

I should have taken this jackass more seriously when I saw him by the road before we dove. The idiot and his band of meatheads set off my red flag radar the minute I talked to them.

With the way Aria's acting, it's clear that trouble runs deeper than meets the eye. And that pisses me off beyond reason.

She makes me possessive. To the point of irrational protectiveness.

As if she's mine.

Fuck.

"The cops removing you would be the easy way. The alternative is going to be much more painful." I let a dark grin tip up one side of my mouth. "For you, that is. Not me."

Without taking my eyes off him, I call out, "You set, Aria?"

She swims past me, placing her secondary regulator on the octopus in her mouth as she nears the center of the cave.

I make a hand signal, asking her one more time if she's ready. She nods. Water splashes off her fins as she flips around in the water and begins her descent.

"If you fuck with anything in this cave, your ass is mine."

He's laughing when I drop below the water's surface. Fucker.

Aria's kicks are choppy and fast as we enter the tunnel.

I catch up to her, wrapping my hand around her calf. She swivels around to look at me through the gloomy water.

I use ASL to check on her.

Mad, she replies.

Fuck him, I sign out the letters one by one. Then I ask if there's anything else.

She hesitates then quickly signs, *scared.* Then she points toward the tunnel.

Jesus. Of course she is.

Now everything makes sense. The way she looked back in the cavern wasn't all because of the asshole showing up, it was because she was still rattled. Kicking myself for not taking better care of her, I quickly sign: got you, baby. Don't worry.

She blinks at me in surprise through her mask.

Baby.

First sweetheart, now baby. I'm going all Hallmark. What's next? Matching sweaters...

That's the last thing I need to be. I'm hard. I need to be hard.

Soft never got me anywhere in fucking life.

I would scrub my hand over my face if it weren't for all the dive gear. Before I do something else that my brain isn't onboard with, I motion toward the cave and sign to her: *five minutes to go.*

She nods and starts swimming.

I stay as close as humanly possible without affecting her kicks.

It's the longest damn five minutes of my life. Probably hers too.

We break the surface of the water at the mouth of the cave to find the clouds darkening and a dozen people waiting on us. Rory, Justice, and Agent Torres step forward to help us out of the water.

Aria goes ahead of me, and quickly walks to the tent without looking at the other group of men. Her avoidance makes me even more concerned.

Rory offers to take our tanks, but I turn him down. "No thanks."

Instead, I move to corner Justice so we can speak alone.

"What's going on with those guys?"

"Agent Torres is trying to get to the bottom of it. I guess you encountered the one that came into the cave."

"Yeah, we did. Keith is his first name, apparently he worked with Aria." As I pull one arm of my wetsuit off, I drop my voice. "Idiot. But that's only part of the problem. I need you to go up onto the mountain. Take one of Torres's agents with you. There's a natural opening at the top of the cavern. It might be hard to find, but you need to see if there are any signs of a struggle or anything weird there. We saw a harness and rope that were dropped into the cave."

Justice's brows go up, he pulls out his phone. "On it."

I brush water out of my hair. "By the way, the cavern walls are covered with ancient art. I need to speak with the professor about this cave system to get some additional details."

Justice scans the hillside. "So it fits that MZ would be interested in this place given that she's in the country to research archeological sites."

"It adds up. But I'm not sure what to make with the harness and rope. I'd help you look, but I'm getting Aria out of here. There's nothing else for her to do here, we're not diving any more today, and I've got a bad feeling about the asshole who came in there. He's got a fucked up attitude. Do you know anything about him?"

"Yeah, he works for a guy named Adam Hill who owns the other dive company." Justice narrows his eyes on the group of men standing by the cave entrance. "I can dig if you want."

"I want you to turn every stone. Also, find out if Marshall or Beast contacted them. I want to know how the other company knew to come here. And look..." I turn my back so no one can see my face, or more specifically so they can't read my lips. "I need you to find out what you can about Rory."

Forehead tensing, his next question is immediate. "Something happen?"

"Aria had an issue with her gear during the dive. Rory handled the equipment. When it comes to her safety, I'm not trusting anyone."

"Fuck, right," he grumbles under his breath. Then his face goes hard as he watches Rory across the opening. "Rory and all of Vik's teams are probably ghosts, but you know that. I'll do what I can. What about that guy Brundage, didn't he handle her gear?"

I swivel my head to look at Justice as I push my wetsuit down to my waist with my mind spinning up. "Shit, I forgot about Brundage."

"He was all over their gear."

155

"You're right." Nerves crackling, I curse the fact that Aria's having such an effect on me. I can't even keep all the moving pieces together.

That's dangerous.

"I'm taking the equipment with me and keeping it under lock and key. I want to get her away from this shit-show before Keith-whoever-the-fuck he is gets back on dry land. You and Rory will need to get another ride, I don't want anyone near her."

"Copy that." He tilts his head, even more concern etching his usually relaxed face. "You good?"

No. I haven't been good since that plane crashed last night. But that's my fucking problem. I've got a job to do.

And now my job includes keeping Aria safe on top of fulfilling our team's mission to find the missing woman.

"Good 'nough." I grab the gear off the ground and turn to walk away.

He calls after me in a low enough voice that others won't hear. "Scout, you wanna talk this out?"

"Nothing to talk about. I need to hustle and get her out of here. I'll check in once I get back to the farm. I'll be working on planning the next phase of searching the cave system with the professor."

He tips his chin, but his eyes say all I need to see. He knows something else is going on and he's not letting this go.

I've taken two steps toward the staging tent when Aria's scream makes me take off sprinting.

Chapter Thirty Four

Aria

Clutching my arms tightly across my bare chest, I glare at my former boss and the man that makes my skin crawl. "What are you doing here?"

His smirk is topped by two unwelcome eyes that are staring at my barely covered breasts.

"Turn around, Adam."

Fear slices through me, gluing my feet to the ground and making my heart flutter like a startled bird's wings.

"What's wrong?!?" Scout storms into the tent with his dive knife clutched in his palm.

Adam chuffs aggressively and crosses his arms.

I used to think Adam was a big man, but he looks so small compared to Scout. And not just in size. Scout has big dick energy. Adam just has dickhead energy.

With contempt in his tone, Adam says, "Talk about overreacting."

The blade glints brightly as Scout's eyes glint like two diamond-tipped drills. "Am I? She asked you to turn around. I don't see you moving."

"I was just going to talk to Aria about her dive."

Low, lethal, Scout commands, "Move out."

Adam's obnoxious chuckle is loud as a fake grin spreads over his face. "Who's this guy, Aria?"

Seeing that horrible expression sends a chill racing over my damp, bare skin. Two damning words rush out of me.

"My boyfriend."

Adam doesn't take his eyes off me, but the veins in his neck bulge. The tension in the tent skyrockets and cold fear makes my hands shake.

Finally, Adam takes a step back.

"I'll be seeing you around, sugar."

Suddenly my body is freezing, but boiling rockets through me and hits my face like I've been slapped. "Don't hold your breath."

But as big and bold as my words sound, I'm barely able to stay upright on the soles of my feet as Adam strides out of the back of the tent.

Oh god. Oh my god. Adam Hill. Christ, I never want to see that man again.

I realize I'm wheezing, clutching to my bare chest.

When I glance at Scout, my breath catches. Nostrils flared, mouth clamped, he looks like he's about to snap, as if it's taking every ounce of his control not to leap into action and rocket out of the tent and bury something sharp in Adam's back.

"Down beast. I'm okay."

Too bad my words don't sound convincing.

I turn away, trying to keep my balance so I don't fall on my face from emotional overload. With angry blood heating my cheeks, I shove my arm in my sports bra.

Scout doesn't say make a sound, but I swear I can hear him calculating murder. Maybe I'm on the hit list too after my stupid remark.

Boyfriend.

Now I've got to deal with that too.

Thank heavens, Scout showed up. Having Adam see a single inch of my bare skin makes my stomach clench.

Rushing to finish putting my clothing on, I make a mis-step in my haste.

As much as it pisses me off to have to ask, I know I'm not going to be able to get it unstuck myself without some kind of contortionist act.

"Scout, my sports bra is caught on my damp skin. Can you help me?"

I fumble behind my back one more time, but blow out a resigned breath.

A second later, I feel him, rather than see him. His warmth softens the air that he stirs around me as he steps close. Cool fingers brush against my back as he very efficiently grabs the fabric and drags it down until it's seated in the right place.

Now I'm not only flushed because I'm mad—I'm embarrassed.

"Thanks. They get stuck like that sometimes."

"You should go without."

I turn around, expecting to find Scout's expression one of humor, but it's not. He's locked on me like I'm some kind of enemy combatant.

After a weird awkward silence he glances down at my hands. "What are those scars on your wrists?"

Uh...

Crap. I didn't even think about that when I asked for his help.

A surge of cold adrenaline makes my veins pulse. My mouth goes dry, my stomach knots and my scars tingle like I've been pricked by icy needles. "Just some... scars."

He tilts his head, studying every nuance of my expression. It feels like a silent interrogation.

Unable to take the intensity, I drop my gaze to his bare chest.

Yes, he's half-dressed too. And the view is fine. If I wasn't freaking out inside, I would definitely appreciate it. The man looks like he does those cross-fit competitions.

Voice low and tight, he presses me for answers. "What are they from?"

I step back, making the mistake of looking at his eyes. "I don't want to talk about them."

The clear blue color flickers hot. "Now that I'm your boyfriend, I think you should tell me."

My eyes round as someone steps into the tent and a male voice booms through the air. *"Boyfriend?"*

My heart plummets to the pit of my stomach.

As if matters weren't bad enough, Brundage is staring straight at Scout like he's got a bead on him in a sniper rifle scope. "Didn't take long for her to spread her legs for you did it?"

Blood drains from my head to my feet in a single whoosh.

Chapter Thirty Five

SCOUT

Seeing a complete haze of red—maybe more than ever in my life—I bite out a command. "Aria, head up to the truck."

I'm so busy focusing on the asshole that's about to find out just how much Aria isn't his fucking business that I don't see Rory slide into the tent behind us.

"What's going on fellas?"

It's not the first time I've wondered how Rory learned to speak such perfect English if he's a Russian mercenary. Or why he's got a name like Rory, but I go by a nickname, so there's that.

I don't bother with a reply to his question.

I may or may not be fantasizing about torture.

Aria takes off, muttering something unhappily as she goes, carrying her boots in her hand as she starts traversing the muddy terrain.

It galls me that she's going to be wandering around with a man that clearly scared her somewhere nearby, but I'm not going to be far behind her as soon as I deal with this ugly-faced fucker.

Another large form appears on my left shoulder. This time it's Justice. And next to him appears Marshall.

Agile's running deep.

Brundage glances across the grim faces—the same men that saved him from me earlier—and mutters, "Bunch of jarhead assholes."

"SEALs," Marshall corrects. "You were leaving town. Didn't know this was on the way out."

"I'm not going anywhere until I speak to Griffon Kane. I work for him. Not you."

Agent Torres joins the party, killing my brief comfort that he was watching Aria as she left. He hooks his thumb behind him. "Mr. Brundage, a word with you."

Seeing as the team has things under control, I don't bother waiting around. With my muscles vibrating, I grab the gear—tanks and bags—and take off up the hill.

Aria's just scrambled up the steep incline, but I have her in sight which eases some of the constriction in my chest. But the reprieve only makes room to let other confusing thoughts bubble to the surface.

Boyfriend.

Why would she call me her boyfriend?

And what the fuck are up with the scars on her wrists?

When you've done the work I've done, you've seen scars like that before. And nothing good makes that kind of mark all the way around someone's wrists. They come from being bound by something sharp-edged.

Maybe she had some kind of accident. But deep down, I

know that's not the answer. Every step I take up the goddamned slick ass slope, I get angrier and angrier.

Who would hurt someone like Aria?

The need to get to the bottom of her mystery grows until it's a pounding drumbeat inside my head.

She startles when I emerge from the trees.

"Just me."

Nodding nervously, she glances around the trucks as if looking for the next assault. She reaches for one of the bags. "Sorry I left you with all the gear."

I set her bags on the ground and set the tanks down. "No problem. I can manage it."

Biting my tongue, holding my questions is harder than I thought.

"What now?" She glances at my bare chest, then quickly away as something repulses her.

It shouldn't hit me hard, but it does. I tug my shirt over my head, regretting not doing it sooner.

"Now we leave."

"But—"

I pick up her dive bag and the bag that Griff's gear is in and head for the back of the truck. "No buts. I'm getting you out of here."

She fidgets with the button on the cuff of her sleeve and stands there barefoot looking rattled but concerned. "Don't you need to go up on the mountain to look at the opening for the cavern? I don't want to keep you from doing your job to search for your missing woman.."

"I did my job. Now we need to make plans for tomorrow's dive. Justice is on the above-ground search."

It takes me a few moments to find what I'm looking for, but when I have the package, I close the rear of the truck and the cap.

"Let's get you cleaned up."

Aria frowns as she looks down at her feet. She wiggles her toes. "I wasn't thinking. I just needed out of there."

I open the door for her. "Hop in, and turn this way."

Making a grimace, she does as I ask her to. "I'm sorry, I didn't think about getting the truck dirty."

I raise my gaze to hers. "I could care less about the truck."

Confusion clouds her eyes.

I pop open the pack of industrial size hand wipes, and lift her muddy foot. "I don't want you to be uncomfortable on the drive back."

This elicits a sound from her, but she doesn't say anything.

When I hold the arch of her delicate foot and clean the mud off, she's very still.

A heaviness settles into the air between us.

Touching her like this feels...

Fuck. It feels right.

I finish one foot, then hold my hand up for the other.

Squirming she says, "You don't have to do that, I can—"

"Shhh. Give me your foot. I want to."

This time when I look at her, she's nibbling the corner of her lip, and the memory of kissing her rocks me.

My throat gets tight, my body grows tight including my dick, and I force myself to concentrate on what I'm doing. I can't make sense of the way Aria makes me feel.

There's no place in my life for a woman.

Especially a woman like her.

As I wipe the last of the mud off the top of her foot, my thumb and forefinger circle her ankle. The pulse is flying, but she's as still as a cornered mouse.

"I'm sorry he scared you."

She tries to pull her foot away, but I keep it in my grip.

"He just took me off guard."

"Care to tell me about the boyfriend remark?"

When she doesn't answer, I drag a finger along the bottom of her foot. She jumps and makes a throaty sound.

"I'll get it out of you one way or another."

I'd like to get a lot more throaty sounds and raspy words out of her.

She laughs in disbelief. "You would, wouldn't you?"

I set her foot on the floorboard. Drop the used hand wipes into the small trash receptacle that hangs from the back of the seat and buckle her seatbelt. My hand gets dangerously close to places I want to touch.

The tension in my groin grows. Goddamnit. I need to get away from Aria Kane.

Voice rough, I say, "When I need answers I know how to get them."

Her eyes flare for a second, then she folds her hands nervously. "It just sort of popped out of me—calling you my boyfriend. I'm sorry. I know that puts you in a tough spot. I hoped it would make Adam leave me alone."

"It doesn't put me in a tough spot. You're brother's already convinced I'm fucking—I mean I'm fooling around with you."

Griff's foul attitude makes me hot around the neck. Yes he should be worried about me being around his sister, but give me a fucking break. I'm trying to keep her safe in the middle of what's clearly turning into a shitshow.

Feeling grumpy, I say, "I'll deal with him, don't worry. Let me get out of this wetsuit and we'll get on the road."

She stiffens in her seat, her brows shooting up. "But

what about the others? Rory and Justice need a ride back, too."

"They're grown men."

She blinks at my response. "Where are we going?"

"Anywhere but here."

I know where I'm going. Straight to hell.

Chapter Thirty Six

Aria

I swear, I need a Scout decoder ring. Anywhere but here?

When he climbs into the truck after changing, I immediately try to find out. "What does that mean?"

Scout tears out of the gathered vehicles and out to the main road. He accelerates and takes a turn too fast, making me bump against the door of the truck. "Hey, speed demon."

"It means I want you away from everyone."

I wish that was for romantic reasons, but given the aura around the man, that's highly unlikely.

Given that I want to get as far away from Keith, Adam, and Brundage, I should be pressing my foot on top of his boot to make him go faster. But instead I sit and watch him driving as fear slithers down my spine.

When Scout was tenderly cleaning the mud off my feet,

I was lulled into a momentary reprieve. But my fear is back and his weird vibe isn't helping.

It's like a switch flipped and gone in the thoughtful man that was just taking care of me, back is the SEAL that's built out of boulders and hard glares.

My fingers tingle and turn cold. I wish the lump in my throat didn't feel like icy gravel. "Why are you acting like this?"

"Because I am."

I look at him more closely, trying to decide if the tic below his eye is a tell of some kind. "That's a non-answer."

He glances at the side mirror and back at the road with his jaw tight, the trim scruff of his beard moving from the pulsing muscle below it.

"Who is Adam?"

Oh, Christ.

I am not ready for that conversation. *Keep it light, Aria.* "He's my brother's competition. I worked for him for a short time."

Scout glances at me, those wintery knives slicing me. "And?"

Lungs locked, I try to sound normal. "And he's a gigantic chauvinistic ass."

"What about Keith?"

Palms sweating cold, slick perspiration, I look out the side window. "Keith is Adam's wingman."

The silence gets so thick, I roll the window down and close my eyes as the humid air washes over my face.

"Why did he call you, *sugar?*"

Oh, the malice in that last word.

It's probably eighty-five degrees outside, but a shiver tightens my muscles, making me cross my arms. "Because he's a pig."

"And you know this because?"

I sigh, fighting for patience. "Scout, are we playing fifty questions?"

If his jaw was tight a moment ago, that was nothing. The cords of his neck stand out like highway overpasses. "My radar is going off, Aria. I'm trying to keep you safe."

"I'm safe," I say. But I do not sound convincing at all. "I mean last night I wasn't, but you handled that. You also handled Brundage. You took care of the crisis on the dive. But now there's nothing to be worried—"

He interrupts me and stops me cold. "I think someone cut the hose to your regulator."

I open my mouth, but the only sound that comes out is a raspy wheeze as my heart drops like a stone to my stomach.

Scout swerves toward the ditch as a white SUV almost takes us out. "Mother fucker," he shouts as he gets the truck back on the road.

Then he jams on the brakes.

An instant later we're in reverse.

Chapter Thirty Seven

SCOUT

Slamming the truck into park, I lunge from out of the cab. "You nearly ran us off the goddamned road!"

Griffon Kane—eyes tight, chest puffed—stabs an irate finger toward me. "What are you doing with my sister?"

"Saving her from your idiotic driving."

Griff tries to storm past me but I grab his arm with a brutal grip. "Don't even think about taking your shit attitude to her doorstep."

The sound of small, running footfalls behind me makes me grind my teeth.

"Griff! Oh my god." Aria throws her arms around her brother. "Are you feeling okay?"

He squeezes her to him, glaring at me over the top of her head. "Somewhat better. You okay, kiddo?"

She buries her face in his chest. "I'm fine. I'm just glad you're well enough to leave the hospital."

He ruffles her hair, and gives her another brotherly jostle. "You're not getting rid of me that easy."

Pulling back, she looks him over, and Griff finally drops his angry gaze from mine.

"How was the dive?"

She glances toward me. "It was fine."

There's a whole silent conversation in the way her expression tightens for an instant as our gazes hold.

Aria doesn't want her brother to know.

Well, fuck that. He's gonna know her line might have been tampered with, and he's going to make sure Brundage never dives again.

"There was a problem," I say bluntly.

"Not now, Scout," she hisses at me before she turns back to Griff. "We can talk about that later, once you've had time to get settled."

Griff's keen attention gets more acute. "What kind of problem?"

"Equipment damage, I suspect tampering."

Aria fists her hands. "Helloooo. I thought we could save this for later."

Griff shifts his weight, his own fisted hands going to his hips. "Whose equipment?"

"Hers."

It takes less than two seconds for his anger meter to peg.

"Come on." He motions for his sister to go to his rented SUV. "I'm not letting you out of my sight."

I step between them and wrap a hand around her upper arm in a possessive move. "Aria's coming with me."

Griff's face flushes red. He swallows roughly, and I half expect to have to do hand-to-hand combat with him in the middle of the road.

It wouldn't be unwelcome.

I'm primed for a fight right now.

Going toe-to-toe with Griffon Kane would be an ideal way to shake off some of the dangerous energy coursing inside my veins.

He growls, "Aria..."

Narrowing her eyes to slits, she huffs and throws her hands up in the air. "Griff, I am not a five-year-old. I have a say in this."

"Not now," he replies flatly.

"No, now." She gives him a withering glare. "I'm tired, Griff. The dive was stressful. I've been worried about you. Scout is taking me back to the farm."

This only makes her brother more angry. If he were a bull, he'd be goring me right now.

The feeling is mutual. Much more of this and I'll be pawing the ground and snorting.

"Griff, I'm getting her out of here."

His anger rises around him like a thunderhead, dark and unpredictable. "I'll take her."

If I were a rational man, I'd push her toward his vehicle, and I'd go back to the cave to help them search. But that part of me vanished somehow in the last twenty-four hours. Now I'm running on pure emotion.

I hate it.

I've never been like this. But damned if I can stop it. Somehow Aria cracked open a door that I can't seem to close.

Before I can tell her brother to fuck himself properly, Aria makes her statment loud and clear. "I'm going with Scout."

Griff's nostrils flare as he takes a step forward. "You're making a mistake, Aria."

She tugs out of my hold and walks away. Doesn't even

look back. The door slams closed on the passenger side of the Agile Security & Rescue truck.

The fist that's been clenched around my stomach loosens.

"Keep your head on Kane, you need to go to the cave and deal with a situation."

Seething, he steps closer, tilting his head. "Besides her fucking equipment being tampered with? Besides her being with your sorry ass? This must be really fucking important."

"Do the names Adam and Keith ring a bell?"

His forward roll stops and he slowly sneers. "Are those motherfuckers here?"

"They aren't just here, Keith showed up in the cavern while me and your sister were diving."

Griff takes off for my truck. He jerks open the driver's door like the hothead I know Griffon Kane to be.

He's about one second from getting a boot in the back. "Kane! Back off, this is your only warning."

Only he doesn't back up, he has the goddamned nerve to raise his voice at his sister. "What the fuck, Aria? Did you know Adam and Keith were coming?"

Chapter Thirty-Eight

Aria

Just when you think the last two days can't get any weirder or worse...

I stare at my brother in disbelief.

"Are you serious right now, Griff?"

If steam really can come from a person's ears, it's about to happen. From both of us. Kane tempers are... hot is too mild of a word. My fuse is just a lot longer than my brother's.

His hand clenches the steering wheel so hard I wonder if it might snap. "Do I look like I'm kidding?"

"There is no reason I would ever talk to Adam Hill again in this lifetime."

Griff's about to open his mouth when he suddenly disappears from the doorway. The truck jolts and I cringe at the sound of someone's breath whooshing out.

I scramble across the console and out the driver's side door.

Scout's in my brother's face. They're both breathing hard, looking like two equally matched wild animals about to tear one another apart.

Shrill voiced, I shout, "Wait!"

As if I've snapped a spell, Scout releases Griff and drops his fisted hands to his sides. He paces in a tight circle, his thin control visible.

Griff's eyes meet mine and regret flashes. "That was out of line. I'll go deal with that fucker and his creep dive buddy."

I have nothing to say. Not a single thing.

I'm so done.

My brother shoves off of the truck. He and Scout exchange one more look before Griff folds his tall body into the SUV and takes off so fast gravel spits from below his tires.

I almost sag to the ground.

When I lean back against the cool metal and press my hand to my eyes, tears sting my eyes as they rush to the surface.

"Hey..." Soft and husky, Scout's voice is close.

Then he's really close. The heat pulsing off him hits me like a cresting wave.

When his hand slides around the back of my neck, warm and strong, I have to bite my lip and close my eyes.

Don't fall apart.

Don't.

Just breathe.

Adam's never going to hurt me again. My brother's not really mad, he's just been through a tough time. I'm safe.

But when Scout whispers, "Hey, beautiful," in a husky tone, I lose the battle.

I fall forward into his arms, burying my face against the strength of his chest.

His heart is pounding below my ear. His breath comes and goes in slow, deep rounds that send heat fanning over my ear, down my neck, softening the constriction in my lungs.

His hand glides over my hair, cups my head to him. "I shouldn't have stopped the truck."

I fist his shirt in one hand as I press my other hand against the heat of his back. "It's not your fault, but I can't understand what is up with Griff. He's completely unhinged when it comes to you."

"He has his reasons."

Scout's thumb brushes over my cheek, catching a tear.

That's when awareness comes slamming into me. I'm touching Scout. He's touching me. I'm equal parts alarmed and relieved.

Nervous, I might do the wrong thing, I ask, "Are you okay with me hugging you?"

Scout's body shifts, his hand wraps around my jaw and he tips my face up. Those pale, fascinating eyes are charged with emotion, and I can feel the weight of the moment pressing down on me, as if he's teetering on the edge of something dangerous.

For a beat, I'm not sure if he's going to kiss me or walk away without a word.

Then he steals my thoughts by leaning closer.

He angles his head as he inhales deeply as if he's about to freedive. Then he's crashing into me, commanding me to open for him with the tip of his tongue.

A rough sound vibrates his chest and slides down my

throat as he presses his tall body against me, pinning me against the truck.

The coarse hair of his beard scrapes deliciously against me. The weight of his pelvis crushes against mine as the length of his cock grows.

He kisses me so hard, so wildly, that I wonder if I might come just from the ferocity of the way he's devouring me.

Then he's gone. I'm panting. And he's clutching the back of his neck, looking at the sky. "Fuck."

I lick my bruised lips.

Heart skipping, core throbbing, I almost laugh at the absurdity of the moment. But something about the way he looks is deeply unsettling.

"Is that a good fuck or a bad fuck?"

He doesn't even reply to my question, or remark about me saying the word I told him I'd prefer he wouldn't use. He sweeps me off my feet and tosses me into the driver's side of the truck.

"We need to talk."

Chapter Thirty-Nine

SCOUT

There's a distinct feeling of falling in my stomach as if I'm slipping below the smooth surface of the water into the current of some unseen, unknown force.

Aria looks shell shocked.

Her eyes are rounder than I've ever seen them. I'm afraid they're only going to look more distressed after I drop a load of reality on her.

"Buckle up, sweet girl."

"Oh, I forgot."

I reach across, grab the belt and shove it home. Then I put the truck into drive and hit the gas.

It takes a few miles before I get up the courage to rip the proverbial bandaid off and lay it on the line.

She's completely silent and the air inside the truck is hot, thick and nervy.

After drawing a breath, I spit out the first fact. "We can't have sex."

The silence gets even more dense.

I glance her way and wish I hadn't. She's more beautiful, more destructive than ever before.

The flush on her cheeks is mine. The color on her lips is mine.

I want nothing more than to own the rest of her.

But that's not fucking happening.

Rain starts to fall from the moisture-laden sky, hitting the windshield in fat, random drops.

"Is something broken?"

I take my eyes off the road and put them on her again. "Broken?"

She presses her lips flat as a deep red blush slides onto her cheeks. "There's other ways to be intimate."

Oh fuck. Now I know what she's talking about. "I thought you felt my cock pressing against you."

"But I guess it could still be broken."

"No, sweet girl. I'm one hundred percent in working order. At least when it comes to my hardware."

She goes silent again and I wish like fuck I'd never started this conversation.

Or kissed her.

I almost choke on my own tongue from telling myself that lie.

Staring through the increasing rain, I curse the fire that changed everything.

Another lie. I was already fucked before that, when it came to intimacy. The fire was just the final straw.

"Scout, remember we said total honesty between each other."

Swallowing deeply, I tighten my hands on the steering wheel. "I can't have normal sex."

Her comeback is instant. "Explain."

"You know I don't like to be touched."

She curls her hands into her lap. "Do you ever have sex?"

Maybe I'm hoping to scare her off because I say. "Yeah, I have sex. A lot of it."

"Explain."

I scrub a hand over my jaw. "Let's just leave it at that."

"Why are you hiding?"

I work my jaw side to side, fighting that falling feeling. Trying to escape the whirlpool that wants to pull me back to dark places I never want to go again.

But the question raps on my brain like there's someone else inside my head.

Why am I hiding?

"I'm not hiding from you, Aria. I want you. I really fucking want you in every way a man can take you. But you deserve more than I can give. Like normal sex."

The farm house that Agile's using for base camp comes into view and I wish like hell I was a different man, because I'd like nothing more than to carry Aria into one of the cabinas and forget about the last twenty-four hours.

"But I'm not that man," I say gruffly as much to myself as to her.

"I see." A quiet, two word reply that makes my fingers twitch on the wheel.

She might think she sees, but the deep layers are where the real me lives. The part of me that's a fraction of the man

I was before I went to war and came back broken, scarred, and a hollowed out shell.

"I'll never be that guy."

Now I've got to deal with this jacked up obsession and need to protect her in a way that makes it clear that this is going nowhere.

When I slow the truck and stop in front of one of the eight cabinas on the property, Aria sits forward. "Is this where we're staying?"

I motion to the small blue stucco house. "That's mine. At least it's my temporary home while I'm in Vandemora for the mission. I put you in the one next door."

Hers is identical in size, but the exterior is painted coral. "What about Griff?"

"He's in the last one on the left—the green one."

"It was nice of you to give me my own space."

Was it? Because I'm thinking that's dangerous.

"We're short a couple of guys right now and I thought you might like to have some time to decompress from all the testosterone."

I climb out of the truck, my feet feeling heavy, my brain a washing machine full of bad energy.

She follows me to the hot pink door that leads into her accommodations.

Turning the latch, I swing the door open and fight the natural instinct to sweep the property before she comes inside.

She notices my hesitation. "Go ahead. Griff always does it."

I don't argue, and stalk through the small house checking the shower, the closet, pantry, and under the bed. "All clear."

Silently, she steps inside, and looks around. Moving

around the room, she touches the back of the couch, then the glossy surface of the small dining table. "Pretty. This is really nice lodging."

"We have a special deal with the property owners. It's a story, actually. My teammate is now engaged to the woman that owns the farm. But that whole story is for another time."

Moving silently, she walks to the bedroom door and stops. I find myself behind her. Too close.

Shoulders tight, she stands silently in the doorway.

"What's wrong?"

"I was just wondering..."

She doesn't move. I brace my hands on the doorframe, a rush of blood racing down to my pelvis from the proximity of the bed.

"Wondering what?"

"What kind of sex you have."

I force myself to swallow my growl. "Don't go there, Aria."

"I want to know."

Sealing my front against her back, I let my mouth dip to her ear. "I pay for it."

She flinches, but she doesn't say anything.

"That what you wanted to hear?"

"No," she replies huskily. "I wanted to know what kind of sex you have if you don't like to be touched."

"The kind where I'm the one touching."

She trembles against me, making my body ache. "And you pay for sex, like prostitutes?"

I should keep my damned mouth shut, but I lean closer to her ear. "No."

"Explain."

"Is that one of your favorite words?"

Quickly, she chuffs. "With you it is."

I trail my nose along her ear and against the sweet spot on her neck that I'm dying to bite. "I pay to be a member of exclusive, high-end sex clubs."

"What's that?"

I chuckle darkly as my cock lengthens. Fuck, this is a dangerous game. "It's a place where consenting adults can have safe sex with people that will agree to their proclivities."

"Are you a Dom?"

"Are you a sub?"

She shakes her head, making her long braided hair dance over her shoulder, causing my hand to tingle with the need to fist it.

Quietly, she says, "I don't even know what that really is."

I could teach her.

"Sometimes, I play the part."

"What do the women do?"

Breaking my vow not to put my hands on her, I trail a finger along her neck, brushing a stray, curling tendril aside. "They come."

Exhaling shakily, she shivers under my touch, making my pulse stall then race.

The thin ice below my feet is cracking at record speed.

Then she wrecks me with a whispered confession.

"I haven't wanted anyone to touch me in a long while. But I want you to put those big hands on me. I want you to show me."

Chapter Forty

Aria

The air around us turns volatile. A lightning storm in the Midwest would be calmer. Any second I expect to see bright flashes from the simmering heat between us.

Scout makes a rough sound behind me. His hand wraps around my left wrist, banding my forearm in a tight hold. "I'm not a good man, Aria."

"You're also a liar."

He makes a deeper, animalistic sound against my neck. "You're making me crazy."

"It's mutual. I won't touch you if that's what you need."

He's still as stone for a few seconds.

"You won't be allowed to look at my body. I'll fuck you without you touching me or looking at me."

Wait. What?

I swallow convulsively until I can speak. "If that's what you need."

"It's what I demand."

Ooookay. That's way hot.

This whole scenario is melting my circuits and making me feel like I'm in some kind of alternate universe. Like a Terminator movie with a lethal dose of romantic tension and a twist of 50 Shades.

Heat pulses inside my chest, scattering out to the ends of my fingers and toes like I'm made of sparklers inside.

Scout makes a rough sound deep in his throat. The tip of his tongue circles the edge of my ear. "You good with that, beautiful?"

God, his voice, so low and rough, is the sexiest sound I've ever heard.

"Yes," I reply with a strained tremble in my voice.

I'm not sure who I am right now. My body is humming with so much need, there's so much adrenaline, so much hunger coursing through me, I feel possessed.

He brings my arm across my body, locking it tight to my chest. "Are you okay with me binding your arms—tying you up?"

The pounding pulse in my chest screeches to a halt. Cold sweat erupts along my spine and coats my palms. Every breath I take for the next few seconds feels choppy.

Scout wants to tie me up.

Why didn't I realize that's what he was getting at?

"Aria?"

A wave of dizziness rocks me. The bones in my melt. "Yes, what?"

"You going to let me tie you up and fuck you?"

Oh god. How can I be so terrified and so turned on at the same time?

I truly am going mad.

But I promised him the truth.

"I'm scared," I whisper.

He inhales slowly against my temple. "Good. You should be. I'm not good for you. You deserve a man that doesn't have the kind of fucked up—"

Argh. I unclench my teeth. "Stop! You're not allowed to talk badly about yourself with me."

He's still for a few seconds, then he laughs huskily against my hair. "You baffle me, Aria. That's the only reason I'm even having this conversation. I don't kiss. I don't fuck women that expect more than a physical relief. I have sex and on my terms. Never while I'm working, and most definitely not with a friend's baby sister."

There's so much in those sentences that I can't even begin to process it all. But one remark sticks. He doesn't kiss? Well you could fool me.

Tell my silly hormones that he didn't kiss me to the point of delirium. Because that's the only explanation for what I ask next. "What would you tie me up with?"

His voice turns to gravel. "Rope, normally, but I'm not going back to the truck, so I'll use your shirt."

Whoa.

I fight the tightness in my throat that feels a lot like my heart is trying to punch my tonsils.

Why is it so damned sexy to think about him trying me up with my own clothing?

My mouth drops open, and out comes the craziest statement of my life. "I'll let you."

He groans, his cock pulses, monstrously large and hot against my bottom.

Burrowing his nose deeper into my neck, he rasps,

"This is the worst, *worst*, fucking worst idea ever. Your brother is literally going to shit bricks."

It's my turn to growl.

"First, don't ever mention my brother in a conversation about sex. That's just ick. Second, let me be the judge of half of this idea. And I'm thinking it's not the worst idea ever. I actually think it might be exactly what we both need right now, because this sexual tension is killing me."

His other arm comes around me, sweeping my right wrist up in his hold as he does. Now he's got me—both arms locked in his grip—crossed over my own chest with me pinned against his abs.

A thrill runs through me at the sheer size of his gigantic body locked against my back, at the control he has over me.

It's freaking crazy that I'd want this—that I'd ever want to be restrained after what happened. But here I am. And I can't stop a train that's already left the station.

I'm not just playing with fire, I'm swimming in it. A raging, burning sea of it.

The only explanation is that I'm ravenous for Scout.

In a deeply primal way that can only be blamed on chemistry. There's no reasoning with my brain over this one. Ten bazillion cells in my body are driving and I'm just along for the ride.

Aching, throbbing. Coming unglued, I melt into nothingness in his arms, consumed by his intensity.

Breathless, I say, "Are we going to stand here and talk about sex, or are we actually going to do something, Memphis?"

The tip of my tongue tingles at the use of his real name.

He groans hotly.

My heart throbs a beat that reaches all the way to my pussy.

"Do you have a safe word?"

It takes me a second to process his question. Then I laugh, sounding a little crazed. "No. Should I?"

He nips my neck, then trails his tongue over the stinging bite, and any semblance of words flies out of my brain.

"Definitely need one. Pick something you won't forget."

My core clenches hard.

Empty. Hungry.

Uh. Uh. "You can't bite my neck and expect me to have rational words."

"Can you remember colors?"

"I can't remember my name with your cock pulsing against my ass."

He pushes me a step forward into the bedroom using his big body like a plow. "Sweet girl, you need to be careful using that word?"

"C-cock?"

He exhales the word, "Ass," against my neck.

I blink at the bed. Oh, lord. This is about to get real. I've never had sex with a dominant man like Scout and I don't know whether to be terrified or overcome with joy. "Tell me about safe words."

He clenches me harder against his chest as he wedges his cock more tightly between my cheeks. "Green. Yellow. Red. Just like the traffic light. Yellow is if you're uncomfortable or want to slow down. Red is stop. No matter what, I stop. You might be tied up, but you are one hundred percent in control of when this stops."

"Okay," I breathe as sweat starts to form on my brow and between my breasts.

Oh god. Glancing down at myself, I frown. I have on a sports bra under my fishing-style shirt. On the bottom I have on hiking pants and panties that I dove in.

So *not* sexy.

I haven't had a shower since only god remembers how long.

I've been in a plane crash, I've fought for my life, and I've been working.

Breathing down at me in a slow, agonizingly sexy way, with every bit of his six foot four body sealed against mine, he asks, "Permission to take over?"

That question is so utterly Scout in every way.

Delirious, I ask, "Should we shower?"

"After."

After I die from adrenaline overdose?

I take a slow breath, say goodbye to my sanity, and jump in with both feet. "Permission granted."

Chapter Forty-One

SCOUT

Before I come to my senses, I walk Aria forward, pushing her with my bulk. Moving one hand to her hair, I fist her braid and turn her mouth toward me.

God, she tasted so good earlier, I can't wait to get my tongue inside her mouth again.

She submits instantly as I bite her lip, melting against me, opening for my thrusting tongue.

As I take what I need, I drop her wrist and move my hand down to cup her pussy. The heat of her is coming through her clothing. A dangerous invitation.

She moans into my mouth as I press the heel of my hand against her clit. "Fuck, baby. You're built so sweet. Perfect for my hands. Unbutton your shirt."

Her fingers fly to her buttons and start quickly working.

Such a good girl. I rip the snap on her pants open, shoving my hand inside the band of her panties. A shudder bolts through me when I find her already slippery. So wet and hot.

Yes.

I take another deep drink of her as I yank her pants and panties down below her hips. When she's bare, I grind my cock, clothing and all, against the sweet curve of her full ass.

Carnal need pulses through me.

"Give me your shirt."

I catch her wrists in one hand as I take the shirt with the other. "I need a green light, Aria."

"Green," she whispers brokenly.

"That's it, sweetheart. I'll take care of you now."

Lashing the fabric around her arms, I tie her hands together. "Too tight?"

She shakes her head, as her breathing speeds.

"Green?"

"G-green."

I shove my hand under her sports bra, making her jolt. When the peaked tip of her nipple scrapes my palm, I take her mouth again.

Fuck. I can't get enough of the taste of her.

So much for rule number one: no kissing.

This should be the giant red flag that makes me walk away. But she's made me lose all control.

Ass bare, plush, warm tit in my hand, she sways against me.

God bless, I need to dominate this woman. I need it like I need air.

I push her down onto the bed, pressing my hand into the center of her back and grabbing a handful of ass cheek with the other. "Color?"

"Green. Green."

As I test the feel of her soft skin with my rough palm,

another thread of control snaps. "God, Aria. You're so fucking hot. Do you have any idea what you do to me?"

Pressing her face against the mattress, she closes her eyes as her lips part. "No."

I glide my hand up the sweet curve of her hip, across her lower back. "Perfect for me. Just like that, bent over with your sweet little pussy hot and wet, waiting for me."

She moans brokenly.

"You on the pill?"

"No."

I grit my teeth. I should be happy.

I should be ecstatic that she's not on the pill, not having bare sex. I should be over the damned moon that I'm not going to raw dog her.

But damned if I can quell the frustration inside of me.

I want nothing between us.

Through my locked teeth, I say, "I've got a condom."

"Good," she breathes, "Because if you left me in this state, I'd have to hurt you."

I find my wallet quickly, and flick it aside as soon as I have the condom wrapper in my fingertips. I lay the foil square on her back so I can use one hand on her pussy, and one hand to free myself from my cargo pants.

Taking my time, I fist my cock with one hand as I slide my fingers between her thighs, finding that hot, sweet, creamy place.

"Oh, honey, you're burning hot." Inhaling deeply, I let myself get intoxicated off her scent. "Look at you. So pink and perfect. Wet as a dream."

"Scout..."

"Right here, Aria, not going anywhere until I find us that release."

She shivers from head to toe, her slit throbs against my

fingers. When I push a finger inside her tight heat up to my knuckle, she breathes my name.

My real name.

Dropping my head back, I close my eyes. Memphis. No other woman in my bed has ever called me that.

The reality of that drives fire into my cock.

The foil crinkles loudly. I bite the edge, tossing the wrapper aside as I roll the latex over my engorged cock. The head is deep purple and pulsing beneath the thin barrier. Veins score the length like vines.

She's got me hard as a steel rod. A pulse of fire runs through my veins as I slide back and forth along her wetness. "You sure you want this?"

Please say, yes.

She nods as her bound hands clench the fabric of her shirt.

"Say it."

"Yes, yes. I want this. Take me."

That's when I cross the line that can't be uncrossed.

With a growl, I thrust my head through her tight open-ing. Clenching her hip with one hand and her shoulder with the other, I shudder, fighting the urge to bottom out on one stroke.

But she's too small. Too tight. Uninitiated to the likes of my power.

I'm not even two inches inside of her and there are stars spotting my vision.

"God. God. Bless. Fucking tight."

"Move, Scout, move. *Please.*"

"You're not ready for all of me. Should have taken more time to get you ready..."

Her breath rushes out as I push in deeper.

"Let me in, Aria."

"Oh, god. Scout!"

I lean over her, taking her earlobe between my teeth as I growl. "Let me in. Relax."

She whimpers and I thrust forward another inch.

"Oh goddamn. Beautiful, you're choking my cock so hard."

"Big...stretching... me."

"Gonna make you come all over me."

I pull back and drive in, deeper this time, but controlled when all I want to do is slam into her over and over again until a loud banging makes my head snap toward the door.

Chapter Forty Two

Aria

Oh my god. Oh my god. Oh...

Suddenly I'm lifted in the air. Scout's raspy voice is a low warning. "Don't make a sound. Someone's knocking on the door. I'm going to deal with it."

He carries me into the bathroom, then he spins me around and sits me on the bathroom counter. The cold tile is shocking. Eyes flashing angrily, he shoves his condom-covered cock in his cargo pants and walks out of the bathroom, jerking the door closed after him.

I'm still breathing heavily when I look down and see my bound wrists.

My pants and panties are around my ankles. The deepest parts of my core are pulsing, I'm so wet, the cream from my pussy is all over my inner thighs.

For a few seconds I stare at my body in disbelief.

Who is this woman?

Not me. I never have wild, dangerous sex with strangers.

Okay, he's not a stranger. But he's wild.

And he's definitely dangerous.

Yeah, this is real. Maybe a little too real.

The heavy glow of pleasure coursing through me suddenly spills out on one big exhale.

I lick my lips, and try to slow my breathing. But it's too late. Something is happening.

Something bad. Tendrils of fear wrap around me like a giant sea creature.

Oh god, is this a flashback?

I've never had one. But my counselor warned me.

Pulse pounding in my ears, my lungs squeezing tight, I suddenly feel cold and hot, and queasy.

The room starts to shrink.

My throat dries. I rock back and forth.

God, no. Not now.

But the scars on my wrists are burning. Throbbing below the fabric of my shirt where. Shaking all over, I bite the knots Scout used to bind me, tugging them with my teeth.

When the door opens abruptly, I look up, but my vision is clouded by tears, my hearing fuzzed by the roar of emotion trapped inside my head.

"Oh, goddamn," Scout says roughly.

"Red. Red..." Two words claw out of me.

His big hands wrap around my face. "I got you, Aria. I'm here. Shhh. It's okay."

"Un-un-untie me." My teeth are chattering.

"Look at me."

I blink furiously, trying to clear my vision. He brushes a

kiss over my forehead as a rumble shakes his body. "I'm right here. I'm going to untie you. You're safe."

"Please, please just untie me."

His hands are quick. Within seconds I'm free and he kisses both of my wrists. Carefully pressing his mouth to my skin. The softness of his touch makes my heart clench.

Then he picks me up and carries me to the bed. Using one hand, he whips the blanket back and he puts me down gently.

Then he climbs in, cocoons me with his body, cradles my head, wraps his legs around me. Scout uses all of him to pull me tight against his warm body. I'm totally surrounded by his strength. "I'm here. You're safe. No one is going to hurt you."

Something inside of me splits wide open. I can't stop the dam from breaking. It makes me feel weak and vulnerable.

"Baby," he whispers softly. "Cry it out. I'm strong enough to take it."

"Oh god, Scout," I breathe.

Stroking my back with his warm hand, he speaks quietly against my temple. "You're safe."

He says this over and over again until I'm cried out.

Every ounce, every tear, every terrible thing Adam did pours out of me. I'm limp, exhausted, and covered in sweat when I'm done.

Scout picks me up, carries me to the bathroom and takes us into the shower.

Holding my back to his chest, he undresses me. With careful, gentle touches, he washes me. His large fingers are surprisingly agile as he unbraids my hair to shampoo and condition it.

Some small part of my splintered mind notices the

lovely coconut smell of products that were already in the shower.

I don't even know where my things are. I'm too broken. Too numb to bother. I just let him take care of me.

"Finished," he says in a husky whisper as he cuts off the water. "Let's get you dry."

A few seconds later, I'm wrapped in a gigantic, fluffy towel.

I'm being carried again, gently placed on the bed when I realize he's still in his clothes. They're soaked. A trail of water leads from the shower to the bed.

"Aren't you going to change?"

"I'll be right back."

"Don't go—"

His pale blue eyes soften, "I'm just going into the bathroom to shed these pants."

When he comes back, there's a towel lashed around his waist. Light catches on the ridges of his abs, and highlights the strong contours of his pecs. Below the towel, his legs are strong and...

I force my eyes up and away.

Burn scars.

Tangles and webs of them cover his knees and his shins. And I bet they go up beneath the fabric of the towel.

Chapter Forty Three

SCOUT

It's impossible not to flinch when Aria's gaze hits my legs. I shove away the reaction and focus on her. Which I should have been doing, instead of leaving her unattended with her wrists bound.

That was an asshole move. Irresponsible. She could have been hurt. You never leave your partner bound.

It takes work to keep the anger at myself out of my voice. "What can I get you, babe?"

"Nothing." She bites at her lip and looks down at the blanket. "I think I just need to sleep."

I carefully move toward the bed. "Do you want me to—"

"I want you to hold me."

Letting out a held breath, I reach for her. Wrapping my hand around the nape of her neck, resting my thumb below her chin. "Let me see those beautiful eyes."

She blinks slowly, then looks up at me. Those big luminous browns are going to be the end of me.

"Talk to me."

"I thought I was ready to have sex. I guess I'm not."

Dropping to my knee in front of her, I reach for her wrists and turn them both over.

"Are these related to what just happened?"

"Yes."

Protectiveness thrums through my body. "Someone hurt you while having sex?"

Her bottom lip turns in and she pinches it with her teeth hard enough to chase the color out. "I'm not sure I'm ready to talk about this."

When I lift one of her wrists to my lips and kiss the pulsepoint she shivers.

"Tell me who."

She shakes her head tightly. "It doesn't matter."

Fuck if it doesn't.

"Does your brother know?"

She freezes, her throat works as she loudly swallows. "God no, he would commit murder."

He's not the only one.

I try to breathe through the need for vengeance that's swirling inside of me. "Did you tell the police?"

Closing her eyes, she sits frozen.

"Sweetheart, did you tell the cops someone hurt you?"

"No."

Christ.

I stroke my thumbs over her wrists. "Did you get counseling?"

"Yeah."

Thank fuck.

"What did he do?"

She quickly pulls her wrists away from me.

Fucking hell. I bound her. I tied her wrists when someone clearly hurt her.

"Did some motherfucker cut you?"

In my heart, I know the scars aren't from cutting, but somehow that seems less terrible than what I suspect.

Aria rocks back and presses her delicate hands over her face.

Sighing roughly, I drop my head. "You don't have to tell me. I'm sorry, I didn't mean to upset you. I promise, I will never get rough with you or tie you up again."

She stops me by putting a hand on my shoulder. "This is my fault. I got carried away. I was so... just really caught up in the moment."

"We were both carried away."

When she looks at me this time, there's a hint of the woman I saw earlier in her eyes. "I can't explain this pull between us."

So I'm not the only one. Huffing, I look at the ceiling. "Well, you're not alone in that."

I put my hand on her bare thigh, circling my thumb. "I've never wanted a woman like I want you."

She pulls her hand back and squeezes her fist closed. "I'm so sorry. I can't stop myself from touching you."

"I don't mind it so much."

Her lashes flutter as she blinks. "It's hard to remember not to touch you because I just want to... I want to feel all of you."

I swallow my growl. "I haven't wanted a woman to touch me in forever. But..."

She nods. "I get it. We're both a lot broken."

When I stand her eyes follow me. "I want to show you something."

I reach for the towel around my waist. "First, I need you to know that it's not pretty."

"You were burned," she says in the softest, most crushing voice ever.

"I was. My thighs are the worst."

"You don't have to..."

"I want to. I need you to know why I am the way I am."

When I open the towel, I let it fall to the floor and hang my head.

I'm a SEAL. I've been to war. I've done crazy, unthinkable things. But I have never felt more exposed in my life.

The sound of shifting fabric pierces the painful fog inside my head.

Then a warm breath dances over my chest. "Permission to touch you?"

A groan rattles in my chest. "Yeah."

Aria's warm fingers, as gentle as butterfly wings touch my collarbone, then slide along my neck, up higher, until the edges of her small nails brush against my scalp.

Keeping her body away from mine, she gently pulls me down until my mouth is in reach. Then she kisses me so softly that something inside of me collapses.

I growl into her mouth. When I reach for her, she leaps up, wrapping her legs around my bare waist. God, she feels good. The weight of her in my arms is perfect. The heat of her wrapping around me feels better than anything I've ever felt.

She kisses and kisses me until I take over and devour her.

"Bed..." she whispers against my lips.

I carry her forward and take us down to the cool sheet.

Our kiss deepens, her hands tangling in my hair, my hands gripping her thighs.

Every breath she takes, rubs her tight little nipples against my pecs. The heat of her skin against me turns my body into an amplifier. The air around us pulses with heat.

My cock throbs between us as her legs tighten around my waist.

Neither of us speak as the kiss turns to nips and licks. Hungry exploration, and the exchange of breath.

My hand somehow lands on my discarded wallet. Thank god.

Making room between us, but not breaking the wild tangle of our tongues, I cover myself.

She shivers below me as her fingers tighten in my hair. I break the kiss, to find her ear. My voice is all gravel, my throat tight with emotion. "Are you ready for me?"

"Always."

Always.

Always.

I close my eyes and push against her tight slit. We both groan as I breach the narrow entrance.

But this time there's no driving frenzy inside me to pound her. I want to take her slowly. I want to feel her. Fucking feel her skin on mine. To look in her eyes and...

Fear squeezes my heart, making my eyes slam closed.

I want her to see me.

All of me.

Every broken, dangerous, unloveable part of me.

Chapter Forty-Four

Aria

Slowly, methodically, Scout takes me. Breaks me, mends me, unravels me. Stroke by deep stroke, he presses me deep into the bed, and I collapse into myself.

Falling back. Tumbling forward. Erasing something bad.

Planting something new.

My neck arches against the bed, my breath leaves in a high pitched keen as my fingers tighten in the thick hair at his nape.

His rough palm scrapes over my nipple, then moves slowly down my body until his thumb is pressed against my clit, making a slow circle.

God. *Oh god.*

Coming apart.

"Memphis," I rasp as I climb unbearably high.

I don't even feel him shift away from me, I'm spiraling toward oblivion, burning bright as a rocket.

"Babe, open your eyes."

I flutter them open and find him above me, braced on one muscular arm, his chest glistening, his expression fierce. "Give me your orgasm."

I have no idea what he means, until it hits me. Until my release crashes into me. Drags me under and flings me to a place I've never been.

I scream, raw and primal, the sound wrenching from my soul as I hold my eyes wide open, with our gazes locked.

Then I know.

He didn't just want my orgasm.

That isn't what he meant at all.

He just demanded my heart.

And I handed it over in a scream with fire tearing through me. Shredding the woman I was.

His expression flashes pleasure, then pain. He swallows roughly as I convulse on his massive cock, his muscled body glistening above me, inside me.

Then he locks still, buried deep in my core. Gritting his teeth, he inhales through his nose. The first pulse of his cock makes me jolt with pleasure. The second drags me over the edge again.

I fall so deep this time, I know there's no coming back.

No surviving Scout, or walking away from this job with any semblance of sanity.

And when he wraps his arm around me, and buries his nose against my ear, he grates out the words that seal my fate. "You're mine now, beautiful. I'll keep you safe. I'll protect your heart and fight your battles."

I lie blissfully in his arms catching my breath with my

body tingling, until he shifts off of me and props himself on his elbow.

His voice is husky. "Tell me everything."

Okay. That was not what I was expecting.

Feeling suddenly prickly, I roll my head until I'm facing him. "You can't just demand that I do that."

He blinks at me once. "If we're going to do this then we have to be totally open with each other."

I sit up abruptly.

This wasn't part of the agreement.

I don't say this to him, because I realize he's just shared the most painful thing in the world with me—his vulnerability about his scars.

"Scout. This isn't going to go well."

I know how men like him react to things like what I'm holding back. It's the reason Griffon Kane will never know.

He sits up and cages me in with his legs. I'm sitting tailor style, and he's wrapped around the outside of my legs. We're face to face.

"Look down."

I drag my gaze away from the intensity of his eyes and look at his thighs. It's bad. Webs of mottled skin. My heart contracts painfully for him.

For a long beat, I don't know what to say.

Finally, I find my way. "I don't see the scars, I see the pain you endured."

He's so still, I'm not sure what to do.

Then he curses and reaches for me. His hand finds my neck, my favorite place for him to touch me. Okay, maybe there are a few favorite places, but something about him cradling my neck in his big, strong hand melts a place inside me that I didn't know could melt.

Sensing he wants to tell me something, I ask, "What happened?"

"Long story short, I ran through a fire."

My heart is so broken for this man. "In the SEAL Teams?"

"Yeah."

His voice is rough now.

All I can think to say sounds so lame. "I'm sorry."

"Don't be."

I look up and let my eyes trace over his chest. All the hard-earned muscles. The dips and valleys, sun line at the base of his neck, the smooth texture blanched by the hard lines. "You're so beautiful."

His throat works. I lean forward and kiss him on the lips again. This time he reaches for my hand, and my heart flutters when I realize what he's doing.

He places my palm on his thigh. I don't move my hand, but I keep kissing him. A few seconds pass then he groans, leans into the kiss, a rough sound in his throat.

When his hands move to my waist, my blood heats. He lifts me onto his lap and my legs go around his waist.

"I've never wanted this," he says in a low rasp.

"Neither have I."

He kisses the side of my neck, as I move my hand to his cock. "I want to feel you..."

He grunts, making a frustrated sound. "I can't reach the condoms from here."

"I'm not ovulating."

"Explain." He uses *my* word on me.

With my heart thrumming and butterflies in my tummy, I whisper, "It's my cycle, I wouldn't be fertile."

His skin burns hot beneath my legs, as if the fire inside him is being stoked to a roar. "Are you sure?"

"Yes. I'm sure. I want to feel you..."

He doesn't hesitate, I'm not even finished saying what I was going to say and he's already lifting his hips, pushing into me.

Then, kissing me slowly, tasting, teasing me with his tongue, he uses his hands to raise and lower me onto his rock-hard length.

It's agonizingly sexy to be upright, face-to-face with him, my body wrapped around him, and the pleasure of being so close with him deep inside of me is the most glorious feeling I've ever experienced.

Something inside of me lets go.

A coiled tension unwinds until I'm liquid light in his arms.

If Scout can let go.

I can let go. I can breathe.

This time he doesn't demand my orgasm, I give it freely to him. Any remaining fragments of my heart that hadn't gone before belong to him.

How is it possible to fall in love in a day?

The old saying, *what the heart wants, the heart wants,* passes through my mind.

Well, what my heart wants—no, demands—is crazy.

I didn't know what I needed. But now I know.

Now that battered organ inside my ribs wants to fit into the broken place inside another heart and become a whole together.

As I try to catch my breath, with my face buried in his neck. My hands resting on his sweat-dampened back, I begin to talk.

"I'll tell you what happened. But this isn't going to be pretty and you may never look at me the same again..."

Chapter Forty Five

SCOUT

Nothing could prepare me for this. Not war. Not carnage. Not walking through the fires of hell in the most physical sense.

But I wouldn't realize how truly unprepared I was to swallow the brutality of Aria's story until much later.

Stroking the long, wavy strands of her hair, I hold her as she speaks in quiet, agonized whispers.

As the late afternoon light spills into the cabina, with only the hum of the air conditioner and the pounding of my heart in my ears, I listen.

"The scars are from being handcuffed," she begins.

Fighting a growl, I tighten my hold on her, forcing myself not to squeeze her too hard.

"It started out so normal. Just a few dates. Then I

noticed that my ex was cruel to strangers. You know, the way someone treats a waitress that makes you pay attention. and not in a good way. I guess those were red flags."

She swallows and her fingers tighten against my back. I'm locked inside my frozen body, anger cinching every inch of me until I'm vibrating with the need to howl.

"He was cruel. Just the way he spoke. And it got worse as the months went by, and I started to question why I was dating him."

"It was harder to have sex with him." Her voice breaks. "I just couldn't reconcile my emotions. I was attracted to him, but his behavior began to cast a shadow on the chemistry. But some lonely part of me didn't admit it was over."

Her nose presses more against my shoulder and I force my hand to move to her neck, unlocking my clenched biceps enough to move.

Hearing Aria talk about chemistry with another man is one of the least favorite topics she could ever bring up, but knowing that this story ends with scars on her wrists makes it the worst fucking story ever.

"Then what happened?" I prompt with gravel—and not the sexy kind—in my throat.

"I guess the first really alarming thing was he choked me one night in bed."

I swallow the shards of glass in my mouth and wait for the stinging sensation to ease in my chest, but it doesn't.

I've been the man choking a woman before. But she wanted it. Got off on it. Even if it never did anything for me.

"I should have stayed away after that." A shiver rocks her shoulders. "But he kept showing up. Kept pushing for more. More of my time. Making me let go of the things I liked to do, only to sit at home and wait for him. But then he'd have some excuse and he wouldn't show up. And all the time, he was getting less predictable. More rash. More hair-trigger."

"This fucker's a real piece of work."

She laughs humorlessly. "Oh that's just the beginning."

Because my stomach is tying a knot around my airway, I have to ask, "He cuffed you?"

"Not until the end."

I press my nose against her temple, force air into my lungs, and kiss her damp skin. "What happened?"

For a few seconds, she just clings to me. The heat of her tears on my collarbone makes me curse silently.

"He's never hurting you again. You understand that. You're safe with me."

"I know," she says softly.

"You don't have to tell me right now."

Her head shakes back and forth. "No, you need to know this. But after I tell you, I'm going to ask certain things of you."

"Whatever you need."

When she leans away from me, I'm hesitant to let her go. But then I realize she needs to see me. Wants to watch my reaction to whatever she's about to say.

I get that.

The split second reaction is one of the biggest indicators of character. And right now, she needs to know who I am.

Licking her bruised lips, her lashes dip down for a second. Then Aria pins me with her luminous brown gaze. "I told him I didn't want to see him again. He drugged me under the premise of having a drink to talk things through. I guess he carried me home to his house, or something. I woke up cuffed. Naked."

Her soft voice breaks. Pinpricks erupt all over my skin and I'm not sure if I want her to continue.

She swallows, never looking away. "While I was drugged, he'd raped me. There was a lot of blood. My wrists were mangled. It looked like I had struggled, or he had been so violent. My...my..."

Grimacing, she tries to inhale, but her chest shudders.

"Stop," I rasp. "It's okay, baby. You do not have to relive this."

Glancing down, she inhales deliberately hard for a few seconds. "It's embarrassing."

"You have nothing to be embarrassed about, baby. You are not responsible for that man's actions."

Tears glistening, forehead drawn, she covers her mouth with her hand. "He convinced me I wanted it."

"He's a monster." My words are growled.

Visions of Aria hurt, bleeding, and terrorized burn into the deepest recesses of my soul. Something dark and dangerous awakens inside of me.

I haven't felt this particular beast before. And that's coming from a man that's got plenty of demons inside him.

Aria's face flushes red, her pulse racing below the thin skin of her neck. "He cleaned me up, drove me home. Kissed me and told me how amazing our night was."

That sick bastard.

"Goddamn, Aria." I close the distance and wrap my hand around her skull bringing her to my neck again, tucking her into the place I'm beginning to know was made for her. "Baby, I'm so mad right now, I want to burn cities. That monster deserves to sit in prison for the rest of his life."

Or face a fate worse than what he did to her. Far worse.

With soul crushing sadness, she says, "That won't happen."

"Why?"

The sheen in her eyes builds until it threatens to over-flow her lashes and I want to kiss every damned tear away.

"Scout, I never told anyone. Not until now. It's danger-ous. Things could go horribly wrong because his father's some kind of federal prosecutor. He'll spin the story. Some-thing could happen to Griff, I can't take that chance because I know how truly evil he and his father are. I over-heard some of the things they talk about."

"Where do they live?"

She pulls away and lunges off the bed, clutching her chest, her expression wild.

"What's his name, baby girl?"

As if the reality of confessing this is too much to bear, fisting her hair, she sinks to the floor on her knees. "I shouldn't have said so much. You have to leave this alone. Someone could die. You promised me you'd give me what I need if I told you."

Chapter Forty-Six

Aria

Scout stands and moves to me, dragging a blanket off of the bed as he does. Silent but clearly angry he wraps me up like a child and scoops me off the floor into his arms.

I lean my head on his shoulder as he walks into the kitchen, where he deposits me in a chair. After making sure I'm cinched in tight in the blanket he kisses my forehead and steps back.

He's totally naked now, and seems to be oblivious to the fact that I can see *all* of him.

"What are you doing?"

"Making you some tea."

"Tea?" I choke.

"Yeah, you need something warm."

I blink at his back. His very naked, sculpted back. I fixate on a dark red puckered scar that looks like a stab wound that wraps around his side. To the left are a lot of smaller holes. Shallower, but painful looking.

Further down are his sculpted glutes. Muscular quads, bulky calves, and strong looking feet.

I'm not sure why, or how I'm lost in this observation when I should be freaking out. *Maybe I'm in shock.*

A lot has happened.

Including a lot of orgasms. Giving up something I didn't know I could give, and confessing my deepest, scariest secret. It makes sense that I would be in shock.

He places a mug of hot water in front of me and eases a tea bag into it with two of his broad fingers. "Do you want honey?"

Fingers that were in my most delicate places earlier. I'll never look at his hands the same way.

"Yes, please."

He returns to the counter and picks up the small glass jar. When he comes back to the table, he takes a seat across from me.

I stare at the teabag in the bottom of my cup. "Who was at the door?" I ask as if we're just two normal people.

He motions to a basket of food on the table that I hadn't even noticed. "One of the Russian mercenaries brought a care package of food."

"Those words do not make any sense."

He laughs briefly. "I agree."

We fall silent as I stir honey into the tea, wondering how the hell we got from point A to B to C to D in the last twenty-four hours.

"Look at me, Aria."

Fighting my nerves, I slowly look up. The first thing I notice are the worry lines around his eyes. He rubs a hand through his dark blond hair and sighs, leaning back into the kitchen chair.

Scout looks like a big, primal animal stretched out before me. The lethal kind who doesn't belong in a small kitchen like this, or with a woman like me.

He watches me look at him.

When I drop my attention back to the tea, he says, "You know I'm not going to be able to just drop this."

Making ripples in the water with the string, I keep my face turned down. "I need for you to do exactly that."

"Not gonna happen."

More than once I've wished to be able to rewind the clock. Now, almost as much as I'd like to go back and change the way I handled things before the attack. But I wouldn't be here right now if the attack didn't happen.

I wouldn't be working for Griff. I wouldn't be sitting here with Scout. But I definitely do not want him or my brother committing murder. No matter how much I hate the man that hurt me.

My vocal cords string tight when I try to talk. "God, what was I thinking when I told you?"

"You trusted me. I can't tell you how much that means to me. We both let down our barriers, I've never told anyone why I couldn't have sex with women in a normal way."

Silence hangs between us.

"Thank you for trusting me with that. But I shouldn't have said things that would make you want to..."

"Go after the bastard?"

"Yeah, that."

He reaches across the table and his hand circles my wrist. The heat of his touch scores my cold skin. As he gently rubs a circle with his thumb over my scar, he speaks.

"Never regret being open with me. I know what you gave me."

I sip the tea, praying for relief from this awful clawing sensation in my throat. But if I'm honest with myself it doesn't stop there. It spirals out to my arms and twists around the scars on my wrists where I carry the horrible reminders of all the mistakes I made.

"These scars can't become symbols for more destruction."

He drops his gaze to the table and a ripple of angry energy pulses off of him. As his jaw flexes, he lifts my mug of tea. As Scout takes a drink, he watches me over the edge.

It feels incredibly intimate. Some kind of statement I can't explain.

"He needs to be stopped. A man that does that once will do it again."

I never thought of that.

My stomach dips, my nape tingles. The narrow scar around my wrist throbs beneath his hold. "I'm scared."

"I'll handle it."

"*No*, Scout."

I didn't mean to tell him about the connection to the feds. Or any other clue that could give away who I'm talking about because I know men like Scout and Griff are deadly. They don't move around under the same code of ethics and laws as everyone else.

He stands up and walks into the bedroom. When he comes back he's dressed in his black cargos and the tight-fitting gray T-shirt he had on earlier. He's putting his pistol into the holster at the small of his back when he takes up a wide legged stance in the kitchen. "Rest. I'm going to make some calls and look over the dive gear."

Stiff with fear, I clutch the mug so hard I wonder if it will crack. "Are you making calls about what I told you?"

He doesn't reply to that question. Instead he says, "I'll be right outside. You're safe."

His expression is so hard and so unreadable that it drives the air out of my lungs, leaving me dizzy. "Please don't involve Griff."

"Your brother would go to war for you, sweetheart."

"It's too much. I can't take it. I already worry about him constantly. Worrying about my shitty ex doing something to him would be too much. And you..."

He looks at me with such intensity, my world starts to spin.

Brokenly, I say, "Scout, it would crush me if something bad happened to you. Please don't do that to me."

Chapter Forty Seven

SCOUT

How am I supposed to handle a statement like that?

Doing what I shouldn't, I clamp my mouth shut and I walk out.

Fuck. *What am I going to do?*

I drag my phone out of my cargo pocket and dial Griffon Kane. It rings at least a dozen times and goes to voicemail as I tug open the truck and pull the dive bags out.

"Griff, it's Scout. Call me now." I glance at my watch. "It's fifteen-twenty six."

When I hit the end button, I prop my phone on the tailgate and start working my way through all the dive gear with a fine tooth comb.

When I get to Aria's lines, my senses rev up. Folding the line back, I inspect the edge of the place where it leaked air. The opening is smooth. Not a puncture. Not a tear.

Bastard.

I don't know who, but someone must have cut this.

After taking a few photos with my phone, I zoom in on them. How did I miss this when we were getting ready to dive?

Irritation makes my fingers tense as I dial Justice. He answers a beat later, sounding out of breath. "Are you running?"

"Yes. There's been a diving accident—"

Static fills the line.

"J, can you hear me?"

A garbled reply comes through. Goddamn these fucking phone carriers in Vandemora. I jog to the front of the truck and grab the satellite phone from the case of gear.

When I call Marshall's satellite phone it goes to voicemail. I shoot off a text to him. **We're on our way back to the cave. J said there was an accident.**

A text comes back immediately. **Affirmative.**

Me: **Who?**

Marshall: **I'm not there, I got a call from J, but it dropped.**

Fuck.

A diving accident. Would Griff go into the cave? That mother fucker. He better not. No one else should have been in that cave. It's our S&R mission.

One last attempt to get information results in more frustration. Agent Torres's cell phone doesn't even ring.

I head for the cabina to get Aria at a sprint, but something catches my eye, and I slow to look across the field. One of the Russian's SUV's is thundering over one of the farm roads.

The one they call Gregor stops behind my truck and rolls down his window. "The cell tower on the ridge just got hit by lightning. Vik just got the information."

Vik, their team's leader, always has truckloads of information.

I give him a thumbs up and take off toward the house. He shouts, "Did you hear about the diving accident?"

"Yeah, do you know who was involved?"

"An American, they think he's dead."

Fuck. Fucking hell.

When I sling open the door to the cabina, Aria jumps to her feet. "What's wrong?"

"Get dressed. We need to go to the cave."

Color draining from her cheeks, she drops the blanket and runs to the bedroom.

Like some neurotic asshole, I clean up the mug, throw away the tea bag, and put away the honey. *Fuck. What if it's Griffon?*

He wouldn't have.

Would he?

The man's been sick. Surely he wouldn't have done something so reckless. It has to be Keith. It has to be. That fucker. It wouldn't surprise me, given that he went diving alone. But still...

What if Aria lost her brother?

"What's wrong, Scout?"

I turn around to find Aria staring at me with wide eyes, her fingers clutched to the bottom of her throat.

"There's been a diving accident. We need to go."

She takes a step back, makes a strangled sound and sprints out of the door toward the truck.

Chapter Forty-Eight

Aria

Every muscle in my body is shaking. *Please let Griff be safe.*

I can't be alone. He's my only family.

He's too young. He's too vital.

Lies. I know anyone can go.

An accident. An illness. A force of nature. But I can't imagine life without my over protective brother.

I still don't have my phone, so I try his number again on Scout's.

"God. I'm scared to death." I close my eyes. "Why can't these stupid phones work?"

As he drives, Scout passes me a satellite phone. "Try this phone. His number is in the call log."

Tears blur my vision as I try to operate a phone I've never used before.

Scout sees my distress. He rests a hand on mine, "Here, sweetheart, let me."

"You're driving." Sniffling, I try to push his hand away. "I'll figure it out."

The truck lurches abruptly as he brakes hard, coming to a stop in the middle of the road.

When he pulls the phone from my hand, he leans over and brushes a fast kiss against my cheek. "Try to breathe, babe. I know you're worried. But don't let your mind get the best of you."

I dissolve into wracking sobs. He holds my hand as he tries to call. It must go to Griff's voicemail because he leaves a curt message with the time.

When he starts to drive again, he keeps my hand wrapped in his warm, tight grip. He tries to comfort me. "I don't think Griff would dive. It's just not like him."

I nod, and wipe angrily at the tears streaming down my cheek. "He's too smart for that. But if Keith didn't come out..."

"Why would that asshole dive by himself?" Scout grunts. "That's the first rule of diving."

I sigh as I press my hand to my stomach where my insides are twisted painfully from worry. "He's a loose cannon. He likes attention."

Scout drops the truck in drive and looks at the road ahead, but continues to hold my hand. "How long did you work with that company?"

Too long.

It takes effort to get my mouth to work because it's pinched to keep my crying to a minimum. "About eight months. It was a mistake. But I didn't know if I could work with Griff when he got out of the army."

"So diving runs in the family?"

"My dad owned a dive business. He was an instructor and we both grew up in the water."

"But your brother didn't want to become a SEAL?"

"My dad was Army."

Scout's expression is stony.

"What about you?" I dare ask.

"Older brother. That's it."

"We're alike."

He glances at me. After a moment of silence, he speaks quietly. "You don't want to be like me, Aria."

That's the last thing he says for the rest of the drive. His thumb circles over my knuckles. I take comfort in the touch. All of his touches.

We crossed a bridge, but I'm still not sure if he wants me to touch him. But something about the sad way he said his last remark makes me want to hold him fiercely.

Maybe it's to anchor me as much as him.

I can't help but tighten my hold when we pull into the road where we parked earlier. The scene makes my blood run cold. There's an ambulance with several people in paramedic outfits standing nearby.

The number of vehicles on site has tripled.

When Scout parks, he slides his hand up to my wrist and turns to face me. "Would you wait here?"

"I... I can't—"

"I don't want you to see anything."

I reach for the door. "If it's Griff, I need to know."

He releases my arm, and strides to meet me at the front of the truck where he takes my hand again and helps me down the steep incline. The entire way down to the staging area I pray as bile burns my throat and my heart skips unhappily.

It's impossible to tell what's happening. There are so many people.

Scout stops abruptly. "Jesus," he mutters and turns to face me, putting his body between me and the chaos at the bottom of the hill.

My heart falls. "What, Scout?"

"I'm not okay with you seeing a body."

He tugs me roughly into his arms.

"Is... is it Griff?"

"I don't know, but they are working on someone in a wetsuit."

My toes tingle and spots dot my vision. But the need to get to my brother is stronger. "Let me go. I need to be with him..."

Chapter Forty-Nine

SCOUT

Things go from bad to horrible in the blink of an eye. One of the paramedics lowers a sheet over the face of the man lying on the ground.

Aria stumbles. I catch her, sweeping her into my arms so I can carry her away.

Crying out, she buries her face in my neck. That rough sound destroys me. I've never wanted to shield someone more. To protect her from all the harms in the world.

Voice shredded, I whisper against her hair. "I got you."

Kneeling on the tarp under the staging tent, I brace her head against my shoulder with one hand and use the other to signal for our team leader.

Looking grim, he trots over to the staging tent.

"Who is—"

Someone shouts, "Beast!"

Taking his attention off me, Beast holds up a finger indicating for me to wait and turns to listen and greet one of the Federal agents.

Beast asks, "What do you need from us?"

"Nothing at this point. We're going to move this guy to the morgue in Carollia."

Before I realize what's happening Aria's scrambled out of my hold and darts around Beast. He makes a failed attempt to grab her arm, but she's on the move.

I get to her just as she falls to her knees next to the body.

Dammit, I reach for her hand to stop her from pulling the sheet back, but another hand stops her. "Don't," a rough voice says.

Griffon Kane. Alive and well.

Thank god.

Her brother pulls her way. Dragging her to her feet.

Aria's so stunned, she stares at Griff through a river of tears with her mouth hinged open.

Relief washes through me, making my knees shake and I rub my eyes to erase the blur. He's alive.

Beast grabs my arm and pulls me back a few steps. "It's the owner of the dive company. He was freediving. Shallow water blackout."

Jesus. I glance at the sheet. He was a dick, but I don't wish death on anyone that doesn't deserve it. Only he was stupid enough to be freediving in this cave. Especially alone. No one freedives alone.

A shrill sound makes me whip my gaze to Aria.

Clutching her brother's arm, she screams, "It was Adam? Oh my god."

Griff tries to keep his hold on here, but she wiggles loose. Three of us watch in shocked horror as she flies back to the corpse.

When the paramedic tries to urge her away, she shatters.

"No!" Her voice breaks. "I have a right to see him. I have a right to—"

With hitching words and trembling hands, she pulls the sheet back before anyone can stop her.

Dead silence falls around us, only to be ripped to shreds by her angry voice. "No. He can't be dead..."

Every sob from her tears part of me that I didn't know could feel. But now I feel everything. All the goddamned pain.

"Aria." I take a knee next to her. "Sweetheart..."

Lifeless eyes stare at the sky. *Shit*. She doesn't need to see this. No one needs to.

My gut twists and it takes everything in me not to drag her away, but I force myself to be still. It's done. She's seen. Now the only thing to do is clean up the damage.

I wish I had words to comfort her, but I know that nothing penetrates that kind of scene. It glues itself into your brain and until you process it, there's nothing anyone can say or do.

A keening cry comes from her throat. Then she slams both fists on the dead guy's chest. "You bastard! You bastard. You stupid, rapist bastard!" And after that she unleashes a torrent of screamed words, tears, and punching hands.

Holy fuck.

Stunned, I grab her, pulling her back. When I pull her away, Griffon Kane's staring at his sister, fisting his hair, looking like he's completely unhinged.

Then yelling erupts behind me. "He's breathing! Quick get the oxygen!"

Chapter Fifty

Aria

Through my delirium voices sound garbled. Scouts arms lock so tightly around me I wonder if he's going to crush me. He carries me up the hill, scrambling deftly up the muddy incline as if it's nothing. Below us I numbly observe people hustling quickly. Equipment being moved.

It all feels so far away. Like a nightmare I'm observing from above.

I'm so astounded at what I did, I feel dissociated from my body.

Scout puts me in the truck and leans his arm on the doorframe. He scrubs his hand over his face, as if he's trying to reconcile what he saw too.

"Are you okay?"

The softness in his tone shreds me even more. But when he then threads his fingers between mine I wonder why.

Why would Scout even want to breathe the same air as a woman that's broken as badly as I am?

I pounded on a dead man's chest.

Full stop.

I'm so far off the rails, I don't even know who I am any more.

As a shadow falls over the truck, Scout pulls away. Moving quickly, he buckles me in and closes the door. Before I can see who is outside, he leans back against the truck, blocking my view.

Also blocking anyone on the outside from seeing how destroyed I am.

No staring at the crazy girl.

I can't hear their words, but the vibe is clear. It's a tense conversation. Scout rubs the back of his neck, and re-sets his ball cap twice.

They're definitely talking about me.

My ears aren't burning. My whole body is. The scars around my wrists are the center of the radiating fire.

Not only did I attack a dead man, I screamed that he is... *was* a rapist.

My rapist.

Fisting my hair, I rock forward in the seat until I'm bent at the waist, staring at my boots.

God. I'm a monster.

And Adam might be alive.

Adam, *my* attacker is breathing. And now everyone knows.

The conflict tearing at my insides threatens to rip me to shreds. When I saw him on that backboard, eyes open toward the sky, his sightless gaze and his pale skin cold and waxy, a dark, broken part of me wanted him dead.

Gone. Forever.

I would never have to see him again.

Yet, I also wanted him alive so someday he might pay for what he did to me.

Rubbing my hand over my chest, I pray for relief from the pain. It's too much. I can't handle it any more.

I collapse back into the seat, the weight of this horrible day crushing me until I'm nothing but ragged breaths, icy hands and trembling muscles. What's left of my heart is throbbing painfully in my chest, the beat uncertain whether it wants to race or stall.

I startle when the door opens and find my brother's worried face peering down at me through the opening.

"I didn't protect you from him."

The agony in his voice drives a stake through me. "Griff, please don't."

There's a thick sheen coating his eyes as he stares at the ground. Outside the truck, I can hear his boot scuffing back and forth against the roadway.

"I'm not letting anything happen to you again."

I reach for him, fisting my hand in his shirt. "You didn't do this Griff. He did. I did. I'm the one who trusted him."

He makes a rough sound. "A brother never forgives himself when something happens to his little sister."

"Well, you have to recognize I'm a grown woman."

Griff reaches inside the truck. His calloused hand comes to rest on my shoulder. "You will always be my little sister."

The tears that were blocking my throat rush to the back of my eyes. "I can't believe I did that."

"You were in shock."

"I'm really angry," I admit. "I need to go back to counseling."

"When did this happen?"

Pained, I press my lips together. "Right before I came to work with you."

Recognition widens his eyes before they turn to angry slits. "I knew something was wrong."

"I never wanted you to find out."

"I want to go down there and choke the life out of him again."

"No!" I tug his shirt. "You have to leave this alone."

His hand moves to my hair and he strokes it down the tangled strands. "You know I won't be able to do that."

When he steps back, Scout quickly steps into the gap. He leans down and presses a kiss to my temple. "The medic is going to take a look at you."

I laugh without humor. "So they can commit me?"

He doesn't reply. Scout, being the guy who seems to be carrying me all the time—picks me up and walks to the ambulance with me tight against his chest. His whole body is vibrating with tension.

When I emerge a while later, I'm medicated. *Sedated.* Given something to take the edge off because they don't like what the heart rate monitor says.

So the thing can read broken hearts—who knew?

I don't even remember the ride back to the farm. All I know is when I wake up in the night the room is dark and I'm alone.

Chapter Fifty One

SCOUT

Pacing the hospital hallway, I look at my phone for the fifth time in half an hour. Impatient as hell, I send another text.

No reply.

My hand curls into a fist and I have to walk away from the wall to keep from putting a serious hole in it.

When I round the corner, Griffon Kane is standing a few feet from the hospital exit. We stare at each other, crackling with the same deadly energy.

"Any word?" he rasps.

I shake my head and walk the length of the corridor again.

This continues until Agent Torres inserts his tall frame in front of my boots.

He looks grim.

"Why are you here?" I demand, pushing my hands into my pockets.

"I was checking on my men."

Bastard put guards outside the emergency department treatment room where Adam Hill's being worked on.

Not that I could get in there with all the people and equipment, but it pisses me off that my intent is so transparent.

He glances down the hallway toward Griff. "Don't know which of you two I should worry about more."

Good. Keep him guessing.

I lean against the wall and cross my arms.

Torres does the same on the opposite wall.

"Are you just going to stand there to make sure I don't get into trouble?"

One side of his mouth hitches up, lifting his dark mustache. "You're smart."

I tip my chin. "We'll see who is more so."

"You can't just threaten that man's life and expect me to let you..."

"Didn't threaten his life."

He chuckles darkly. "It's in the eyes, man. Words are petty. It's the quiet ones with cold eyes that you have to worry about."

I just give him a flat stare.

He laughs again even though nothing about this situation is fucking funny. I'm so blinded by rage, I'm surprised I'm not smoking out of my ears.

He casually pulls out his wallet. "Let me buy you a coffee?"

Keep thy enemy close?

I like Torres. I don't like him impeding my own brand of justice.

I nod toward Giff. "You buying him one too?"

"Yeah, get his Delta Force ass and meet me in the cafeteria."

I shove off the wall and stride to the other end of the building where Griff is scaring the staff with his crazy muttering and death scowls.

He stops in his tracks. "Any word?"

"Torres is buying coffee. Come on."

Griff's eyes turn to slits. "He's not getting rid of me."

I turn and walk away. "Me either."

In the cafeteria, Agent Torres is holding court with a few nurses. *Shit, that didn't take him long.* He says something to them and the three women toss frowns our way before heading off. But not before one of them passes him a piece of paper.

"What was that about?"

He lifts his brows. "I told them I needed to go take your asses to jail, and I'd have to come back another day."

"They looked like they'd haul us out in a trash bin if you asked them to."

Again Torres grins. "Never piss the nurses off."

Griff takes a cup of offered coffee.

Torres passes me one and motions toward the table by the windows.

I'm not up for a fireside chat, but questions have been pressing in on me for hours. Torres will have the answers.

Griff looks like he's seconds away from stuffing his fist into someone's face. Mine or Torres's, I don't know.

I get it. The man lying in that hospital room hurt his little sister. The same man I'm determined to make pay. Through legal channels or through other means. I don't care.

Torres stirs a pack of sugar into his paper cup and leans back in his chair. "She's going to have to press charges."

Griff's fingers tighten around his cup, threatening to crumple the shape of it. I keep my hands on my thighs, but I also clench them.

I'm the first to speak. "I don't want her to testify."

"I get that." Torres nods. "No one wants someone they love go through that."

I take a drink of the craptastic coffee, trying to wash down the acid churning through me. "Is there any other way... you know, some other option here in Vandemora?"

He considers his words as he stares into his cup. "There could be. I've been thinking about something."

My phone dings in my pocket. "Excuse me, I need to talk with my team."

By talk, I mean text as there's no guarantee a fucking signal is going to work here. I stand up from the table and move to the other end of the room.

Justice: ***Sorry, I was driving. Bad signal.***

Me: ***Driving where?***

Justice: ***The Professor is taking me to the next cave for recon. Beast put me on this.***

Worry slices through me.

Me: ***Who is with Aria?***

Three little dots appear, they blink. And blink. And blink.

Me: ***Repeat, where is Aria?"***

Justice: ***At the farm.***

I run down the mental list of our men. Beast is in a meeting in Karma. We're two men short. Justice knows better than to leave a sedated woman alone.

Which means if Justice isn't at the farm, then that leaves the Russians.

Agent Torres and Griff whip their heads in my direction as I shove between two tables, knocking a chair over in my haste.

"I've got to get to the back."

Chapter Fifty-Two

Aria

Sedation is great, until you have to wake up.

And you realize there is a stranger in the house.

One that looks like he eats puppies or chews on the bones of innocent people for folly.

My scream is loud in my own ears.

I stumble backward, my foot catches on the chair and I fall on my butt behind the small loveseat.

Scrambling to my knees, I bolt toward the door like I'm a toddler on crack.

Two, big, very rough hands land on my arms and haul me upright, lifting me so high, my feet don't touch the floor.

"Let me go!"

I'm plunked onto the floor and turned around to face a man that's easily six foot six, and two-seventy. But as scary as his size is, the blackness of his eyes is what makes a fist of fear clench around my stomach.

I feel like I'm staring down the grim reaper. And I thought Scout's icy eyes were disarming.

Gone mute, I consider whether kicking him in the balls is smart, or will it just get me snapped like a twig.

Maybe I can talk my way out of this.

Whatever this is.

All I know is I've never seen this man, and he looks like the kind of person you never want to wake up with in your house.

I blink, my vision not exactly right, and I know it's from the drugs. Which makes me wonder if I could hit his balls if I tried.

"Where are you going?"

The man's voice is like thunder and he isn't bellowing.

"Um... I don't know who you are."

His eyes narrow as he grins. "So you're Scout's girl?"

I stare at him, too confused to answer. But the fact that he knows I'm Scout's... Wait. I'm not Scout's girl. *Am I?*

Straightening, he crosses his arms. "You're a little thing, but you got some lungs on you."

"I do?"

"Not too steady are you?"

I sway to the side and his hand shoots out and wraps around my upper arm. He's got calluses and his skin is burning hot. Like he chops people up for fun.

Tremble in my voice, I whisper, "Uh, I guess not."

"Those drugs will do that to you."

He leads me toward the sofa and I still have the sense I'm being led around by a wraith that's here to claim my soul.

I give my head a small shake. Something is not right in my brain.

"Did Adam Hill die and come back from the dead?"

When I drop onto the sofa, he takes the seat across from me. "I don't know his name, but some guy did... uh wake up after visiting a watery grave."

Crass. God.

"Way to sugar coat it." I groan and press a hand to my uneasy stomach. "So this isn't a bad dream."

More staring from the reaper.

"Does anyone ever tell you you're scary looking?"

He studies me for a beat then grins. "Usually not the ladies. Being 6'6 has other affects on them."

I give him a small eye roll, even though I question whether taking my eyes off of him is safe.

"Where's Scout?"

His lips press into a firm line.

Uh oh. I don't like that look and he's not saying, so that's bad. Heaving my unsteady body up, I try to climb off the couch and he gently pushes me back down. "Nope."

"I need to talk to him. Where is he?"

"The boys are off working."

Working as in exacting a slow and painful death on someone? The gurgling in my stomach intensifies. "On the case?"

"Working."

So much for getting answers out of Grim.

My stomach twists around itself at the thought of what working might mean.

He unfolds from the seat, rising to his ginormous height and looks down at me. "You need to eat."

"Who are you?"

"You can call me Grim if you like.

My eyes shoot open. "Did I say that out loud?"

He chuckles—a dark sound—and strolls off toward the small kitchen.

"Is my brother here?" I call.

"Don't know your brother."

"Griffon Kane."

He stops and pivots with military precision to look at me. A strange expression washes over his hard features, then disappears behind a wall of concern.

Um. I don't like that look.

"You know him?"

He turns back to the kitchen and jerks open the fridge.

Feeling unsteady, I keep my butt planted on the couch. The last thing I need to do is crack my head on the coffee table. "What's wrong?"

He gathers some items out of the fridge and places them on the counter. Fruit, yogurt, something I don't recognize.

"Are you another of the silent brooding types?"

His eyes flick to mine across the bar, but then he silently focuses on his work.

"Come on now," I plead with frustration in my tone. "If you know Griff, then just say it."

He reaches for a bowl, rattles around in a kitchen drawer until he has a spoon in his hand. "I know him."

"Jesus. Who are you?"

"Truck."

I glance at the door and rub my forehead. If this guy expects me to get in a vehicle with him, he's nuts. "Hell no," I mutter. "I'm not going anywhere, I don't even know you."

He makes a face. "What are you talking about?"

"Truck?"

He goes back to working on the bowl of yogurt as he

shakes his head for a few seconds as if I've lost my mind. "That's my name."

Oh. Truck—like Scout and Beast. Dropping my head back on the couch, I grimace. "Either I'm really drunk off that medication they gave me or this conversation is completely messed up."

After some thunking sounds fill the kitchen, he returns. There's a slight limp to his gate that I didn't catch before. For a beat, I wonder if he has a war injury too. Not going to ask. Just like I don't want people to ask about my wrists.

When he puts the bowl on my lap, there's chopped bits of melon on top of the yogurt and sprinkles of shredded coconut.

For some reason this causes tears to spring to my eyes, making me feel ridiculously vulnerable.

"Oh brother, it's just a bowl of yogurt," he says gruffly and he takes a seat in the chair in front of me again. "Eat."

I weirdly obey, maybe hoping it dissipates some of the fog in my head, or the emotions clawing at the inside of my chest. I'm exhausted too. Like the weight of the past two days is a heavy blanket draped over my shoulders.

He—the guy called Truck—watches me in silent tension. As if he's looking for some kind of clue.

Well, good luck buddy. I'm clueless right now.

When I've finished most of the food, I place the bowl on the small end table and fold myself up in the corner of the couch. I feel small and out of place under his hawk-like observation. "Are you just going to stare at me?"

After rubbing the back of his knuckles over his chin, he starts to speak. "Do you know how Scout and Griff met?"

My brain is foggy, but not that foggy. "Yeah, they met on some kind of mission, I guess. I mean I don't know the specifics. But Griff is a Delta, which you know, and of course you know Scout is a SEAL, so they work together sometimes."

I find myself frowning at his stern expression. "Do you have something to add?"

"What has Scout told you about himself?"

I blink at Truck, the big, impossibly dangerous looking man, and realize that this is territory that I'm not comfortable entering. "Some things. But I'm not going to discuss those with you."

Weaving his hands together, Truck cracks his knuckles. "Do they act jacked up toward each other?"

"Oh yeah." I curl my arms around my knees. "Like they're out for blood. Or they don't trust each other. Or...I just don't know."

His eyes glint then he looks away. "You need to know what happened."

Chapter Fifty-Three

SCOUT

I'm not sure if I'm alarmed—more alarmed—or relieved when I crest the hill and see there are no trucks parked in front of my cabina where I left Aria sleeping.

Surely she's not alone.

Justice would not do that. *No fucking way.*

He's way more honorable than that.

But the Russians... they might not be in a vehicle. They're staying in one of the farm's cabinas too. The agave farm is Vandemora's grand central station for operatives these days.

Fuck. And I don't even know who they really are.

Any one of those big bastards could have walked over to stay with Aria.

My anger surges hotter than a volcano and threatens to uncap my head. I told Justice about my suspicion about the damage to her lines, but would he trust one of the others to watch over Aria as she slept?

The thought of Rory being near Aria makes my hands clench, and my brain pulse with murderous rage. Gregor is a complete unknown.

And where the fuck is Vik? Their leader has been MIA for the last two days. It drives me crazy to have so many unknown variables.

Driving way too fast, I tear past the big wooden barn with 'DonAzule Agave' painted on the side and slam to a stop in front of the little blue stucco house. That's when I see a shadow looming through the curtain. Not just a shadow, a big shadow and a small shadow.

Dammit. Aria. *Someone has Aria.*

When I flip open the glove box, the first thing my hand lands on is a knife. It'll do. I bolt from the truck.

The element of surprise went out the window with my noisy arrival. So I go right for the one and only door and kick the fucking thing so hard one of the hinges breaks.

Everything happens fast.

A hand chops down on my arm, a punch lands in my ribs, knocking the air out of me. The knife flies, but I land a solid punch to a steel jaw and catch the big bastard's arm, swinging it behind him.

A white ceramic bowl soars past me and bounces off of the guy's head.

Wait what? The fuck?

Truck and I both start laughing.

Shit, I drop his arm and shake out my hand. "You son of a bitch. I didn't know you were in town."

He rolls his shoulder, stretches his neck, and looks pointedly at the bowl on the floor. "Aria, who were you throwing that at?"

245

Standing by the front door, her hair is tousled, she's wearing one of my t-shirts and a pair of my boxer briefs—the ones I put her in when she was asleep—and I've never seen a more beautiful sight in my life.

She makes a small grimace and fists her hands next to her thighs. "I don't know. I just... I just thought you were going to hurt each other."

Truck slaps me on the shoulder. "She's got cajones, I'll give her that. She even thought about kicking me in mine when she woke up to find me in the house."

I narrow my eyes on him. "Did you scare her?"

Aria kneels to pick up the bowl and its spilled contents. "How could he not, looking like that?"

"Good point. He does have a way of terrifying women." I grab a towel from the kitchen and crouch down to help her with the yogurty mess. "I'm sorry I wasn't here when you woke up. How are you feeling?"

"I'm fine. Groggy. But Truck claims the ladies don't mind that he looks like he's come to claim souls. All he needs is the cape, and a big knife thing."

"Depends on the kind of woman," Truck quips. "There are plenty out there that like to live dangerously. Have you ever looked at BookTok?"

I shake my head and toss the kitchen towel toward the sink. I don't know what BookTok is, but I know one story. "Like the paramedic girl from the earthquake?"

"Shit, that girl," he snorts and shakes his head. "She wanted to play doctor and it wasn't my *left* leg she wanted to look at."

Aria's looking between us like we're a tennis match. But there's definitely worry in her eyes. And I don't like that one bit.

Course Truck is being Truck.

He grins, but it's always more like a wolf's snarl. "Good to see you, man."

I shake his hand. "Welcome back. We could use the help. You heal up okay?"

A quick shrug, and Truck picks up a black backpack from next to the front door. "Well enough. Now that you're back from...uh... taking care of business, I'm going to go hike that mountain to look for MZ."

Aria looks alarmed and I'm not sure if it's because... well, hell. Hard to tell why at this point. We have a lot to talk about. But first, I need him gone but I'm also worried about my teammate. "You sure your leg is well enough to go?"

A somber expression darkens his already nearly black eyes. "You know we've both dealt with worse. Did you take care of business?"

"Not yet."

He tips his chin. "Is that where her brother is?"

I nod.

His head swivels toward Aria. "Nice to meet you. Remember what I said."

Chapter Fifty-Four

Aria

As soon as the door closes, I lose my composure. Hand shaking, I drop into the closest chair. "Is he alive?"

Scout stands perfectly still. I'm not even sure he's breathing.

"Is he?" My voice cracks.

"For now."

I turn my face away, and chew hard on my lower lip. I hate the part of myself that wants *him* dead. I also hate the part of myself that wants vengeance.

But one emotion rises above both. I don't want Scout to murder Adam.

"What business was Truck asking about?"

Hollow. My words sound like I'm inside a tin can. Somewhere lost deep inside of myself.

Scout just stands there. Almost as if he's at war with himself too.

Aren't we quite the pair?

"I was surprised you were gone when I woke up."

He flinches. I catch it out of my periphery.

The timbre of his words is a low rasp when he replies. "I didn't know Justice would leave you. He had to take the Professor to the next cave. I came as soon as I found out."

I let myself look at Scout again. He's wired. But circles darken his cheeks, and his face looks gaunt. "Did you sleep last night?"

"No."

Worrying at my fingernail, I look past him out the window. God, how I wish anything between us could be easy.

"Have you eaten?"

"No."

"Let me guess. You've been main-lining coffee?"

He watches me with a guarded expression as I walk past him toward the kitchen. "I'll make you something to eat."

But he catches up to me and presses a hand to the refrigerator door, his body close enough that I can feel the heat from him, but not touching me. "Your scars..."

A shudder wracks me.

He continues in that rough tone. "Calling me your boyfriend..."

I drop my head, and my tangled hair drapes around my face. I look like a feral animal. But more importantly I feel like a cornered one.

"He's my rapist. Is that what you want me to say?"

Scout leans into me, cocooning me in his arms, pressing his mouth to the top of my head. After exhaling raggedly, he half growls, "I want to kill him."

How crazy is that?

"No. No, please promise me you won't. He's not worth it."

Scout's scary, silent, and vibrating with the most dangerous energy I've ever felt around him.

"I need for you to stop being a barbarian over me."

His body tenses. "I don't know if I can do that."

"Well you need to. It's time for the authorities to handle this. You were right, he shouldn't ever be able to do what he did to me to another woman."

He rumbles.

I take a breath. "I am sorry you found out who it was that way."

"It's okay, sweetheart. But you shocked the fuck out of me and your brother."

I jolt and try to pull out of his arms. "Wait, where is Griff?"

Scout rests his palm against my cheek, his eyes search my face, then come back to hold my gaze. "I rather not talk about that."

My heart plummets. "Is he—" My throat contracts and works, trying to swallow. "I need to talk to him."

"You need to let this play out."

"Play out!?" I shriek and back across the kitchen. "If Griff kills Adam, he'll go to prison."

Scout leans against the fridge, a look of cold uncaring on his face.

I'm appalled. "You don't care if Griff gets in trouble?"

He looks affronted. "Of course I care. It would hurt you."

Clutching the island, I stare at a man I hardly know, but one who knows all of my darkest secrets. The one who also allowed me to touch him when no one else does. But I have no idea what the darkness swirling in his hard gaze is about.

I pull back, curling into myself. "You don't care if Griff murders someone? I can't stomach that. I would never look at him the same."

"I've killed."

So blunt. It's a punch to my gut. Of course I know this. Scout is a combat hardened SEAL.

But it still unsettles me.

"Aria, your brother and I are both special forces. We've taken the lives of bad people. A lot of them."

I fight flinching.

Scout takes a step toward me, putting him in my personal space. A shiver works through me as I tip my face up so I can see his eyes. Everything about his expression is fierce.

"That fucker lying on that backboard hurt someone I care about. This is personal."

Tears crest over my lashes. The trails they leave are strangely cold.

I know they've killed in the line of duty. I really, really know this. But when you see someone living and breathing and you think about someone you know taking the life out of them, that hits differently.

This whole situation is a nightmare. The fault is squarely on my shoulders. If I had only seen the red flags with Adam.

I shake my head. No, I saw them. I just didn't heed them.

Pinching my lip between my teeth, I fight the urge to sling my arms around Scout and beg him to leave this alone.

But I don't. And I still feel weirdly drunk from the meds

and my emotions are so wrecked, I don't know if I'm coming or going. Angry or hurt. Scared or relieved. *Raw.* I decide that's how I feel. Completely raw and vulnerable.

Hurt seeping into my voice, I demand, "Why do you care about me, Scout? Is it because I dropped my panties for you? Or is it because I'm submissive? What is it?"

Chapter Fifty Five

SCOUT

A knife to the gut would have hurt less than Aria's words.

"You want to know why I care?"

She's shaking, her eyes wild, damp and hurt.

Fucking hell.

"Other than one of my team members, you are the first person who has ever touched me because you care."

Her eyes flash with disbelief.

I nod, as my chest tightens. "I never had a loving parent. A sibling. Anyone that would touch me with tenderness. But you slept next to me. You checked to make sure I was breathing…"

My throat works with a rough swallow.

She makes a small, pained sound. "Scout—"

"My father was a gigantic fucking prick. He thought a belt to the ass was caring."

"But what about…" Her voice falters as even more water gathers on her eyelashes. "Your mother?"

"Never had one. And the women that my father brought around wanted to touch me for the wrong reasons."

"Oh god."

"I grew up fast. I was big. By the time I was a teenager, the kind of women he ran with wanted me as some kind of conquest."

"That's disgusting." Aria shudders.

I look down at the floor as the old memories make my skin crawl. "You can see why I had certain sexual… preferences."

When I raise my gaze to hers again, she's nodding slowly. "That all makes so much sense. Then the fire?"

"Yes, then the fire."

A tear drops onto her cheek and rolls down the velvety skin. It takes everything in me not to catch it. To wipe it away. "Don't cry for me, Aria. I'm not worth it."

"You're so wrong," she says hoarsely. "You can't see who you are, but I can."

I fight and fight the urge, but I can't stop myself. I reach for her, dragging her against my chest as a growl builds in my chest.

"Why?" My voice sounds ancient.

"I don't know."

Burying my face in Aria's dark hair, I try to catch my breath. It's impossible. My world is collapsing around me.

"Please don't love me." I hold onto her as I feel like I'm about to shatter. "I'm broken. So fucking broken. You deserve more, Aria. Someone that's not a monster."

"Stop, god, Scout. *Stop! You are not a monster.*" She makes a choked sound and takes my face in her hands. "You can't tell me not to love you, because it's too late."

Her thumb traces over my jaw as she leans up on her toes and pulls me down toward her.

My hands tighten around her waist as blood thrums through my veins. I need this woman. The best thing for her would be to push her away. To make one of the other team members guard her while she's in Vandemora, then to send her on her way back to her life in the states.

But then the sickening thought of Adam Hill going back to the states makes me want to scream.

No. I'm not letting her go. Not leaving her safety to anyone else. Aria Kane is mine now.

When her lips brush across mine, I take over. She pushes closer to me, letting me dominate her mouth with deep, twisting thrusts. Soft whimpers pour gasoline on the fire.

"Unless you tell me to stop, I'm going to strip you, kiss every inch of you, and bury myself hilt deep inside your perfect little body."

"Please," she rasps, pressing herself tighter, rubbing her nipples against my chest.

When I lift her, she instantly wraps her legs around me. God bless, the heat at the vee of her legs presses tightly against my engorged cock, making the breath hiss out of me. "See what you do to me, I'm consumed with you, beautiful girl."

Her kiss grows frenzied, her nails scoring the back of my neck, knocking my hat off as I carry her toward the bed. "Seeing you in my clothes does something brutal to my control."

"I like wearing your things, they smell like you," she murmurs as I lay her down onto the bed. Her eyes are burning liquid, and only for me.

How did this happen for me?

I lower myself onto her as she opens her legs for me, cradling me against her. With my weight on my elbows, I make sure not to be too rough with her smaller frame.

She watches me with open love in her gaze as I take her face in my palms. When I lower my mouth to hers and kiss her slowly, she closes her eyes and sighs happily.

That little sound unravels thousands of tight muscles in my body. Softens me in a way I never knew could happen.

When I pull back, her gaze is dreamy, her fingers are soft against my back, pressing against the skin below my shirt, and I'm feeling more vulnerable than I've ever been in my life.

That's when I see it. A sign from the universe. As if I've ever believed in anything like that before now. But this is a sign.

Smoothing my thumb over the tiny tattoo tucked just behind her ear, I feel a deep sense of peace lodge itself in my chest.

"It's a compass..." she says quietly.

"It's perfect."

"It is a symbol of luck for me. So I'll always find my way even in the darkness..."

My heart tries to work its way up into my airway.

For a few seconds I stare at that the small mark and wonder if Aria's a gift from something much larger than any one of us can understand. When I speak, my voice is smoke and gravel and my bone marrow is on fire. "You know what maps meant to me. The compass I bought with my allowance was the most precious thing in the world to me."

Stroking her fingers in a slow circle against my skin, she holds my gaze. "Do you still have it?"

"No, it was lost somehow over the years, but now I have *this one*."

Her breath turns shaky and catches as mine fills my chest with light.

"I love you, Aria. I didn't know I was..." My throat seizes up. It takes a few breaths before I can go on. "Nothing like this, nothing good like you has ever happened for me."

"Oh Memphis," she whispers as she holds me tighter. "I'm going to show you just how much you deserve to be loved."

Unable to take that sweet expression on her face any longer, I drop my forehead to hers. "I'm not an easy man."

"You're perfect."

"I'm—"

"Going to be quiet now and use your mouth to show me how good you can make me feel while I do the same."

Chapter Fifty-Six

Scout

I groan and take her mouth again, drinking in the sweet essence of her, then I pull back and slide my hands under the shirt she's wearing. Pale soft skin glows beneath my darker, scarred hands.

Every breath she takes seeps into me through my hands, working some kind of deep magic on me.

When she pulls at the shirt I'm wearing I reach back and grab the neck, ripping it off of myself. A playful smile brightens her eyes. "That's a handy trick. Can you do that with your pants?"

"I can do it with yours." I hook a finger in the waist of my boxer briefs—the ones she's wearing and yank them off in one hard pull.

After a little gasp, Aria laughs. It's a warm, husky sound that makes my pulse stutter and race.

"Fuck, you're so pretty." I reach forward and sift my

fingers through the dark array of hair spilling around her head. "Mmmm... I love this."

Then I trace a finger down her neck and spend a few seconds enjoying the dip at the base of her throat. When I lean over and lash that little hollow with my tongue, she goes crazy.

"Oh god, Memphis, your tongue..."

I press her breasts together, lifting both mounds until they're plump and ready for my mouth. When I press my lips at the top and delve my tongue between them Aria squirms and fists my hair.

"You like that?"

"God, are you crazy? Yes!"

I chuckle and move lower, wrapping my hands across the softness of her stomach. "So fucking sexy."

She doesn't even notice me dropping the f-bomb any more. At least not when she's so wet with her arousal that I can smell the cream leaking from her pussy.

When I nip at her hip, her moan is long.

"I want to touch you, to lick you and..." her voice trails off. "Oh god, what are you doing?"

Pressing my thumb to her clit, I swirl my tongue in her belly button. So fucking cute and sexy, that little divot makes me crazy.

"What were you saying?"

She reaches blindly for me. "Cock. Hand. Mouth."

It's my turn to groan. "You sure? I have plans for you."

An unhappy sound is followed by her smacking my shoulder playfully. "Lay alongside me, the opposite way."

"Listen to you, little sex kitten."

"Not, but it's the only way I can think to...you know."

"I can show you some other tricks."

She shudders as I slide my finger through her soaked

labia. Voice rising to a sharp tone she says, "For the love of god, just humor me!"

I chuckle and stand up next to the bed while keeping the pad of my thumb on her clit, working slow, wet circles. With my other hand, I jerk open my cargo pants while I kick off my boots.

She lifts her head and gazes appreciatively at my cock which makes me burn hot from the root to the tip. Her focus never falls to my burned thighs, not once. She's locked on, with a hungry light blazing in her pretty brown eyes.

Unable to stop myself I stroke my cock, from base to head with one hard stroke. Aria's hands go to her breasts, tugging on her nipples, making my mouth go dry.

"Look at you, sexy girl. So perfect. I can't wait to be inside you again."

As I climb on the bed, her hands drop from her tits and reach for me, scrambling over my skin with featherlight touches. As I lie down next to her, my feet toward her head, she rubs her whole body along mine. The sensation is fucking delicious. Skin to skin.

My nervous system goes haywire.

I never knew how good this felt.

"You may use your mouth again," Aria announces with breathy humor in her tone.

"Oh, I can?"

"Please."

Fuck. How can I not? I spread her thighs and wrap the creamy soft heat of them around my face as I seek out the sweet scented wetness that's got everything tantalizingly slippery.

Curving my hands around her ass, I bring her pussy to my mouth, spreading her open with my fingertips from the back. A swift jolt from her thighs tells me exactly what I want to know.

But when she wraps both her hands around the base of my cock and presses a tiny kiss to the head, I groan into her pussy.

Oh, fuck.

Can I do this, or am I going to lose my control?

She wiggles on my face as she takes my throbbing head into the heat of her mouth. Oh. Oh. God.

Then she begins to lick and suck along the length of me. I'm groaning, stabbing her pussy with my tongue, nuzzling her clit with my nose as she gets even wetter, hotter.

A series of slow contractions hit her core. As I trace the tips of my fingers around her slit, she starts to shiver under my hold. Her mouth tugs harder at my cock.

I will not come. I will not—

I focus on her.

All her.

Dragging my finger through her slickness, I seek out the tight circle of muscle at her rear. Licking, sucking, nuzzling her, I make a slow glide around the ring causing a strong contraction to tighten around my tongue.

Her hands still on my cock, and I feel the heat of her breath scoring across my skin. She's close.

So am I.

I'm close to pushing my finger into her sweet little ass, but want her to let me know she's down with it. So I pull my mouth away, lick my lips and rasp, "Tell me what you want."

Pushing her pussy toward my face, Aria whispers brokenly, "More, everything."

One of her hands goes to my thigh, over the scar and I flinch.

Chapter Fifty-Seven

Aria

Scout stiffens against me and I realize where I have my hand. "Please don't stop," I say as I lean into his cock and offer a slow lick to the crown.

"You taste so good," I murmur, and Scout relaxes against me. "Mmmm, I love the saltiness of your precum."

He growls and buries his face against my aching pussy again. *Thank god.*

I close my eyes and lick him with delight as he works me up with his fingers, his tongue... and god, is that his nose?

It's heaven.

The way he teases me all over, all the way to the back makes my pussy clench. I've never—

"Ohmygod! Right. The-*there*." I gasp and moan and make some other kind of weird sound as Scout pushes one of his thick fingers into my rear entrance.

But that's not all. The pressure of another finger hits my g-spot, his tongue swirls over my clit and I nearly crawl out of my skin. "Ye-ohmygod!"

That's the last thing I remember before I wrap my legs around his head and ride his face like a rodeo bull until I'm somewhere in outer space.

My mind is a haze of buzzing pleasure, my limbs out of my control. My pussy flooded with golden, liquid heat.

I don't know how long I'm lost.

But I come back to a deep masculine chuckle and realize I'm on top of Scout, my thighs spread around his head, and I've got a deathgrip on his rock-hard cock.

Flushed with embarrassment and the power of my release, I blink at the thick, dusky head crowning his erection. "Holy cow. How did I get here?"

He gives me a slow lick that causes me to moan and my everything to twitch. When he slides a finger into my pussy this time, it starts all over, like the orgasm switch has been flipped and I can't get off the ride.

This one is fast and brutal and makes me scream.

And while I'm in my blissed out black-as-night nirvana, Scout flips me around like I weigh four pounds and am made of jello until I'm on my back, one of my legs is hooked over his elbow, and the other is down between his thighs.

His veiny cock is hovering delightfully close.

I'm a shivering, soaking wet shell of a woman with an ache inside me that can only be described by two words—desperately empty.

One of his big, rough hands goes to my breast, where he touches me like a man that knows how to make a woman's body sing. My nipple leaps to attention, as if it wasn't already tight and I moan.

Then he slides his hand down and palms my pussy with a possessive glint in his eyes. "I don't share, Aria."

I blink at him, my skin slick with my orgasms. "Good, because I don't either."

He growls and closes his eyes. "Fuck, woman. You don't know what it does to me to think about that."

Without thinking, I reach for his cock, and align the head to my screaming vagina. "Now, Memphis. Claim what's yours now."

He flicks his gaze to me. It's a thousand burning watts of raw desire mixed with pain.

Lowering one hand to the bed, he braces it against my shoulder and dips down. When I expect him to kiss me he bites my lip, and murmurs hotly, "When you come on my cock this time I want your eyes open and your hands on me, I want you to love this monster back to life."

Then without preamble, Scout shoves his ten inch cock into me. He doesn't bottom out and I thank god because I need a second. I need to catch my breath. And I know he's done just that. He's taken care of me.

But when he tightens his hold on my leg, and locks my bottom leg to the bed with his thighs, he makes a rough sound in his throat.

Keeping his control is costing him. And I know he won't hold back long.

I can't wait.

Spread open like scissors for him, pinned to the bed, open and vulnerable, I've never felt more safe. More able to let go.

I plant my hands on his chest and meet his hot gaze head on. "Memphis..." It's a low, groaned version of his name that wrecks his control. Because after that he's pure animal.

Deep, hard thrusts, rough breathing, sweat slicking his skin below my palms.

He takes everything.

My mind shatters, my heart swells, and I come like I've never come in my life. It's a rolling wave of heat, a tidal wave of pleasure. The emotional release that will leave me changed forever.

This time, Scout follows me. Eyes wide open.

I press the tips of my fingers into his thighs. "I love you. I love you. I'm here for you."

He shouts—a harsh guttural sound—then collapses onto me, fusing our mouths together. I don't need to hear words. His heart screams at me.

Scout holds me for a long time. His silent tears dampen my hair, run down my cheek, trace over my neck, fusing our heated skin together. I take a deep breath and realize that I feel utterly safe.

How long has it been since I've felt this?

Pressing my body closer to his, I let his powerful body cocoon me, and I realize that I've never felt this.

This completion.

The insatiable need to help this man know love. To hold him. Heal him. Walk by his side.

Squeezing my eyes closed, I soak in the sensation of his emotional surrender. Today is the first day of forever.

I'm lazily stretching two hours later when Scout presses a kiss to my temple and unravels his long legs from mine.

Darkness has fallen outside, and the little house feels like a tiny, safe escape from the world. It's only temporary. We need to work. His teammates and my brother need to be dealt with. But for one more moment, I want this more than I want anything else.

"Starving. Are you?" His voice has a sexy rasp I've never heard before.

I reach my arms overhead and for the first time in a year, the scars don't tug tightly on my skin. "Twinkies?"

He chuckles softly. "I'm fine with never eating out of another vending machine again."

I roll onto my side and enjoy the view of him stretching as he stands next to the bed. Completely naked.

"God, you're beautiful," he says in a husky tone.

"I was just thinking the same thing. My heavens, how did you get all that muscle?"

He shrugs casually and swipes his pants off of the floor. "Hard work."

As he strolls out of the bedroom, I slide from the bed and walk to the bathroom, a silly grin on my face.

When the reflection in the mirror catches my eye, I see a new Aria. Cheeks tinted pink, hair in sex-tangles, nipples peaked.

Scout appears behind me, wrapping an arm around my waist. He feeds a slice of orange into my mouth.

The bright, sweet flavor bursts on my tongue and I close my eyes and moan. "So good. Way better than Oreos."

He kisses my neck, then takes a slice for himself.

We take turns until the sweetest orange I've ever tasted is gone, then he flicks on the shower and drags me inside.

Chapter Fifty Eight

SCOUT

What the hell is that noise?

It's a ringing phone. Not mine. The ringtone is some song. I open my mouth to grouse about the interruption to my long needed sleep, but my lips won't part. Fuck.

My head is heavy... and there's a piece of tape—

No!

No! No! No! *Fuck no.*

I shake my head as I force my bleary eyes to focus.

I'm in the bedroom. The bed is empty. It's night.

I'm naked and bound to a chair.

Aria.

My chest nearly explodes from the sudden thrashing behind my sternum.

Goddamnit. No.

Jerking one hand, then the other, I test the tape around

my wrists, bellowing against the duct tape on my mouth like a raving lunatic.

I've never seen red so dark. So consuming. I'm alive with rage.

The chair scrapes against the floor with every jerk, but the tape holds.

Mother fuckers. Someone used a whole damned roll on me.

Blood. There will be lots of blood for this.

I throw the chair over onto the floor, crashing on my side and begin thrashing like a wild animal against the tape around my ankles.

This. Goddamned. Chair. Is no match for me.

Gathering a head of steam and feeling the strength coursing back into my body, I buck wildly and snap one of the legs off.

One more wild thrust—channeling a kicking mule—I splinter the other side of the chair.

I'm coated in sweat by the time I get to my knees. An oily feeling churns in my gut. Fucking poison. Probably some cheap date rape drug, or tranq.

As I climb to my bare feet, the remainder of the chair clings to my back held by the tape around my wrists.

Panting through my nose, I ram myself into the wall, over and over until the wooden chair splinters into jagged shreds.

A chair arm dangles from each of my wrists, at last allowing me to tear the tape off of my mouth.

For a few seconds, I gulp air that's scented with Aria's sweet scent, our sex, and the rinds left from the fruit we shared hours ago.

With every breath my head gets clearer. The fruit must

have been tainted. We shared every item, so she would have been poisoned too. She's much smaller. She could still be unconscious.

They could be doing god knows what to her right now.

I tear the room apart looking for my phone and my sidearm, but they're gone. Whoever did this made sure I wouldn't be a problem.

The phone that woke me is ringing somewhere in another part of the house. It takes me several moments to find it in one of Aria's bags.

"Hello," I rasp, praying this is some fucked-up ransome and that I can buy Aria's safety.

"Hi this is Melanie calling from Florida Dentistry, is Aria available? I need to confirm her appointment."

"No!" I roar loud enough to echo off the walls.

Disconnecting with a viscous stab, I try to remind myself to breathe.

You have to keep your head. Get your shit straight.

Aria's counting on me.

I dial Beast's number from memory.

"Calder here."

I storm through the house, dragging on my clothes, shoving my feet in my boots as I yell into the phone. "It's Scout. Someone has her."

"Her? Aria her?"

"Yes. The truck's gone too."

"Are you sure she didn't just—"

I shove open the front door and storm into the darkness with a viscous pulse pounding through me. "Unless she drugged me and taped me to a chair..."

"Holy fuck. I'll rally the team."

"I'm going to the Russian team's cabina."

"I'll meet you there."

As I sprint up the hill toward the other lodging, I vent my fury. "Rory could be involved."

"Justice told me. Wait on backup."

I snort at that stupid request, "This is personal. There's no way I'm waiting a single second."

Chapter Fifty Nine

Aria

Well this sucks. I pretend I'm still asleep as I stare at the man behind the wheel through slitted lashes. He's unfamiliar, but I'm still a little woozy. My brain is by whatever drug this dickweed gave me.

Fortunately, my neck is propped in a position where I can at least some of his shoulder and I don't have to try to move my overly-heavy head.

He's stinky. Sweat and alcohol are pumping out of his pores.

Scout wouldn't like him sweating all over Agile's nice truck.

Oh no. *Scout, where are you?*

He wouldn't have let someone take me if he were physically able to stop them.

But maybe they drugged him too.

Please let him be okay. My chest squeezes painfully, twisting with emotion that's bigger than anything I've felt. *Please let him be okay.*

He'll come for me.

His team will too. They won't let this man get away with this. *Whatever this evil idiot has in mind.*

But reasons for taking me are not good. Ransom would be the easiest. But the rest...

A cold shudder runs through me, making my bound hands twitch. I never thought I'd find myself bound, at the mercy of a monster again.

But here I am. And I have to keep myself together. I need to get free.

I practice controlling my breath and listening. Oblivious to me, the man's been talking on the phone in rapidfire something that sounds kind of like Spanish, but not.

Of course, I didn't finish my Babel course on Spanish, so maybe I just don't know. But something tells me it's just a little off.

Or maybe it's me. My brain feels like it's swimming in molasses right now.

But I don't have to think hard to know I'm in trouble. The tape around my wrists is all the clue I need.

Without moving my head, I open my eyes a little more and scan the floorboard. I need a weapon.

Surely there's something in here...

A bunch of SEAL's drive this truck. There's got to be deadly objects inside.

The driver hits a bump in the road and my body rocks on the rear seat, changing my angle enough to see something new...

Something big and black and perfect for inflicting pain.

Yes.... I grin into the darkness.

But how am I going to get it without Captain Asshole finding out?

He swerves slightly and I rock again.

Oh my god. I know! This is perfect.

The next bump he hits, I throw myself onto the floorboard, stifling my groan. He needs to think I'm still asleep.

A muttered curse comes from the front, but nothing else. We're still driving on a rough road, and based on the sound of the rain on the roof, there's a hell of a storm outside.

I carefully wiggle my hands up and wrap them around the MAG light. It's heavy and cool against my palms. A machete would have been better, but this sucker has to be two feet long and weigh ten pounds.

Thank god, whoever bound my wrists did it in front.

Probably thinking I'm a weak female. *Well, guess what? I might not be strong, but I'm determined.*

He's got another thing coming and it's full of D-Cell batteries.

I wait and wait for the next rumble in the road, and when it comes, I sit up. The driver doesn't look back. He's still yelling at someone on the phone.

Please let this work.

I take a few seconds to clearly picture what I'm about to do. Then I realize he might wreck the truck when I knock his head off.

But this is it. This is my chance.

I lunge forward, swinging the light until it makes a satisfying thunk against his skull.

He grunts. The truck swerves. His foot mashes the gas.

Tree branches slap the sides of the truck as we rocket off the road.

Oh, Christ!

For a split second we're airborne.

A scream tears out of me as the truck hits the ground. Wham!

Everything comes to a terrifying stop with the most violent bone-rattling jolt I've ever felt. Even worse than the plane crash.

Lord, is this the week from hell, or what?

I grunt as my face bounces off the back of the driver's seat. But I'm surprisingly unscathed.

The truck? I'm not sure.

And him... not so much. There's a gaping wound in the side of his head and he's making a weird sound.

Gross. My stomach herks.

Before I have time to think about what I've done or what might happen now, I scramble out of the back seat and onto the wet leaves that the truck has trampled into the earth.

A shiver wracks my body and I look down. Reality sets in. I'm naked as the day I was born. No shoes either. *Nothing.*

Reaching back into the truck and fish around until my hand lands on something fabric. Okay not fabric. Mesh or something.

For one single second, I'm seriously bummed. *Oh, come on.* It's a mesh vest—the reflective kind when someone's working on the side of the highway.

But it's more than I had before.

After shoving my arms through the gigantic garment, I dare peek in through the window of the truck at the driver. His eyes are open, he's blinking. Looking into the forest that is now lit by the wayward headlights.

My first thought is—maybe I should hit him again...

Think, Aria. Think.

You need to figure your way out of this. If you can get him out of the truck, you can take it back to the farm.

And surely the guys left the satellite phone in here, I can call for help.

But that means I need to get rid of drunk-breath first.

Fudge. This sucks.

I shiver again, the reflective vest doing nothing to keep the rain off of my skin. And while it's tropical, it feels like I could get hypothermia.

As I'm wracking my brain, I climb over some small downed trees and make my way to the back of the truck. There's tons of gear in there if it's like the other truck. *If I can get it open.*

Given that my hands are still bound—I need to deal with that too—I squeeze the flashlight between my naked thighs and try to open the latch on the back of the truck.

Ugh! Why can't anything be unlocked when I need it to be?

I guess I'll just have to knock the glass out of this too—

What was that noise?

I swing around and jolt. Drunk-breath-guy is leering at me. He literally looks like a zombie. One of his eyes is bulging. His teeth are broken. He's covered in specks of something and rivulets of blood.

Good grief. Whatever is wrong with him did not come from the Mag Light Special. Dude must not have had his seatbelt on. Come to think of it, I didn't see an airbag, but I don't have time to think about that.

He makes a noise. Clearly not too messed up to growl-snort like a bull that's about to charge. And it's all the warning I get before he leaps at me, bloody hands outstretched, having zero problems with his legs.

"No!" I stumble back and scramble away. Panting, I scream, "Help!"

You fool, I chide myself. There is no help.

You're in the middle of the Vandemoran jungle with a real live zombie chasing you.

Wet tree branches and gigantic tropical leaves slap my face and arms as I take off. The sound of his heavy breathing and stomping feet aren't far behind.

Chapter Sixty

SCOUT

Why bother with the doorknob when I have a perfectly good foot? I kick the door in and stalk inside.

The house is still a church on Friday night, but I stride down the short hallways, hungry for blood.

"Rory!" I bellow.

But it's not one of the Russians that appears in the open doorway. It's my teammate, Truck. His weapon is in his hands and wearing his get-down-to-fucking business face.

"No one here," I kick a boot that's sitting by the couch. It flies across the living room, crashing into the wall.

He looks around, his nearly black, hawk-like eyes taking the whole scene in at once. "Marshall told me about Aria and you think it could be Rory. I thought the teams were working together, are you sure he'd—"

I nearly plow over him. "Do you have a company tablet?"

"In the truck, in my duffel."

Thank fuck. I'm out the door when he yells at me.

"You need the password."

He rattles off eight digits and I leap into a blue Ford pick-up that was sitting in front of the house with the door ajar

I almost collapse to my knees with relief when I get the machine in my hands. The small, armored tactical tablet boots up right away, has a full battery and connects instantly to his satellite router.

Thank you. Thank you and thank you.

Truck is a solid operator. Of course his shit would be charged and ready to go.

I hold my breath as the icon spins on our team's tracking software. Just looking at the map brings a kind of deadly calm into my chaotic system. Those topo lines have been my anchor since I was a kid.

But the small compass rose icon that blinks on at the corner of the screen hits me like a lightning strike. I hope it's an omen, because it's just like the tiny tattoo Aria has behind her ear.

Truck jogs to the truck and climbs into the driver's seat. "Someone was here recently. How many trucks does Vik's team have?"

"Three black Expeditions, plus Vik's Suburban. None are here as you can see."

He taps his finger to his jaw as he considers this. "Then why would they take our team truck?"

"To slow us down?"

"We'll find them and get your girl back."

That hits me in the chest so hard, I fight to keep the sound of despair that tears through me locked inside me.

Finally, a blue dot flashes on the screen—Amen—and I

zoom in with my stomach in my throat. "The truck is outside Karma, roughly 8 klicks."

We're moving fast just seconds later. As he tears down the driveway through the agave fields, he cuts a look at the tablet I'm clenching with white knuckles.

"Is it moving?"

"According to our software it was recently. But now it's stationary...

"Are they at some kind of house?"

I zoom in and turn on the terrain features.

"No. Looks like jungle," I say with my panic flaring and stomach clenching. "Nothing for at least three klicks.

He doesn't look at me again, but I feel him processing what I've just said.

The jungle is dense and unpredictable here in Vandemora. Bad things happen in places like this.

Hang on Aria. I'm coming baby.

Truck calls Griffon Kane and the rest of the team and somehow keeps the Ford on the road in the driving rain.

My mind is locked on. Nothing other than my determination to get Aria back.

She's coming home safely.

Come hell. High water. Or fucking anything.

I watch as we get closer to the icon that marks the truck. It hasn't moved in five minutes.

Five fucking minutes is a long time. Anything can happen in five minutes.

Truck hangs up and shoves my shoulder with a meaty fist.

"You solid?"

No, but I tip my chin.

He reaches behind him and pulls another gear bag from the floorboard. "That's got—"

279

"I don't care what it's got. I'll use my bare hands. I'll use a kitchen knife. I'll fucking shove my goddamned boot so far down somenone's throat—"

He holds up a hand. "Point taken. But if you want it, there's a nice sharp K-bar in there."

I take his offer on the knife and take a handgun too.

"Your head clear enough?"

I turn to look at him, feeling the murderous rage coursing through my veins. "Do I look like I'm not clear?"

He lifts a brow. "You, my friend, look unhinged."

"You would be too."

His gaze flicks away. "I'll never feel that fear again."

Truck is a loner. Our team knows it was bad—whatever happened to him—but he's never had more than one night with a woman since we met years ago.

Sounds familiar. Only I got blindsided.

Aria Kane.

I fist my shirt over the center of my chest. "I can't take this. From the moment she got here, I've been worried sick about her."

His expression hardens, the ghosts of his past flashing behind his stone façade. "You're a good SEAL. I got your back, brother."

I turn to stare out the window at the road in front of us through the hellacious rain.

A good SEAL?

"A good operator wouldn't let their girl be stolen in the middle of the night."

His hands flex on the wheel. "Did you do it on purpose?"

"Fuck no!"

He snaps back viciously. "Then get that shit out of your head."

"I need my anger right now. It's fuel." And I'll use it to burn the world down until Aria's back.

We pass through a curve on the road and de-ja-vu hits me.

It's pouring rain just like it was a few nights ago. Lights are pointing in weird directions at the sky.

Only this time it's a truck and not a plane.

Chapter Sixty One

Aria

I'm a diver, not a jungle warfare specialist. But, boy, do I wish I could channel me some SEAL or some of whatever Rory studied when he said it was 'everything.' Because I'm freaked out.

Thank god I have a light.

At least I had the wherewithal to cover the light with a leaf so it would dim the shine, and hopefully hide it from zombie stalker.

I offer another prayer to the jungle gods—because it seems right for the situation as I am in the thickest, most remote place I've dared set foot. *Please let these batteries hold.*

The light might lead my attacker to me, but there's no way I could move through Jurassic Park without it. This human girl needs all the tech help she can get.

The guy chasing me must have had his phone light, because there is no way with his popping eyeball and his concussion he could navigate this place in the dark.

Unless...

I shiver and a choking sound comes out of me. Unless he really is a walking dead man.

With that thought, I speed up, hoisting myself quickly over a fallen tree, and down a small incline.

This place feels...snakey.

Another choking sound escapes me. Give me sharks, electric eels, fish with poisonous barbs any day. No snakes, no way, no how.

When a twig snaps behind me, I jump so high my feet leave the ground.

What was that?

Heart thrumming the back of my sternum like a heavy-metal guitarist, I shine my light around. Probably not the brightest move, but I'd rather see what's coming. At least I can hit him again if I know where he is...

A flicker of light through the dense foliage makes my whole body lock up.

Oh good grief! Him again.

Definitely using his phone's light.

Now my prayer to the jungle gods is for his battery to run out.

But in the meantime, I need to disappear. Sliding behind a tree, I make my breathing shallow and listen.

Uncoordinated footsteps, more like thrashing, is barely audible over the rain and jungle sound.

He's close.

Turning the light off, I clutch it to my chest with my taped hands. The last thing I have time to do is gnaw through the duct tape. That comes after I know I'm in the clear.

Minutes go by.

My adrenaline peaks and starts to wane. It's a miracle I have any left after this week.

I pause a while longer to listen, holding my breath. Now it's been a long time since I've heard him. His light isn't visible from where I'm hiding.

A cold drop of water falls off a leaf above me and lands on my nose, runs down my chin and drops onto my chest through the mesh vest.

If I wasn't so freaked out I'd laugh.

Yep. I'm ready for this night to be over.

Chapter Sixty Two

SCOUT

The Agile Security truck is both wrecked and empty. *Goddammit.*

The driver's door is open, swaying in the wind. Rainwater pools in the cab. Diluted blood streaks the steering wheel. The metallic stench of blood mingles with the humid rot of the forest.

My gut cinches tighter as cold fear wraps around my mind.

Our clues are fading.

Mother nature destroying any evidence.

I take a step back, scanning for signs of a struggle. Desperate to know more. Terrified of what I might find.

But there's nothing. No footprints or scuffs, nothing but Aria's faint scent clinging to air inside the cab.

Truck opens the passenger door, leaning inside. A rough

sound rumbles out of him. "Something about this doesn't sit right. It's a MVA, but what else is going on here?"

"Fuck." I clench my teeth. "Who the hell did this? And where did they take her? There's nothing around for several klicks."

"Maybe she got away." He opens the glove box and pushes the contents around.

The satellite phone is there. He pockets it and asks, "Is the thermal tracking equipment in the back?"

Truck's tone is steady, but tense, when I'm anything but. I'm a downed electrical wire.

"Should be." I tear my gaze from the blood as I search the rest of the cab. Just the usual equipment—no keys, no pack, nothing personal. No goddamned clues.

But I'm hit by her scent again, faint but undeniable. It's the soap we both showered with.

I tense, fighting the stinging pain in my throat. "She was here."

Truck scans the floorboards, running his handheld light over the interior. "No signs she was forced into the back. No signs that she resisted."

The words hang in the charged air.

I have to swallow twice before I can speak. "Unconscious would be my guess."

He looks at me and I see the question in his eyes. *Or dead.*

I slam my fist against the leather driver's seat, making water fly off of it. "No. She's alive."

But the thought grips me, twisting my insides until I'm forced to step back, doubled over. Bile scorches up my esophagus. My stomach heaves as the forest floor spins below me.

I let the nausea wash over me before vomiting into the mud.

Truck rounds the hood and stops next to me, his muddy boots in my field of view. "No keys here?"

I spit on the ground, wiping my hand on the back of my wrist, appreciating that he's not handling me with kid gloves. "Affirmative."

He stalks away and seconds later I hear the muted sound of shattering glass. Truck muffled the sound, and the rest was covered almost completely by the drumming rain that's washing every goddamned thing clean.

Once I've thrown up everything in my system, I get on the tablet again, looking at terrain features as he passes me the gear.

"I found the NVGs, thermal system, plus comms gear. I'm calling Beast to tell him to search the road before reporting here."

"Copy."

"Come on. If she's out here, we'll get her back."

The forest sounds grow as we leave the wreck behind. Wet leaves, rivulets of water, mud. Dense undergrowth. It's a goddamned tracking nightmare. The thermal imaging will be almost useless.

Truck's conversation with Beast comes through my in mouth-bone conduction speaker.

Ignoring them, I tune in, going deep to a place that I haven't been in over a year. The part of me that tracked and killed in the worst places in the world. Truck has the same skills.

If anyone can find her, it's us.

I'm coming for you and we're getting the hell out of this country on the first plane I can find.

"Got her tracks," Truck mutters in my comms gear as he crouches.

Yes. Sweet relief loosens my clenched fist.

I scrub my hand over my face. "What do you see?"

He swings his hand over a small area. It's there. One print. Small, exactly Aria's size. Nothing else.

The sight cuts through me.

Truck tips his chin. "Take her trail. I'll keep looking for the other."

Presuming there's another.

Fuck. Something about this is off.

In my coms gear, Truck's voice is a rumble. "Maybe someone picked up the abductor on the road. He could have called for help."

"Or maybe something ate him."

He chuckles. "Or that."

I don't laugh. I keep moving, slowly scanning for the fading footprints.

The forest closes in. Suffocating. The rain is a constant barrage, falling through the thick canopy at an impossible rate.

Fuck rain.

Fuck the mud and goddamned flooded caves.

After I get out of here, I'm taking a year to live in the desert. We're taking a year. Because Aria's going to be with me. Griff can bite my goddamned ass. She's my future.

I push forward, scanning the trees, the ground, looking, listening.

Hoping for another sign of her.

"Anything else? Over." I check in.

"Negative. Over."

As much as I don't want Aria to be with a damned man,

the thought of her alone in this jungle makes my heart thud erratically.

"Scout."

I freeze, worried about Truck's tone. "What?" I rasp, "Over."

"Do you think she did this on her own? Over."

Narrowing my eyes, I see a small divot. I bend and brush my finger over the slight depression but my mind racing with questions I can't fathom.

Could she have drugged me and bound me?

Chapter Sixty-Three

SCOUT

"Brother," Beast grips my arm. "You need to lie down."

I shrug off his hold. "The team has this. Griffon and Agent Torres's men are on shift.

"Two fucking days." My voice is brutal. "She's been in that goddamned jungle for two days. I'm not stopping."

He shoves a pair of dry boots into my hands. "Take care of your feet."

Grudgingly, I jerk them out of his hands. He's right. I've been soaking wet for days. I can't afford for the flesh to fall off my bones now. Not when my woman is out there.

As I stalk under the staging tent that the feds brought, Beast is hot on my heels. He's on the phone, talking fast as fuck and in a low tone. "Are you sure?"

Something about that question makes me whirl.

The boots thud to the ground, forgotten. "What did they find?"

He holds up a hand.

Rory stalks into the tent, mud smeared on his face. He shakes his head. "No sign of her to the east."

Boiling anger makes my hands clench. "What are you doing here?"

He holds my gaze with a cold, flat look. "Looking for your woman."

I take a step toward him. "Did you cut her air hose?"

Rory tosses his raincoat over a chair. "Now why the fuck would I do that?"

"Who the hell knows?"

We're yelling, the tension as thick as lava.

Then he chuckles softly. "Back down. I like her. I would never do anything to hurt her. She reminds me of my little sister, full of fire. When that asshole Brundage went after her at that meeting, I was the second person with my hands on him."

I don't know if it's exhaustion or something else, but I blow out a hard breath as some of the rage leaks out of me. Rory's background was pretty much empty, but clean. Like I knew it would be. "Then who?"

His expression darkens. "Doesn't Brundage make much more sense? He had access to their gear. I just carried it down the hill."

Wrapping my fingers around my forehead, I curse. "And he had a motive."

"Glad you're getting your shit together. But who took her? That's the question now."

"Brudage and Keith are on their way back stateside. Confirmed by Agent Torres."

"Then who?" He tilts his head. "Someone who had access to the cabinas since you were both drugged."

I groan and drop my head, tucking my chin to my

muddy jacket. "Truck asked me if I thought Aria would have done this by herself."

Rory's face contorts. "Her? Tie you up and leave? Why the hell?"

Truck steps into the tent and glances at the two of us. "What if she did it so she could go after Adam Hill?"

Beast hangs up and digs a hand into his hair. "I have news. Adam Hill is dead."

"How?" I ask immediately.

"Asphyxiation."

I don't know exactly what the feeling inside of me is, but I look around at the team, hoping someone will tell me what the fuck is going on.

"Suffocated?" Truck asks.

Beast grunts. "Yeah, but that's not the only dead guy. Griffon just found one in the forest. But the asshole's going to be hard to ID. Something ate his face and hands."

Static fills my ears.

I might have passed out before from exhaustion, but this is far different. This is the blood leaving my brain.

A cold sensation takes root inside my stomach. Someone pushes me into a plastic chair and drops the boots in front of me.

"Get him some food," someone says behind me.

The next few minutes are a blur as I change into dry gear and shove some kind of tasteless food-product into my face. God knows I need my strength. After chasing the rations and some electrolytes with water, I'm on my feet hustling with the team.

Beast holds the truck door open for me—probably because I'm so fucking freaked out. "Agent Torres is meeting us at the body. It's definitely a male, that part didn't get eaten."

Chapter Sixty Four

Aria

I'd give a million dollars for a compass. Looking overhead, I try to use the sunlight that's peeking through the clouds— yes sunlight—to figure out which direction I'm heading.

At long last a break in the rain which is good because I'm over it. I blow out a tired breath and look around. The jungle is less dense here. Maybe I'm getting somewhere.

Stretching my back, I long for a bed, a hot bath, and an all-you-can-eat breakfast buffet.

Who knew I'd be dreaming about eggs and french toast when I was running for my life?

With that thought I scan the jungle one more time, listening and looking for anything out of place. The guy that was after me probably gave up. And I'm betting his phone battery died before my Mag light which is still hanging on.

Something purple catches my eye and I crane my neck forward.

Oh my god, is that a passion fruit?

Maybe it's a hallucination. I'm so freaking hungry.

I climb over a small fallen tree, my bare feet protesting. Prune feet is something Griff and I used to laugh about when we were kids. This, not so much. The soles of my feet look like hundred year old raisins.

For the tenth time, I wonder if I could turn leaves into shoes. *After I check out this fruit...*

When I finally reach the tree where the fruit-laden vine is climbing, I'm so happy, I laugh out loud.

"Thank you!" I tell the jungle gods, sounding a little breathless with awe. Once again, I have been blessed. The gods have become my steadfast imaginary companions through this hellish ordeal.

It really is passion fruit!

I step closer, careful of where I'm walking and reach out to grab one. The fruit is so high off the ground, I can just barely reach it. My fingers brushing over the smooth, purple skin. Come on! I jump, making me wince in pain.

God, I can't imagine what the pedicure lady is going to say when she sees my feet.

At last, I grab one. Wiggling my bare but cheeks, I do a little victory dance. Everything feels like a win right now.

I'm alive. I've survived two days. My hands are free. And I have food.

Next up, leaf shoes.

Then I'm following the sun until I get somewhere.

I pick my fill of fruit, and study my feet as I eat. They are a mess. Covered in cuts and bruises. But my thoughts drift to Scout and Griff.

They have to be safe. I won't allow a single thought that

doesn't align with that. My will to keep going would just evaporate if I did.

Longing fills me. I can't wait to see them.

And we're figuring out how to fix whatever's wrong between them. I don't care how bad it is. I love them both. I want them both in my life. It feels complicated but not. Scary but right.

Maybe Scout will move to Florida with me.

Could he be based out of there for his job?

With thoughts of him filling my head and warming other parts of me, I find leaves to tie around my feet.

After testing a couple of configurations, I start to make my way, following the sun. The weight of my flashlight—now named Hammerhead—a little less now that I have food in my belly and thoughts of Scout to push me forward.

Too bad my new 'shoes' are slippery.

"Oy!" I scream as the light goes flying out of my hand and I slip down a long ravine like a turtle in a luge.

Chapter Sixty Five

SCOUT

I'm looking at a map on the tablet when Beast slams on the brakes. His voice booms inside the truck. "What the fuck am I seeing?"

The device flies out of my hands, landing between my feet. We're still rolling when I leap out of the truck like I've been shot out of a gun. Behind me there's a whoop of relieved laughter.

In front of me...

Heaven.

Aria climbs to her feet, brushing her hand over her dirty face, a wobbly smile on her sweet lips. "I guess I found you."

"Babe." Choking out a relieved sob, I grab her and bury my face in her damp, tangled hair. She smells like fruit and mud, and my forever girl.

"Are you okay?" The words shake out of me, like rocks tumbling down a hillside.

"A little ragged, but I'm fine." Tightening her arms around my neck, she whispers, "So glad to see you."

I rock her, holding her off the ground for several minutes until my hands stop shaking and I can finally breathe.

She wiggles against me. "Um. We have an audience and I'm kind of not wearing much."

As I set her down, using the width of my back to block everyone else, I take her face in my hands.

"They can wait." I press my mouth against hers for a searching kiss. Proving to myself she's real. "All goddamn day."

When I pull back she smiles at me as she touches my cheek. "God, Memphis, you look exhausted. We're taking a vacation to somewhere very quiet..."

"And dry," I add as I grip her shoulders. "What do you have on?"

It's orange and white and muddy, hardly recognizable as a safety vest.

"It was all I could grab out of the truck before I ran."

I laugh at her cute expression as relief courses through all of my cells like warm honey. "A reflective vest is not the best thing to hide in, but lord, I wish I could have found you with a spotlight. I have half-a-mind to put a tracker on you, sweetheart. I'm never going through this again."

"Fine by me. Oh—" She pulls back. "I lost the big Mag light right up there! Can you go get it? I'm kind of fond of it now. I even named it Hammerhead."

I loop my hands around the back of her neck and bring her mouth to mine for another swift taste of her. "I'll buy you another and I'm not worried about that damned thing."

Studying her pretty face, I rasp through tight vocal cords, "You're the only light I'll ever need from now on."

Her tears nearly crush me. But her words are the sweetest sound I've ever heard in my life. "I missed you so much. I was worried sick about you."

I scoop her into my arms. "You don't even know how crazy I went when I woke up and you were gone."

"I'm sorry."

I press my forehead to hers, trying to push out the memory of seeing our bed empty. "You didn't do anything wrong. You did everything just perfectly."

"It was crazy. Scary. Crazy. Exhausting."

Fucking hell. I can't imagine what it was like for her.

Hungry for revenge, I fight snarling like an animal. "Do you know who it was that drugged us?"

"He was speaking a language I didn't know."

"A dead male was found in the woods, but there's no ID on him."

She nods and hugs me tighter. "I wondered if he made it. The wreck... and I hit him pretty hard with the light."

"God." I rasp, refusing to picture that scene in my head.

"Take me home, please. I just want to forget about it all right now."

Over my shoulder, I call out to the guys. "I need a blanket STAT."

She laughs softly. "Actually, we need a bed."

"Oh, that's guaranteed. This time I'm staging armed guards outside of the house."

When a blanket is tossed over my shoulder, I snug it around her without letting her go. "Let's get you dry and get your feet taken care of."

She wiggles her legs where they're dangling over my arm. "I would say I want a massage later, but truthfully I don't think I can stand it."

A growl rumbles through me. She's been through hell.

"We'll get a doc to clean you up." I don't trust myself. Not with the risk of her getting an infection. I want an expert. Even if I have to carry her all the way to Carollia in my arms.

The team is gathered around the truck when I stride back with her, barking orders about having Agent Torres send a doctor. Justice, Beast and Truck close in around us, ruffling Aria's hair, giving her a squeeze on the shoulder, offering words of praise for her survival skills.

Aria waves it off. "It was dumb luck. The worst part was the duct tape on my arms."

Anger rolls through me, making my eyes narrow.

"Easy tiger." She nuzzles into my chest as I climb into the truck with her in my arms. "I hear you growling."

"I was afraid that you had been bound."

"I wasn't scared of that, weirdly, as long as I could run or hike, I was fine. I even managed to knock the bad guy out with the flashlight with my hands bound."

"You knocked him out?" I ask, shocked.

Beast looks at me in the mirror, his eyes narrowing as he grins. "Boy, you're so toast."

I roll my eyes as Truck chuckles next to me and Justice covers a laugh with a cough.

After the laugh, silence fills the truck as Beast drives toward the farm. I rest my chin on Aria's crown and watch the scenery passing.

Everything feels so right.

Aria.

The team.

My life. *What the hell?*

I never thought I'd have someone. Letting someone hold

or touch me was so far outside my scope, I just didn't think it could happen. But with Aria... I want it all. I want the future that I tried to end.

That's something we need to talk about. I don't want anything between us.

Chapter Sixty Six

Aria

I drop my head back with a purr in my throat. "Your hands are amazing."

Warm water sloshes around us as Scout kisses my wrist —the one he just cleaned along with every other part of me. Some parts twice.

When he deposits my hand on his thigh, on his scars, I let myself look at the unevenly-colored, tangled lines in his flesh. He doesn't seem to notice where my hand and my gaze is at all, his hands are busy lathering my other arm.

"You make them feel better," he says huskily.

A warm flutter in my tummy makes me shift. "Same for mine."

I barely even thought about the scars around my wrists this afternoon after he found me. Well, I sort of found him. Thanks to my leaf shoe antics. *Thank god.*

If they had passed that part of the road, lord knows when I would have been found.

Scout's promise to embed a tracking device in my arm was in jest, but I would have gladly offered my flesh if I'd known what was going to happen.

"How do your feet feel?" He draws me out of my rambling thoughts back to the present where I'm warm, safe, and very much feeling loved.

I purr in my throat, *mmm,* and lean my head back against his large and very comfy shoulder. Who knew a human pillow could feel so good? I think we're going to need a big tub like this wherever we live.

"I can't even feel them right now, in a good way."

Smiling, I wiggle my legs where they are sticking over the edge of the tub so my bandages don't get wet. "Whatever you guys put on them is amazing."

He chuckles softly. "Secret sauce."

"Well, it's far better than Mickey D's secret sauce."

This makes him laugh again and it vibrates all of my cells.

God, I love that sound. So rich, and warm, coming right from the deepest part of him. I'm totally addicted.

With my heart glowing, I look around, feeling *all* the love. "You didn't have to get this hotel room for us. It looks expensive."

He makes a chuffing sound. "It's nothing. And you weren't getting in the shower with your feet."

"And I definitely needed a shower or a bath, I smelled like swamp."

"We both did."

"Is it okay if I wash you?"

His hand pauses on my elbow. "Do you want to?"

"Of course. You're my man. I want to take care of you too."

It feels my soul to take care of Scout. He's never had that and I want to give it all to him. Every sweet, gentle gesture I can so I can replace all the bad things with good feelings.

"I'd like that." He exhales softly against my hair and a shudder vibrates the muscles of his abs against my back. "But you can't wash my dick."

I crane my head around to meet his frowning expression. "And why would that be?"

"Because you're resting tonight and if you touch me there, that won't be happening."

A wicked little grin tips up my lips. "We could...you know...between naps."

"Naps..."

"You know the kind where you wake up to your girlfriend with her mouth on—"

Blue eyes flaring, He snaps, "Aria!"

Getting back to taking care of me, he mutters something under his breath.

"What's that big guy?"

"You're making my cock ache."

I sigh longingly. "Thank god. Because all I've been able to think about is you deep inside me, filling up this empty ache."

I guess I did it.

Pushed him over the edge, because Scout somehow magically stands up with me in his arms, snags two towels and drips water all the way back into the hotel room. We're halfway to the bed when a knock on the door stops him dead.

"Room service?" I ask as he growls like a feral beast.

"Not until nineteen-hundred hours. I had specific instructions on the time to deliver."

That's so very 'Scout like'. He likes things orderly. I've lived with my brother so I know what I'm getting into, but I also know I'm going to drive him a little bit crazy because I'm not like that.

I barely know what time it is, but the clock on the dresser says five thirty. "Could it be your team?"

He lays me gently on the bed and kisses my forehead. "No fucking way. They know the consequences. Stay here."

He tucks a towel around me and lashes the other around his waist. He's looking through the peep-hole with his gun in his hand when he groans loud enough for me to hear it across the room. "We're going to have a come to Jesus meeting."

I stiffen and push to my elbows. "Who is it?"

"Griff."

He flips the latch on the door and jerks it open. The pistol is still in his hand.

Chapter Sixty Seven

SCOUT

Griffon Kane looks down at the gun, then back at my face.

Hollow cheeks, overgrown scruff, shadowy eyes with a few new ghosts. He looks like I feel. Any other time I might tell him to take a damned nap. A dirt nap.

"Where is she?"

"Resting."

"I need to see her."

Fuck you. "Later."

"No, I need to talk to her now."

I consider my options. Shooting him isn't the best choice. I slam the door in his face instead.

Aria shrieks and rustles around on the bed. "Wait! What did you just do?"

I stalk to her and drop to a knee next to the king size frame. She blinks rapidly at me, her pretty brown eyes full of concern. "Memphis..."

Warmth shoots up my arm as I gather her hand in mine and kiss across her knuckles. As I do this, she searches my eyes.

I lay it all out there. Man up like a motherfucker.

"I want you to marry me."

"Holy... what?" She hinges up off the bed, her wet hair sending droplets flying.

Hope fills my chest as her cheeks start to take on that nice shade of pink she gets when she's excited. I also know a few other shades of pink she gets too. But that's not this.

"Now?" That one syllable has a shake to it. The vibration matches the nerves in my stomach.

"The wedding can wait a little while, but I want us to start forever now."

She closes her eyes, a small smile playing at the corner of her lips.

Warmth fights against anxious energy in every cell, in every muscle in my body.

"What do you say, beautiful, will you make this beast whole?"

A loud bang against the door makes her eyes fly open. As she stares nervously across the room, she presses her free hand over her heart. "Oh my! He's really going to be furious."

"Don't worry about him."

"Sounds like he's got a battering ram."

"He'll get his turn in a few minutes. Right now, you're mine and mine alone."

Smile gone, she meets my gaze as she traces a finger along my jaw, teasing the days-old growth of my beard.

That simple touch unravels so many of my broken circuits and wires them back together again.

Solemn, she asks, "Will you two be able to get along if you and Griffon are brothers-in-law?"

I lean up and kiss her, tugging gently on her bottom lip, then tasting forever with a decidedly possessive swipe of my tongue.

I don't know how long this goes on but there's another ridiculously loud thud on the other side of the door.

When we break, I press my mouth to her temple for one more feel of her silky skin. "Anything for you. Now, tell me yes, so I can go deal with him."

There's a happiness in her gaze that feels fresh as a spring morning. "Yes, I'll proudly be Mrs. Memphis Silas."

The sudden ache inside my chest makes me wonder if I'm dying of happiness.

I cup her face in my hands wishing I could climb onto the bed and show her just how special she is to me. One slow stroke at a time.

If only...

But that's not happening with her brother doing a wrecking ball impression out in the hallway.

There's gravel in my throat as I make a promise to my fiancée. "I will do my best—"

She shakes her head, stopping me with her own words. "You already have."

An all new level of possessiveness sears through me. "I'm serious about tracking you."

She plants a kiss on my cheek. "While that would sound a little stalkeresque to most women, I'll happily appear as a little blue dot in your tracking software because I know that would make you happy. But I get to have one for you."

"Like I said. Anything for you."

I lean in, pressing her hand to my chest beneath my palm. "We'll go ring shopping—"

A big ass grin splits my face, stopping my own words when Griffon Kane crashes through the door. He's going to go ballistic when he hears the news.

Chapter Sixty Eight

Aria

No one got murdered. But talk about bad timing. I need to wrap my arms—and a few other body parts around the hottest SEAL on the planet.

My SEAL.

Forever.

The dreamer inside me squeals with delight. I might have spent an hour or three hundred looking at Pinterest wedding trends. But the practical side of me never thought about who he would be...

Especially after what happened.

But now? I'm wondering how I ever thought there could be someone else. He's perfectly imperfect and so loving in his rough and tumble way. Which right now involves him tucking me in like he's making a bed for a military inspection.

I suppress a chuckle at the ridiculousness of the moment.

The man who stole my heart in a matter of a few days is making a big production out of tucking me into bed as Griff watches with murder in his stone-gray eyes.

Is my life resigned to two over-protective alphas trampling all over my freedom? This thought makes me smile like I just won the lottery.

I'll gladly sign up. I didn't know I had so much room in my heart, but now that they're both there it feels good. Really freaking good.

"Why don't you sit?" I pat the bed and they instantly glare at each other.

"There's room for all of us." I scoot to the middle.

The two men laugh roughly in unison. There's not an ounce of humor in the gruff sounds.

"That's never going to happen," Griff says as he drags a chair over to the edge of the bed since I can't join him in the sitting area of the gigantic hotel room. My feet are bandaged up like two Michelin men.

Overkill, but hey, Scout made sure the doctor did EVERYTHING and then some. But the special sauce he and his team carry for injuries... that was the icing on the tootsie cake.

"How are you feeling?" Griff asks as Scout sits on the side of the bed within arm's reach of me.

Protective much?

"Tired, but good. I'm really happy to be clean."

I don't tell my brother how I got so clean, or that as soon as he leaves we're going to get really dirty. Instead I deflect. "How are you?"

His answer is instant. "Angry."

I let his reply hang.

Wait 'til I tell him I'm marrying Scout. *Boom.* His head might explode.

We'll wait for another time. The hotel room is too nice.

When the silence gets painful and I get alarmed at the stare Scout is giving my brother, I break the seal. No pun intended. Carefully, I say, "I'm sorry. What's going on?"

"Angry at myself. I should have done more when I recognized the signs that something had happened to you. Just never thought it was that bad. You know, maybe a typical break up. But rape—"

Oh. *Oh, no.* That.

Glancing down at my bare wrists, I nip my bottom lip. "You weren't supposed to know. I tried to hide the signs."

"When you came to work for me and moved into my guest room, I should have realized something *big* had happened."

I glance at Scout, he's deep, deep inside his head right now and it's not a good place.

"I was safe with you. I didn't need to worry any more."

Griff buries his face in his hands with a stifled curse. When he drops them he gives Scout a searching look. "Does she know?"

Scout's head shake is tight as his shoulders stiffen. "She doesn't need to know that right now."

Hm. Know what?

Now they're driving me mad. "You guys can't do that. You have to tell me whatever you're hiding."

They exchange a long, calculating look.

My nerves flutter, the heat from the bath taking flight from my body like frightened doves. "You should tell me whatever it is."

Scout speaks first, but they basically both tell me at the same time. "Adam's dead."

311

I flinch reflectively. *"When?"*

"Earlier today."

A weird, numb sensation washes over me like a wave of tepid water. It reminds me of when you touch liquid that's the exact temperature of your skin. It's almost undetectable.

My attention is dragged back when Scout's strong hand slides up my arm and loops around the back of my neck. "Love you, sweetheart. It's okay to feel however you feel."

Soothing.

His understanding is so comforting.

Fresh tears pool in the corner of my eyes—a mix of relief, and maybe some disbelief, and also grief for a life that ended too young. But I can't think of a single thing to say.

Griff fills the void for me. "None of us want to see someone die from a diving accident, but Adam made his own choice and you had nothing to do with that."

"It was reckless, but he was always that way. I never really understood how he ticked."

My brother's silent for a few moments and the haunted expression in his eyes makes me wish I could go to him.

Scrubbing his palm over his face, he sits back into the chair. "I failed you, A. I was too busy caught up in my own bullshit."

Scout takes my hand in his, lacing his fingers with mine. "You're right, Kane, you should have known."

An unhappy sound comes from my throat. "Hello, you two. It was my secret to keep. I didn't want you to know, Griff. I knew you'd unalive Adam and turn him into fish food."

Griff's expression darkens as he wraps his hands around the back of his neck. "You're probably right."

Scout's looking at Griff in the weirdest way. I look back and forth between them.

"What's going on?"

"Nothing." They both say.

Oh my god. Twin nightmares. "How did Adam die?"

This question earns a very uncomfortable silence, one that might crush the whole darned hotel.

Oh no. My heart flops around inside my chest as a really yucky thought slams into the back of my mind. "Which one of you did it?"

They both answer. "Not me."

Okay, this is good. But still, someone did. Argh. "Who then?"

"I thought it was you," Griff says to Scout as he throws an arm over the back of his chair.

Scout fires back. "I was searching for Aria."

"So was I."

Are they really going to argue over *everything?* "Boys! Boys!"

It sure didn't take long for them both to get red-faced.

"So someone kill—killed." My throat constricts on the word.

"Suffocated," Griff says, blunt as a sledgehammer.

Scout rumbles, "Who then?" as my blood rushes out of my head. I don't feel so well.

Chapter Sixty-Nine

SCOUT

Two hours later

It's a good thing this joint has room service. I didn't know we were having a fucking party.

Another knock sounds at the door for the second food delivery. We're going to need more chairs soon too. It appears operations for the team have been temporarily relocated to our room so Aria, Griff and I can be part of the planning.

And of course there's some debriefing to be done.

Not the way we used to do in the teams. This looks more like a late night college hang-out session only it's not late at night, and we're not college kids.

Beast and Camile occupy one of the oversized chairs, all lovey dovey, like I want to be with Aria, but I'm busy playing damned host.

Rory and his sidekick, Gregor, are camped out on the floor, looking as tired as the rest of us as they shove tacos into their mouths.

Justice has plunked his ass down on the bed—yes the bed—and is talking about something with Aria.

If he wasn't my buddy, I'd be removing him with force, but right now, I just feel...

Satisfied.

Like I'm home.

Home in my skin.

But more importantly in my heart.

Even though I'm thousands of miles from the house I never use, I feel more grounded than ever.

The house is something else Aria doesn't know about yet. But it doesn't matter much. I'm hers. I'll be where she wants to be.

Griff is camped out near his sister, stuffing his face. "Pass me that stuff," he motions with his fork.

"You mean the pico de gallo?" Truck asks, balancing his plate in one hand to reach across the coffee table for the bowl Griff wants.

Griff nods his appreciation, and turns the conversation to business. "What's the latest on the missing woman?"

I tune in to the team with a generous side dish of guilt weighing me down.

There's a woman we've been paid to find, but more importantly, she could be in danger and the team has been fully engaged in the chaos around myself and Aria.

"Yo, man. Are you coming to sit down?" It's Beast calling for me.

I give him a flat look. "When I'm done playing Martha Stewart, yeah."

Camile laughs as I hand her a bottled water. "Calling room service was so hard."

I feign an expression of insult, clutching my chest.

"Oh, I see how you are. Someone had to secure this event venue and plan the perfect seating arrangement for the rude guests," I quip with a smirk. "Even if I didn't invite a single one of you."

She gives me a big smile. "Touché. And it's good to see you smiling."

"Ditto, teammate."

Camile and Beast went through their own hell when our team first arrived in Vandemora to look for Allison Westerly. I thought they were crazy for falling so fast, but damn if I didn't fall faster.

Oh well. I'm definitely in it to win it now.

Giving into the smile my face insists on wearing, I get back to my job. *Jobs.*

Catering to our team of tired, hungry, operatives at the moment. Which comes in below taking care of Aria. But I do still have my position with Agile and Team Falcon and the work we do is important.

"Justice, did you find anything on the mountain around the opening at the top of the cave?" I ask as I empty my armful of water bottles by passing them out to everyone.

The smile drops from his face as his hand stops midway to his mouth. For a beat the food on his overstuffed fork looks dangerously close to sliding off on my bed.

Jerk.

"There were some signs of recent activity, but nothing

definitive. The rain has ruined any evidence of who it was. But the good news is we've got a dive set up for tomorrow at zero-six-hundred at one of the other caverns. This one isn't as prone to flooding and the professor said it would be a good candidate for MZ's research so she could have been there recently since her belongings were found closeby."

"So the rain won't make this one as dangerous?" Aria asks, concern tightening her brows together.

"Devil's Belly, they call it," Truck says as he smirks. "Sounds like fun, doesn't it? And the rain doesn't have to make it more dangerous. It's already incredibly dangerous. It's known for filling up with water once a year and it's a trophy dive. Only the best of the best do it."

A fog of silence slides into the room. All cave dives are dangerous, but when divers come from around the world for the challenge—that's serious.

"Are we sure it's worth the risk?" I ask to get inside Beast's head on this decision.

"We don't have any other leads and until we can rule out her being in the caves, and given her research specialty..."

"What is her specialty?" Rory asks.

I reply, "Geoarcheology with a specific interest in metals."

I get a few raised eyebrows.

"English, please." Aria bumps me with her elbow. "What do you think she's looking for?"

Beast rubs a hand along Camile's back as his expression turns to frustration. "If we knew, we could probably find her more quickly."

"So the cave has to be explored. Who's diving?" Aria asks with a tone of caution in her voice.

Griff lifts a hand, "Me."

"And me," Justice adds as Aria gives her brother a biting glare.

Beast whistles. "Down girl. You're brother's not diving."

Griff flips Beast off. "And when did you become the boss of me?"

"When I hired your ass." Beast teasingly presses his palm over his girl's mouth and I know what's coming. "I'll be diving."

Camile's eyes flare over the edge of Beast's big hand. He's going to be in some serious hot water for not clueing her in on that little announcement.

I throw my own hat in the ring. "I could go. Just so you know. I'll be good to go after a night's sleep."

"Just don't give him any Twinkies," Justice says with a snicker.

"Great. I'll never live that down will I?"

Aria grins beside me. "It's a pretty great story."

"Yeah, it is." Voice husky, I admit that I'm completely besotted. "Truth is I'd gladly do it again."

A collective groan fills the room. "Back to business, Twinkie King," Rory tosses out with his own smirk, but there's something understanding in his gaze.

Beast, taking control of the conversation again says, "No additional information on MZ has been found, except Camile ran down all the financial leads. She went underground right about the time her father hired us."

Camile, still frowning about Beast's announcement, twists her water bottle in her hands. "That means one of two things to me—either she's being held against her will or she knew her father was hunting her."

As the team bounces ideas, I fill up a plate with a criminal amount of food. No Twinkies or Oreos in sight, but I did hide the slice of chocolate three-layer cake for just me and my girl.

My eyes land on Aria. She's smiling across the room at me, ignoring everything else going on and it makes me feel like a single ray of sunshine has burst from the sky and pinned me in the spotlight.

All else fades to black and that insane rightness inside my chest gets even bigger.

Except for seeing Justice in that damned bed even if he's just talking. I'm going to let him know if he ever gets in bed with my fiancée again he's going to find out just how short my temper is and how long my reach is.

I can hardly form a coherent thought beyond—she's *mine*. Those long, dark locks have dried in long ringlets around her shoulders and she looks good enough to eat.

Which I plan on doing for a long damned time when we get rid of these fucking yahoos.

My stomach makes a loud rumble, snapping me out of my imagination. This week stressed about forty-thousand calories right out of me. And I need my stamina for later... for after the nap...

Aria's eyes flash with heat as I walk toward her. Oh yeah, she knows what I'm thinking. She scoots so I can sit beside her on the bed.

She leans in, pressing a kiss to my ear before whispering, "Should we tell them?"

I chuckle, picturing how this could go. "Yeah. Go ahead."

To get everyone's attention, I whistle.

The room falls silent, except for a nervous laugh next to me. But she lays her hand on my thigh and the warmth of her touch goes straight to my marrow, bypassing my old wounds.

"We have news."

Camile sits up abruptly in Beast's arms, her eyes widening brightly. "Oh boy!"

The rest of the room looks clueless. Until...

"We're engaged!" Aria says breathily and turns to look at me. "Scout asked me to marry him and I said yes!"

A second later, Truck's on his feet, beating Griffon Kane on the back trying to dislodge something that went down the wrong way.

Chapter Seventy

Aria

As I fall back onto the giant stack of hotel pillows, I sigh. "They are a lot."

Scout, standing next to the bed, leans over me, planting his hands on either side of my head. When he looks down at me with serious eyes, my heart doubles its pace.

"Hi," I whisper.

He continues to search my face and when I place my hand against his scruffy jaw he leans into my touch.

Scout is shockingly gorgeous. Rugged, but so handsome my brain can hardly process him. Maybe it all did start with the eyes.

I've never seen eyes like his, just a shade bluer than diamond. But the depth in them now rocks me.

The man before me is a different animal than when we met.

Loving. Open with his admission of his feelings. Like we've cracked the seal on our dark secrets and now we both can finally breathe.

"I couldn't wait for them to leave." There's a sexy rasp to his tone.

It feels so good to touch him, to show him the affection he's deserved his whole life and never gotten.

"I'm glad they came though. It felt right."

Without looking away from my eyes, he lifts my hand and brushes the softest touch of his lips across my knuckles. "This feels right."

I feel happy tears beginning to press at the back of my eyes. But a tendril of doubt chases them like a wisp of smoke. "Are you sure you want to get married? I mean we can feel this out if..."

He presses my hand over his heart. Heat from his body melts into me through the thin cotton of his t-shirt. "Feel that?"

"Yes."

"It's never felt so strong."

Only by sheer will can I swallow. "It's all been so fast."

"You can't stand in the way of a force of nature."

Those little tears squeeze out of my eyes when I smile. "God, and you are one."

But I need to get something off my chest. Worried, I lower my gaze to Scout's chest, feeling bad that I need this right now. "I need to ask you something."

Keeping my hand over his heart, he's quick to reply, "Ask away."

Tracing the fingers of my other hand over his thigh, a worry line forms between my brows.

"Talk to me, beautiful."

"What happened between you and Griff that made him so...angry with you?"

Scout tenses, his heart speeds below my hand. But he quietly answers me. "Look at me, please."

Without hesitation, I do.

"When the fire happened, I didn't want to live. Griff was the one who got me out of that shit show and when he and I were alone, I asked him to end me."

My world screeches, tilting on its axis. "Oh god. I'm so—"

He shakes his head once. "It was bad, but here I am. I'll never regret any of it now. But there's something else you need to know and I feel like I'm treading on telling you something that's your brother's private business."

Nervous energy skates along my nerve endings. I pull my lip between my teeth and force myself to hold his gaze. "Then don't tell me."

"No. I think this will help you understand why he thinks I'm not suitable for his baby sister."

"O-okay," I reply feeling very unsure.

"Griff knows what kind of sex I like."

Swallow.

"How?"

"We ran into each other..."

I feel that frown line deepen—the one that could be a canyon one day. "Where?"

Scout clears his throat. "I'd rather not say."

Realization hits me. "Oh my god. At a sex club?"

"I plead the fifth."

Closing my eyes I shake my head. "Please don't tell him I know this. I do not want to ever have that conversation with my brother."

He laughs softly, holding my hand more tightly to his chest as if letting go even a little could let me slip away. There's something in his expression...

The need to be reassured.

"Scout, I do not judge you for what you've done. I'm glad you found a way to...have pleasure."

This time his vulnerability shows in full force. "You sure about that?"

"I'm so sure. And who knows, maybe one day we can go somewhere sexy together. Don't couples do that sometimes?"

"NO one is seeing you naked. *Ever.*" A growl forms in his throat as his hands tighten on me. "This is for me only. But yeah, we could definitely go somewhere that we could play in the private cosplay rooms."

My pulse quickens with as my imagination kicks in. "Like dress up?"

He brushes a thumb over the rise of my cheek, speeding my heart rate even more. "I need a second. I'm letting my mind entertain all the kinky ways we could get dirty together. Role playing. Other things."

A little thrill races through me and he studies me as my tongue quickly slips across my lips. "I'd like to do that with you. I'd like to do everything with you and only you."

"Aria Kane, you never cease to surprise me."

A heartbeat later, he's crushing my mouth with hungry, searching lips. When he pulls back, it's only long enough to whisper, "Fuck, I love you."

Yes. *This.* All of this.

My happy meter blows completely apart as the needle pegs so far to the right it's never going to be the same.

Then he's delving both hands into my hair, climbing on

the bed, to crouch over me with his thighs on either side of mine.

As he deepens the kiss, my hands seek him out, shaking with the need to touch his skin.

He groans into my mouth when I find the tight muscles of his abs. Heat scorches my fingertips, making my body sing in response.

I've never felt that response to touching a man before. He elicits so many first time responses, I've lost count. Like the bone deep need to make him mine, to love him, hold him, show him how special he is. Have his back. Take his pain.

These realizations tighten my insides, starving me for air. *No, not air.* Him.

I need him skin-to-skin on me. Deep inside. Fusing us from head to toe and everywhere in between.

When I drag his shirt up his back, he reaches up and tears it off and over his head in one violent move. Then he's gloriously naked from the waist up for me to see.

I saw him only hours ago, but I already forgot how much I love his body.

"It's yours." His rough reply rumbles in the quiet space between us.

"I love all of this. I love you."

He trails a finger down my neck, across a sensitive spot on my collarbone, pushing the neckline of the t-shirt down. Every place he touches goosebumps. "I love you in my shirt."

"Except that first time." Grinning, I tease as my pulse flies.

"Oh, I loved the way you looked, all warm and sexy as fuck, but I was furious I didn't remember touching you. And goddamn, I wanted to touch you in the most..." His palm slides under the fabric, stretching the neckline as he finds my throbbing nipple.

Voice low, he finishes, "Dirty ways."

And my shirt vanishes in some magic trick that involves hot hands all over me.

"On your back." It's a grunted command.

"I am on my back."

He knocks the pillows off both sides of the bed. "No sweetheart, that was not on your back. "This—" he leans down and devours my nipple until his lips are damp and dark red. "Is on your back."

Then he trails that mind wrecking tongue of his down the centerline of my stomach. When I start to arch, he flattens his hand over my lower tummy, spanning all of me with the width of his palm. "No, this is on your back. My feast. My playground to enjoy."

"*Oh.* Scout." I latch my fingers on the corded muscles of his shoulders as he breathes on my bare skin. No panties under that shirt, the entire time his team was here.

Just bare wet pussy that's now below his gaze. I'm so aroused I can smell my own scent perfuming the space around us.

For a few seconds he inhales me like I'm fine wine, then he brushes his mouth over one hipbone, then the other. "I want you to have a baby with me."

Wait! What?

I'm pretty sure I heard something screech to a halt.

I'm stunned speechless, my fingers digging into his shoulders, but apparently he's not out of words.

"I want our child to grow here." The warm ridge of his nose nuzzles across the soft spot below my navel and I can't stop the clenching of my heart.

"*Memphis...*"

He pulls his eyes away from my skin, looking up from where he's resting between my legs and sears me to my marrow.

Hope. Raw, unabashed hope brightens those diamonds to a shine so powerful it lights up my whole world.

With my throat aching from all the love that's trying to squeeze out of me at once, I say, "I really want that."

A family with Memphis.

I was always one of those girls...the kind that loved kids. But after what happened I shelved those dreams. I was going to be a great aunt—if Griff ever finds a woman that will put up with him.

But this... would be a beautiful new chapter for us both.

Nipping my inner thigh lightly, Scout's voice dips to a husky whisper. "I'm going to worship you now, fiancée." He flashes a hot, proud grin.

"I'm so ready."

He very carefully lifts my legs until my knees are over his shoulders and settles between my spread thighs, pushing me open wide to fit his massive width. "Keep your feet on my back so we don't make them worse."

I shake my head once. So darned sweet to me. The big badass SEAL with the ice eyes and the heart of a lion.

My protector.

"Babe, I'm good. Really good. I don't even have feet right now. But I do need—"

Chapter Seventy-One

SCOUT

My Aria will never need for anything. A vow inside my head as I drop my mouth to her with a growl.

Heaven. Help. Me.

How is it possible Aria tastes even sweeter, even more perfect? Dragging my tongue through her lush pussy, I groan in the back of my throat.

This is mine. *All mine to cherish.* To pleasure.

A possessive fire grows inside me, pushing blood in hard waves into my cock, making my hand move down to it.

Hello and hell yes. I'm thick as a tree trunk right now.

As I fist my girth, I swipe broad licks across Aria's pussy opening, pushing my way up until my tongue brushes her clit. Taking my sweet time to explore the pressure and pace, I swirl around there.

Once I find what makes her moan, I repeat this until she's breathing fast, my cock is throbbing and my senses are filled with nothing but her. Every little movement, the sound of her raspy breathing, the shifting of her against my face as she seeks release.

Stroking myself keeps the animal at bay long enough for me to get her really fucking close.

My signal to take things up a notch, her thighs tremble around my shoulders. Gliding a hand from my dick up the sweet pale skin of her inner leg, I find her juices running over everything. Soaking her, my face, the tempting crease between her ass cheeks.

"God, Aria. So damned wet for me."

"Memphis," she whispers on an exhale. "I'm close."

I know that. I've got her right where I want her. Slipping two fingers around in her hot wetness, I tease her slit. "I want you to be nice and open for my cock. I'm going to drive into you in one hard thrust."

Aria whimpers, her body moving restlessly against me. "Yes...I want that."

"Now come for me," I rasp against her clit, and graze it with my teeth, before I suck it gently as I work her deeply with two of my broad fingers.

Her body responds like a dream.

She lets go on a scream that's low and ragged. Her pussy clenches over and over against my fingers, coating me, driving me wild. My cock throbs, the skin hot and tight as I return my fist there as I lick up her come with greedy sounds coming from my chest.

"Oh my... what did you do to me?" She shivers and pants as her fingers dig into my hair. "Come up here."

"Oh, I'm coming sweetheart."

I crawl up her body, biting her hip, and grazing my teeth over her budded nipple as I go. Each time my mouth hits her skin, she whimpers below me.

As her legs wrap around my waist, I kiss her, sharing the taste of her on my tongue. Definitely my two favorite flavors. Better than any Baskin Robbins cone. And all for me.

A throaty purr from her breaks my control as I fist the lush waves of her hair and prop myself on an elbow. With my damp hand, I guide the head of my cock back and forth across her clit, making her jump and cry out in little whimpers.

"God, I love how responsive you are."

As her fingers dig into my arms, then move to my back, I close my eyes and try to slow my overactive ticker. Her touch is so fucking sweet, like someone is mashing my gas pedal to the floor.

When I look down at her, she's smiling. "I love wrecking you."

"Wreck away. I'm ready and willing any time day, night, morning, noon."

I've seen her smile now a dozen times and it will never be enough. Not this special, intimate smile. *No, I'll never get enough of this.*

"Bare okay again?"

I told her I wanted to have a family with her on impulse, and she said yes, but that doesn't mean we have to do it now. I'll follow her lead. Any damned where.

She reaches between us and wraps delicate fingers around my cock. "Always."

Fuck. Me.

Bare and raring it is.

I notch the thick head against her, then I do as I promised. I lose myself deep in the sweetest place I've ever known in one deep stroke.

We both groan. Mine deep. Hers as soft as a velvet purr.

I settle my weight on her welcoming body. We find just the right position, her wrapping her legs more tightly, then I begin another slow, deep stroke. Whispering against her ear.

"Love you, Aria Kane."

Pulling back and thrusting again.

"You're my true north."

Another slow, hard stroke.

"Love this."

Pulling back slowly. "Feels so fucking good."

Kiss against her ear.

"So perfect."

Thrusting deep. Slow and so fucking deep. Hitting the bottom.

"I'm so glad no one else touched me."

Pressing my face the curve of her neck.

"This body only wants your hands."

Pulling back, dragging against her g-spot.

"Now give it to me, Aria. Give me that sweet heart and body."

The delicious sting of her nails in my skin, she keeps her eyes wide as her tongue slicks across her parted lips. "For you. For your and only you, Memphis."

And when she comes, she pulls me down, drowning me so fucking sweetly in her love.

Chapter Seventy-Two

Aria

My voice bounces with every step Scout takes. "Oh my god, you're really strong."

He chuckles between my legs, making my very happy pussy tingle. "You said the same thing last night when I held you up against the wall."

I blush so hard I can't think of a reply. He's right. I did compliment him on that. And a lot of other things.

One big thing in particular.

He squeezes my hips and looks over his shoulder at me with a heavy dose of hunger in his crystal blue eyes. "We have to stop talking about this right now."

I'm grinning as I press my cheek against his back,

feeling the cool damp raincoat against my heated skin. "We'll save that for later."

We leave it at that as he makes the final descent to the staging area for the Devil's Belly cave entrance. Ahead of us, there's already a flurry of activity even though daylight is just starting to break.

Griff spots us first, or maybe he's the only one that stops what he's doing and watches Scout carrying me.

After the choking incident last night, Scout's team gave him so much crap, I think it helped ease some of his disbelief that I was swept off my feet.

Which was one of the reasons I told him how I did. Not that I knew he'd inhale a chunk of tomato.

He studies us as we approach until I feel like crawling out of my skin, but Scout never even tenses. Instead he pokes fun at my brother.

"Morning, Kane, snorted any tomatoes this morning?"

Oh snap.

Griff shakes his head. "Fucker."

As Scout places me on a chair, and fixes a second chair to elevate my feet, I remind Griff that there are lots of other words he could use. But my brother doesn't take his eye off what Scout's doing, as if he's cataloging every movement.

When my man steps back and crosses his arms with a satisfied look on his face, my heart squeezes. The big brute has been taking care of me since we met. Not always happily on his part, but he's always been keeping me safe, reassuring me, making me comfy.

Really comfy. Like boneless and hoarse from groaning his name comfy.

A wave of heat hits my face. That my brother also watches. He shakes his head, ruffles my hair and shoves his hands in his pockets.

There's a thickness to his voice when he says, "When did you grow up on me?"

Oof. A movie plays in my head of my big brother always, always looking out for me and when we lost our parents a few years apart, he became my anchor.

"A while ago. You were on a few deployments."

He nods and goes silent for a beat.

I grab his arm. "It's not a bad thing. I'm just saying. I was busy becoming the woman I am today while you were off saving the world. It's just what it is."

His sad smile makes my emotions climb up my throat leaving a stinging trail.

Before I can say anything too sappy, Griff huffs. "So you're marrying this fuc—I mean—this jerk?"

There's no bite to his words now, they carry almost a teasing affection.

"That's my plan."

He chuckles. "Scout, when I told you to stay away from my sister, this is why. I just had a bad feeling she'd fall for those damned spooky blue eyes, and then I'd be stuck with your annoying ass."

My irritation starts to rise, but he quickly sticks his hand out to Scout. "Welcome to the Kane family. I'm happy she didn't fall for some Air Force dork."

Scout's brows go up, and he starts to laugh. "Me too."

They share a hearty handshake followed by a violent back slap. "Thanks, man."

"Break it up, you three." Justice hustles into the tent. "Time for huggy-huggy later. It's game time."

Motioning around to different things, Justice puts the guys to work before winking at me. "Figured you could use a break from those two."

I shrug, a hint of a smile sneaking through. "I don't

know. It's kind of like watching a car sliding on ice—there's this strange fascination. You're just waiting to see if it'll glide to a safe stop...or if something gets dented with a bang."

When I finish my weird analogy, I realize Justice is looking at me with his complete focus. "That's so weird you said that."

"Why is that?"

Truck limps into the tent. "What are we talking about?"

"About—" I start, but a whistle cuts through the air.

Truck holds up both hands. "Hold that thought, I'll be back."

Only I don't see him again and I realize there's some kind of big discussion going on over by the water. Beast and several men are motioning toward the cave. The professor is there. Someone's voice goes a few decibels louder.

I growl in frustration. *What is going on?*

Stupid feet. Being bundled in gauze was fine as long as I was in bed with Scout. But now, I'm stuck waiting until someone comes back.

It seems like a petty problem though. Everyone is in mission mode at that point and I don't want to be a distraction.

Justice and Beast suit up in record time. There's no sign of Camile this morning, and I wonder if she's staying away because she's upset. From what the team said about the cave last night, I'd be too.

Is it greedy of me that I'm happy Scout's not diving?

Yes, I decide, but I'm lucky this morning that he's not. Griff too. But soon my brother will be back doing what he does. Rescue diving is Griff's life.

Scout... I'm not even sure what Scout's life is.

I scrub my hands over my eyes. "I can't believe I don't...

335

Scout appears at my elbow. He drops down on his haunches and looks at me with those cool, pale blue eyes that did have a hand in stealing my heart.

"You talking to yourself now, sweetheart?"

Before I answer, he's pressing his lips to my temple. "I'm going to pick you up."

"Where are we going?"

"As much as I want to carry you back to the truck, I'm not. I'm taking you over to the water's edge with the rest of us. I don't want you here by yourself."

So thoughtful. But there's an undercurrent to his voice that makes my forehead crease.

"Is everything okay?"

"We'll see. There's been a development."

Justice jogs past us in his wetsuit. Beast is already by the water, propping his mask and snorkel on the top of his head. The others have stationed the dive tanks around the edge of the water.

The energy is focused and heavy, leaving no doubt, something is happening.

Scout carefully puts me down on a tarp that's been placed over the wet ground. He covers my feet with the raincoat he brought for that purpose because he's obsessed with taking care of my foot injuries.

Then he turns even more serious. "The professor and his student were using a UUV in the first part of the cave and they spotted some women's shoes."

"Oh no," I breathe as I cover my mouth. "I hope they don't belong to her..."

"Me too." He looks toward the water, his brow drawing down tightly.

The surface is the color of mercury, and dotted with pockmarks from the rain. It's deceptive. Water like that looks so calm, but it can be full of secrets and hidden dangers.

Scout folds his fingers over mine. "The other situation is that conditions are far worse than expected in the cave. It's going to be a very hard dive. There's a lot more current than anticipated."

Fear strikes me, stealing my breath. The cave is already known for being incredibly difficult due to the narrow passages. I squeeze his hand as a shiver builds in my muscles. "Don't let them go."

"What if MZ's trapped? It's been days since the caves filled with rain. We are her last hope if she's trapped in one of those chambers."

Cold sweat peppers my skin.

"I don't feel good about this," I say, pulling him closer.

"Stop! Stop! Don't!" A woman's frantic voice echoes off the water and the walls of the cave, making all eyes snap toward the origin of the sound.

Standing between the trees, she looks almost ethereal in a ghostly operative kind of way. Pale blond hair hanging in long wet pieces, a dark coat, dark tactical pants and boots.

"Who is she?"

"Her," Scout rumbles and stands to his full height. "That's Allison Westerly, our missing woman."

"Thank god," I rasp as relieved tears fill my eyes.

Chapter Seventy-Three

TRUCK

Nothing ever fully prepares you to come face to face with a ghost.

I'm vaguely aware that there's a pain behind my sternum. Any doctor would probably be alarmed, but I know I'm already dead inside so there's nothing left to break in that particular cavity.

Out of all the people standing around staring at the woman who just shouted, my team leader shoves me. "Go get her."

As if there's a disconnect between my brain and my feet, it takes a moment to get all six-foot-six inches of my skeleton moving.

It's damned hard to walk toward the thing that could put you in the grave. Again. This time maybe for good.

My long strides cover the ground with some momentum once I get on a roll. I need to get this done and figure out how to dig myself out of the dirt for the second time in my life.

Or hell, maybe I'll just stay there.

"Allison?"

Shit, I sound like I feel. Hollow and wrecked.

The apparition folds her arms over her frame—her too thin frame—watching me warily as she stands in the rain. I'm reminded of a deer, all delicate and nervous with luminous oversized eyes.

She doesn't just look ethereal, she wears her exhaustion like a veil.

"Who are you?" She asks instead of answering my question. This biting reply comes just about the time I'm turning from stunned to angry myself.

Not angry.

Furious at the world for bringing her to my fucking doorstep looking like the one person that haunts my sleepless nights. The one person I'll never see again.

"Our team's been looking for you."

She tightens her hold on herself. "I know."

I'm not really sure what the fuck is going on here, but an uneasy feeling works it's way into my gut right alongside the paralyzing grief that's been there for too fucking long.

"It's all a scam."

Weird remark.

I'm not sure why, but I get close enough to reach out and grab her if she decides to take off. "What's a scam?"

"All of it. Whatever my father told you."

I'm not sure why, but her attitude is all over my last nerve for no good reason. Or maybe for every good reason. But there's a tornado inside my head right now and I can't see clearly for the debris.

"Oh really?"

The woman stares at the center of my chest as if there's something interesting there. Maybe the black, smoking fucking cavern where my heart used to live.

If she stares long enough she'll probably see a curl of smoke.

The whole 'not meeting my gaze' irritates me too. Women look at my eyes and fall in. That takes care of the other mixed-bag of body language my soulless carcass gives off.

"Hey, I'm up here."

She mutters, "Tall men are such tools."

I smirk at that stab. I don't know about all tall men, but I'm well acquainted with my assholeness. I pull it out regularly.

"I know a few remarks about blond women. Shall I share?"

Boring her gaze into my pecs, she sighs dramatically. "Spare me. I've probably heard them all and something tells me you're not very original. The taller they are, the smaller the brain."

Oh, damn. This woman's got a razorblade behind those straight white teeth.

"Okay, let's cut the bullshit. Where have you been?"

Shifting between her feet, she frowns, causing a crease between her delicate brows. "Around."

"That's damned cryptic."

I'm living up to her expectation that I'm a tool.

Grumbling, I jerk my chin toward the party of onlookers that are leaving this shit up to my ass like I'm the greeting committee and interrogation team all rolled into one.

"Come with me."

She takes a step back, glancing around nervously. "No, I should go."

This is when I do reach out and snag her.

My arms are way fucking long and she probably thought she was out of range, but I grip her wrist in a lose ring formed by my long fingers.

No need to use force. She's easily a hundred-fifty pounds lighter than me and she's got nowhere to go. I'd chase her down in four seconds flat.

Or maybe I'd just chase her away so I wouldn't have to ever look at her again. But I'm more honorable than that.

"Hold on a hot minute. We've got questions."

A look of alarm transforms her face, blanching her pale color even more and I realize she's looking up at a 6'6" stranger with a scowl that's been known to scare grown men so bad they piss their pants.

A lot of people.

And some begging for their life too.

For a fraction of a second I feel human like I never do during interrogations of tangos, and I feel sorry for her.

"Look, I'm not going to hurt you."

She tugs her hand free—I let it go with my hand stinging weirdly from the contact.

Okay. Allison Westerly is not an apparition. This is not a bad dream, but it is a nightmare. She's warm, and delicate, and fucking with my head seriously hard.

She looks even angrier now as she wraps her arms around herself again, pinching her black raincoat to her middle. "You and your people need to stop looking for me."

Taking my time to look her over, I take in all of Allison Westerly, the woman our team refers to by the initials MZ. The target we've been hunting for weeks. She's a walking, talking page right out of my past that makes me realize just how fucked up I am.

I really am dead on the inside and I hate her for reminding me.

When I looked at the photos in her file, I tried to ignore that she was very, very similar to Hope's likeness.

This isn't similar. It's...unthinkable.

A shudder rolls through me, leaving behind a longing so destructive, things inside of me creak and break like rotten timber that can't hold the weight of my existence any longer.

But I'm not so fucked that I don't see that she's suffering. Scared too. Alone. Caught up in something if our intel is right.

Not that we have much. The woman isn't just the ghost from my past. She's an enigma, so elusive a whole damn team of SEALs haven't been able to locate her. Until she locates us.

"Are you alone?"

There's not another person in sight that isn't part of our team or associated with the dangerous cave diving rescue we were about to attempt to find her.

More elusive silence follows.

I press, "Do you have a guard?"

She blinks at me, her soft green eyes widening a fraction, before she flicks her gaze away. "I um...I did. Not now."

"You're not going anywhere then."

A swirl of panic flares behind her eyes. Her voice rises an octave and the image of that frightened deer returns to my brain.

"No, you don't understand."

"Ma'am, I don't think you understand. We've been

hired to make sure you're safe and right now I'm looking at a woman that's ten pounds thinner, a whole lot paler than her photo, and skittish as fuck. She's also alone in a country with dangerous rebels. So you can forget about us stopping this mission until we know what's going on."

This time she meets my gaze and there's something blazing there. Anger?

Biting words come out of her pretty mouth. "You need to leave me alone. You could die. All of you could die because of talking to me."

Like that's going to happen. "You're not walking away until you give us answers."

Closing her eyes, she mumbles something under her breath that ends in a snarl of her broad, pink upper lip that makes cold sweat bead between my shoulder blades.

"What was that, ma'am?"

"I shouldn't have come."

Too late for that. She's caught now.

"Why did you?"

She exhales, and shakes her head causing her damp hair to cling to her cheek. "I couldn't live with myself if something happened to innocent men who dive in that lethally dangerous cave because of some bullshit story my father sold you on."

I know I'm staring, but there's nothing I can do. And when tears build on her lashes, I curse silently. *Don't cry. Don't fucking cry.*

I might not trust myself to keep my act wired together when a woman that looks like my former fiancée is crushing my careful façade, but she will be safe with our team.

That's guaranteed.

"You can trust us."

The first tear falls. Then I do.

"I don't have anyone that I can trust."

+++

That's all for Aria and Scout's Story! Thank you so much for reading.

Secret Mission (Allison & Truck's book) is up next.

Reserve your preorder copy now. https://readerlinks. com/l/4420878

Hungry for another protective SEAL + strong woman romance now?

Covert Mission and Stealth Mission are available, and so are 10 other books in the Agile Security & Rescue Series. All are in Kindle & Kindle Unlimited.

Use this link to start reading Book 1, Covert Mission now. https://readerlinks.com/l/4419960

Use this link to check out the Agile Security Series books. https://readerlinks.com/l/2688641

Also by Jenna Gunn

The Jenna Gunn Romance Library

Jenna Gunn's books can be found under her name and the pen name Maris Night. Below is a partial list of her books.

Agile Security & Rescue Series

Lethal Threat (Formerly titled Forgotten Soldier) - Cole & Sierra's Story

Deadly Rescue (Formerly titled Dr. Trouble) - Scotch & Simona's Story

Off-Limits Protector - Andre & Willow's Story

Forbidden Knight - Wolf & Kate's Story

Clash Landing - Mako & Erika's Story

Lost & Found - Mikail & Gina's Story

Guarding Secrets - Marshall & Danee's Story

Dangerous Secrets - Dozer & Candy's Story

Lethal Secrets - Eli & Mia's Story

Dangerous Ties - Beckett & Madeline's Story

Seth- An Agile Security & Rescue Novella

Agile Security & Rescue Team 2

Covert Mission - Beast & Camile's Story

Stealth Mission - Evan and Marianna's Story

Dangerous Mission - Scout and Aria's Story

Secret Mission - Truck's story

Guarded by the SEAL - is free when you join my newsletter and features the origin story for Agile Security & Rescue.

The Eden Mountain Firefighters Series

<u>Saving Sophia</u> - Liam and Sophia's story

<u>Saving Skye</u> - Larson and Skye's story-

<u>Saving Summer</u> - Carter and Summer's story

<u>Saving Savannah</u> - Caleb & Savannah's story

<u>Saving Valentine's Day</u> - A Novella- Mr. & Mrs. Strong's story

Jenna Gunn Standalone Books

Rocked - Gage, Julian & Winter's story

Kieran & Carra's story (Not currently available)

Avery's Hero - Brock & Avery's story

Archer Brother's Series
(Now Under Maris Night Pen Name)

<u>Boss Rules</u> - Bryce and Raven's Story

<u>Faux-Ever Rules</u> - Christian and Maddy's Story

<u>Broken Rules</u> - Brandon and Anya's Story

<u>Do-Over Rules</u> - Bishop and Mia's Story

<u>Friend Rules</u> - Tyson and Abby's Story

Get updates on Jenna Gunn's new releases,

book sales, and free books.

Join her newsletter on her website.

<u>www.jennagunn.com</u>

Made in the USA
Columbia, SC
10 April 2025

56451515R00193